FLESH AND GOLD

Praise for Ann Aptaker

Advance Praise for *Flesh and Gold*

"Devilishly dark and rough, this quest mystery brings 1950s underworld dyke Cantor Gold to pre-Castro Havana. Aptaker brings vividly alive the era and the mob-, gang-, and rebel-infested city. The battered hero says it best herself: 'I came here to find the woman I love, but all I've found so far is blood and betrayal.'"—Lee Lynch, award-winning author of *The Swashbuckler* and *Rainbow Gap*

Criminal Gold

"This is author Aptaker's first novel, and if this is an indication of what she can do, we need to welcome her to the canon of gay literature."—*Reviews by Amos Lassen*

"Hey, doll: You look like the kind of girl this book was written for—willing to take a few risks, sit in a stylish watering hole with a suave woman in a suit, explore the night and all that New York can offer, not caring if the sun rises or not. Pour your favorite libation, sit back, and get ready for a hell of a ride."—J.M. Redmann, Author of the Lambda Literary Award–winning Micky Knight Mysteries

"A brilliant crime novel set in New York City in 1949 featuring Cantor Gold, dapper dyke-about-town, smuggler of fine art and savior of damsels in distress."—*Curve Magazine*

"An author can make a time and place come alive, and this was certainly true of Ann Aptaker's book *Criminal Gold*. We're plunged into the heart of 1940s criminal New York with a thrilling tale of murder and deception...Aptaker has set herself up for a cracking series not only because of the character of Cantor Gold but for choosing a period of time that is fascinating to read about."—*Crimepieces.com*

Lambda Literary and Goldie Winner *Tarnished Gold*

"Cantor Gold is an inimitable and larger than life tour de force...This is a triumphant second book in a series that is likely to be nonpareil!"—*Rainbow Book Reviews*

"Aptaker's background as a curator of art and professor of art history is more than apparent, and without being overwhelming, that perspective adds a whole other dimension to her storytelling...[I]f you haven't read the first book, you should, you really should. Not only to catch up, but for the sheer joy of reading beautifully crafted historical novels and noir crime."—*Curve Magazine*

"It's rare that I picture a book as a movie in my mind, but the entire time I was reading *Tarnished Gold* I kept picturing a classic black-and-white noir film, with the dapper and cunning protagonist hunting down clues to save the day."—*Just Love Reviews*

Genuine Gold

"Cantor Gold is still completely mesmerizing, as she talks and struts her way through the story, wearing hand tailored silk suits, with woolen overcoats, caps, and fedoras. Aptaker uses words like thick oil paint, sweeping them across the page. The criminal underworld, with gang bosses, crooked cops and prostitutes, is painted expertly."—*The Lesbian Review*

By the Author

Criminal Gold

Tarnished Gold

Genuine Gold

Flesh and Gold

Visit us at www.boldstrokesbooks.com

FLESH AND GOLD

by

Ann Aptaker

2018

FLESH AND GOLD

ISBN 13: 978-1-63555-153-2

THIS TRADE PAPERBACK ORIGINAL IS PUBLISHED BY
BOLD STROKES BOOKS, INC.
P.O. BOX 249
VALLEY FALLS, NY 12185

FIRST EDITION: OCTOBER 2018

CREDITS
EDITOR: RUTH STERNGLANTZ
PRODUCTION DESIGN: STACIA SEAMAN
COVER DESIGN: PHILOMENA MARANO (WWW.PHILOMENAMARANO.COM)

Acknowledgments

Writing this book presented a lot of hurdles, some creative, some personal. I overcame both through the love and friendship of Jody Gray, Jacquie Hawley, Allan Neuwirth, Debra Solomon, my wonderful sister Yren Berry, and with special appreciation to Cora Jane Glasser.

Life challenges. Love challenges harder.

Chapter One

Idlewild Airport, New York City
January 1952
11:15 p.m.

The red jacketed barkeep in the cocktail lounge is giving me the same sort of less than friendly look-over that I got from the airline's ticket clerk, pert and pretty in her blue uniform and cute little cap. But here in the cocktail lounge, just like at the ticket counter, money talks, so my cash for a first class ticket and a big tip for my tumbler of Chivas scotch—neat—put those nasty look-overs back into their eye sockets. It didn't hurt my feelings much that the pretty ticket clerk still didn't like me, still cringed at the sight of a dame in a gentleman's suit. And I don't care that the barkeep isn't any chummier when he pours me another, even takes his time wiping the spillover on the bar. The clerk gave me my plane ticket and checked my luggage, and the barkeep pours my scotch, and that's all I give a damn about right now. The two of them can enjoy their contempt in peace. I didn't give any lip to the ticket clerk and I won't slap the barkeep around. I won't do anything that would cause a scene, disturb the other patrons in the cocktail lounge, and bring a bouncer—or worse, a cop—my way and jeopardize my getting on the midnight plane to Havana.

I've got an envelope stuffed with cash in my inside jacket pocket, the kind of cash I'll need to open tight lips. The cash is comforting, though not as comforting as a photo I pull from that same pocket, look at it while I quietly sip my scotch. The photo came from my office, where it sat in the safe for over three years because it hurt too much to keep it on my desk and see it every day. It's a picture of happiness, of two people in love. The beautiful woman with long, dark, tousled hair and zest in her eyes is Sophie de la Luna y Sol, my Sophie of the Moon and the Sun. The grinning idiot next to her is me.

I've never loved anyone like I love Sophie, will always love her. From our very first night together to our very last morning six months later, my heart, my soul, were hers. I'd even considered giving up my racket—I steal art and other treasures and smuggle them into the Port of New York—if that's what Sophie wanted. If she'd wanted a country cottage with a white picket fence, I'd have chucked my big city ways and lived a peasant's life in the sticks. If she'd wanted a palace or a Park Avenue penthouse, I'd have given her those, too. Hell, I would've climbed the Empire State Building to grab the stars right out of the sky, used them as jewels for her sparkling crown.

I've waited a long time for this night, three and a half years of hope and misery, of false leads and no leads, since the night Sophie was grabbed off the street and forced onto a flesh boat that took her away. Years of lousy sleep and empty days, full of rage for what she's been forced to do, forced to be, and me helpless to do anything about it.

Until today. Until I finally got the goods on that flesh boat and where it went.

Three and a half cold years. That's how long I waited for Sig Loreale to make good on a promise he never kept, a promise to get a line on that boat and where it took Sophie, because if anyone could get the story, it would be Sig. His underworld web stretches from the docks of New York to the docks of California and beyond. And besides, he owed me a couple of favors. Big favors. Favors he welched on.

So when a deal for the information on Sophie's whereabouts showed up at my door, I jumped at the chance to pay the high price of ten grand to get it. A business deal is more reliable than a favor anyway, a lesson I learned long ago from the tough old lady who came to my door today wearing mink and sensible shoes, sat her ample body down in a big chair in my living room, and gave me the name of the boat—the *Belle Caribe*—and where it took Sophie. That old lady is Esther "Mom" Sheinbaum, the Lower East Side's Empress of Crime, for over fifty years the city's top fence of stolen swag, often including mine. Mom's got her own contacts on the docks and in the precincts, maybe not as wide afield as Sig's but enough to learn that the boat sailed to Havana. But that's all Mom had. Just the town. Not the street. Not the house. But I'll find it. I'll pay off or kill off whoever I need to if it helps me find Sophie.

Another scotch eases these thoughts, helps squelch my rage so I can think clearly about what to do when I get to Havana. The first thing I'll do is go see a guy I telegrammed on my way to the airport, a guy who's moved goods for me—

"Forget about your drink, Gold," comes a gruff voice from a bulldog-faced lug in a big gray overcoat and low slung fedora who's suddenly on one side of me, taking my coat from the next barstool and shoving it at me. On the other side of me, a potato-faced lug in another big coat and a hat pulled low says, "Put your coat on. Mr. Loreale wants to see ya."

I slip the photo back into my pocket. It's not for these mugs' cheapjack eyes. "Why am I not surprised you boys are here," I say, once again face-to-face with the fact that there's nothing on this earth Sig Loreale doesn't know. His tipsters, killers, flunkies, and thugs keep him up to date on everything that goes on in the underworld, and since I'm part of that world, it's a sure bet he knows what goes on with me.

Or maybe Mom Sheinbaum tipped him off. Who the hell knows? True, she's no fan of Sig's, wasn't crazy about it when her daughter, Opal, took up with him instead of some square jawed American dreamboat Mom groomed her for. And when Opal was killed, Mom never forgave Sig for dragging her precious American-born bundle of joy back into the crime world and to her death. But Mom does what's best for Mom, and now that my ten Gs are tucked away in her handbag, if chummy-ing up to New York's most powerful crime lord has something in it for her, she wouldn't bat an eye to betray me. She might even tell him I've stopped waiting for him to make good on his broken promise to help find Sophie. It wouldn't be the first time Mom's betrayed me, business deal or no business deal.

Or maybe it wasn't Mom at all. I'm in a tough racket, and there's no end of louses who'd sell me out for a buck, a bribe, or just the sheer hell of it.

But it's Sig's thugs I'm faced with now. "Listen, fellas, I've got a plane to catch. Tell Sig I'm not missing my flight just to go all the way back to the city to chitchat with him. Tell him I'll call him from Havana. He can say whatever he has to say to me over the phone."

The bulldog-faced lug on my right says, "You ain't goin' to his place. You're just goin' outside to the curb." The next thing I know, the guy grabs my coat from my hands, throws it around my shoulders, and says through an ugly sneer across his big, tobacco stained teeth, "It's cold outside. Wouldn't want you to catch the sniffles." He has all the sincerity of someone who wouldn't mind if I died of plague.

I've suddenly got a hammy hand under each arm and I'm lifted off my barstool.

The barkeep grins, enjoying what he's sure is my comeuppance. For the first time tonight I really do wish I could slap him around, because even if I flashed hundred-dollar bills at him, it wouldn't wipe that smug smile off his face.

I tell the lugs on either side of me, "Thanks anyway, but I can get outside on my own. I don't need training wheels."

But they don't let go. I'm sure Sig told them not to. So they pull me across the cocktail lounge, to the bewilderment of the other patrons, ladies and gentlemen on sofas and at little tables, everyone smart enough to look away and just keep sipping their martinis.

Outside, Sig's big black Cadillac idles at the curb, the polished body and heavy chrome reflecting the thugs dragging me out of the terminal. The car's curves contort the three of us into shapes I used to laugh at in the fun house mirrors of my Coney Island childhood. But what's waiting for me inside that car is no fun house.

One of the thugs opens the rear door. The other guy pushes me into the back seat.

It's warm inside the car, and dark except for a small overhead light that shines on the black homburg shadowing the fleshy face of the man in a big black coat seated next to me.

Sig Loreale.

"Cantor," he says, accenting each syllable in that slow, threatening way of his. Sig's carefully articulated speech has been giving me the heebie-jeebies since I was a tomboy kid and Sig was muscling his way into the Coney Island rackets. I've learned to control my urge to cringe whenever he opens his mouth. It's safer. "It was not necessary to sneak out of town," he says with as much threat between the words as in the words themselves. "I would not have stopped you from going."

"What do you call this curbside kidnap? Bon voyage and drop me a postcard?"

That actually gets a small laugh from the guy, if you can call that creepy, open-mouthed-but-silent chuckle a laugh. "Don't worry, Cantor," he says after the laugh. "You will not miss your plane." He says it with such certainty, I get the feeling he's already made arrangements with the tower to hold the flight. He can do it. He's got the airport officials and the unions that run the place by the throat. "I want you on that plane, Cantor. Now that you've decided to go to Havana—"

"No thanks to you," I say. "You made a promise to me, Sig. You knew you owed me a favor, a helluva big favor—two, as a matter of fact, for finding the person responsible for Opal's death, and handing you a work of art which should have gone to someone else—and in return you were going to get a line on the flesh boat that took Sophie. But you lied." By throwing his lies at him I've just dropped my life into his cold lap. But years of pent-up fury is finally oozing out, and I can't stop it even if I want to. And I don't want to. "The world was too big to find one little boat, you said. Well, what you couldn't—or wouldn't—do in all that time, it seems Mom took care of with a few hours' worth of phone calls. So I don't owe you any favors, Sig. Not anymore. Now if you don't mind, I really *do* have a plane to catch." I move to get out of the car, but the lug outside has other ideas and keeps his meaty hand against the door. I'm not going anywhere until Sig says so.

I guess he really does want me on that plane, because I'm still alive despite my little outburst. After a silence that feels longer than a prison stretch but shorter than death, he says, "I did not lie to you, Cantor. I wanted to get you more accurate information, not just the name of the town. And now you're going to Havana"—there's a subtle sneer on his fleshy lips, barely visible in the shadowy light of the car but razor sharp with ridicule—"where you'll have to pull back the covers of every bed in every brothel, with many dangerous people trying to stop you. You should have waited for me, Cantor. I wanted to make it easier for you, but you have no patience. In all these years, since you were a kid doing mischief under the boardwalk, I have not been able to teach you patience."

I can do without the lecture. "Why don't you just tell me what's on your mind, Sig."

He reaches into his inside pocket, pulls out a sealed envelope. His movements, as slow and deliberate as the way he speaks, have the tempo of a dirge. "I want you to give this to someone."

"Why don't you just call them on the telephone? They'll get the information faster. You don't need me to run your errands."

"You should know better, Cantor," he says like he's scolding a kid who doesn't listen. "Telephones can be bugged. I do not trust the telephone lines in Havana at this time. And there is violence brewing all over Cuba. The Havana men doing our business down there are having difficulty keeping certain factions under control." He hands me the envelope but keeps his fingers on it. "It is understood you are not to open this."

I give him a nod, the kind that lets him know I'm not stupid.

He finally releases the envelope. "The man you are to give this to lives in a penthouse suite on the eighth floor at the Hotel Nacional.

He is expecting you. And he can be of help to you, too, Cantor. He knows quite a bit about what goes on in Havana."

That's the first helpful thing Sig's said to me in years.

He turns off the overhead light, a signal for his thug to open my door. In near darkness, with just the light of the terminal seeping into the Caddy, he says, "I believe you have a plane to catch, Cantor."

CHAPTER TWO

The Hotel Nacional is a landmark spot—in more ways than one—above Havana's seaside promenade, the Malecón. But I'm checked in to another joint, a little less flashy but a lot more convenient, at least for what I came here to do. I'm in the Plaza Hotel in the Habana Vieja neighborhood, Old Havana. The Plaza's a nice place, lots of history, with that wedding cake Baroque architecture the colonial Spanish brought with them. The architecture's pretty, but it's the location I'm crazy about, convenient to Havana's Colón Quarter and its red-light district. I'll prowl the Colón's every house and room, from the fancy to the fleabag if I have to, to find Sophie. And if some pimp or madam or whoever's got her tries to stop me, I'll kill them.

But maybe Sig's Cuban Señor Big Shot at the Hotel Nacional can help me cut through all that. So after a shower to wash off the staleness of five hours on a plane, a change of clothes into a linen suit of eggshell white and a crisp panama hat—the necessary duds for Cuba's tropical climate, even in January—a bite of breakfast, and strong Cuban coffee, I'm in a cab on my way to the other side of town. Sig's envelope is in my inside jacket pocket. So is the envelope of cash. So is the photograph of Sophie and me.

❖

Depending on how you live life, Havana in the early morning is either a sweetly scented princess just waking, or a fleshy, perfumed harlot staggering home after a long night. It's been ten years since I was last here, during the wild smuggling days early in the Second World War, but the town still seems to have those two personalities, their aromas—one delicate as fresh flowers, the other heavy as overripe fruit—alternating on the breeze through the open windows of the cab.

The city's seaside boulevard hasn't changed much, at least where it runs along the edge of Central Havana, except there are fewer American sailors stumbling around after all night wartime binges. It's mostly Habaneros out here this morning, sleepy men and women on their way to work, shopkeepers getting ready to open, and a good number of local shufflers still getting over the night before. It's a crowd whose skins tell Cuba's history; the brown of the native Taino; the white of the Spanish conquistadors and their plantation owning descendants; the black of the slave trade; and all the tones resulting from all the couplings across the centuries. The morning sun seems to adore every one of them.

The morning sun still loves the sea and the street, too. The light on the Caribbean waters is the same pink it was ten years ago. The reflection throws a fairy-tale glow on the pretty if a bit tawdry little buildings lining this end of the Malecón, which has always reminded me of a movie set ready for Rudolph Valentino's Latin Lover period. But the old Malecón changes the closer we get to the Hotel Nacional in the Vedado district, one of Havana's moneyed parts of town. There's a lot less peeling paint.

The Nacional sits on a bluff overlooking the sea on one side and the villas and grand apartment houses of the Vedado on the other. My cabbie swings us off the Malecón and up the bluff to the hotel's entry drive, a two lane affair with a line of tall palm trees down the center, their fronds swaying like tropical traffic cops directing all the comings and goings. The hotel's arched entry and two arched and red-tiled towers give the place the feel of a gigantic Renaissance villa, the perfect touch of class to satisfy the hotel's champagne cocktail clientele. But like most classy things, there's darkness at its core, giving the hotel's polished reputation a smokier patina.

The darkness in the Nacional's story is an epic that stamped the place as a gangster landmark. During Christmas week of 1946, the American Mob's biggest big shots assembled here to divvy up Cuba's moneymaking activities for their own profit, with the support of a Cuban government whose higher-ups would take their own cut. With the war over and plenty of tourist money flowing again, the plan went into full swing. These days, the Mob's hired hands shuffle the decks at the newer casinos, choreograph the splashy shows at the nightspots, carve the roast beef at the restaurants, pour the rum at the cafés and saloons, and host the tourists and junketeers at the hotels they've either built or are taking over. The boys are muscling in on a country. What they're planning is a Caribbean empire, one island at a time. And Sig's fingerprints are among the other big shots' whose thumbs are all over it, as surely as his fingerprints are on his envelope in my pocket.

Of the two penthouse suites on the eighth floor, I don't have to guess which door leads to the suite where I'm expected. As soon as I step off the elevator, I see two tough customers—why do these guys always come in pairs?—standing guard on either side of a door at one end of the hall. These two aren't as thuggish as Sig's airport lugs. They seem more stony than meaty. The guy on the left could pass as the hotel's house detective, leather-faced and cold-eyed, but the house dick would probably be wearing a wrinkled suit and scuffed shoes, not a natty pale green double-breasted number and brown-and-white wingtips. The guy on the right looks like a politician's bodyguard, his conservative beige suit keeping him low key in a Havana crowd, his hard gray eyes alert for trouble.

I take off my panama as a show of courtesy, run my hand through my always unruly crop of short brown hair—it's been compared to everything from an old broom to a tangled mop, but Sophie loved it, said it made me look charmingly naughty—and say, "Buenos días, señores. Me llamo Cantor Gold," trotting out my limited Spanish.

The gray-eyed, beige-suited guy on the right says, "And my name's Santa Claus," in an accent right out of Flatbush. "Whaddya want?"

Actually, I want to thank the guy for relieving me of any lingo gymnastics, but he doesn't seem like the joking type, so all I say is, "I'm expected."

Both boys look me over as if I'm a disease carrying insect they'd like to step on.

I've seen that look so many times in my life—y'know, the go-put-a-skirt-on look, most recently back at Idlewild Airport—it's getting boring. Last night it was annoying. Today I simply sigh at the unoriginality of humankind.

"Look," I say, "I have something for your Señor Big Shot, something that came all the way from the big shot in New York."

Snappy Dresser in Wingtips extends his hand, says, "Give it to me. I'll deliver it."

"Nope. The envelope's sealed, the contents confidential. I'm not about it give it to any old Ike and Mike."

Now it's Politician's Bodyguard who pipes up. "Yeah? On whose say-so?"

"Sig Loreale's."

There are names that earn smiles, names that get you a good table at a restaurant or front row seats at the theater, but mention Sig's name and even tough guys suddenly get polite.

Snappy Dresser turns to the door, raises his hand to knock, but stops and says to me over his shoulder, "What you say your name was again?"

"Cantor Gold."

He knocks, and when the door opens partway, he says to someone I can't see, "Got a—I'm not sure what the hell she is, but says her name is Cantor Gold and that she's here from Loreale in New York."

The guy I can't see says, "Yeah, let her in. She's expected."

I give the boys a smile as I walk past them and into the suite's vestibule. "I'll put in a good word for you with your señor," I say, "tell him you were on the job."

The boys aren't amused.

The guy I couldn't see turns out to be another well-dressed Yank, this one in a gray sharkskin suit with a small white carnation in his lapel. His dark hair's barbered to perfection, his blue eyes set in a chiseled face that's Hollywood handsome with an expression that tells me he's in love with himself.

He says through a smile full of his inevitably perfect white teeth, "I'll have to take your piece."

"I'm not carrying," I say and open my suit jacket to prove it.

"Pockets?"

I take out my keys, spare change, and a small penknife from my pants pockets, but Mr. Hollywood's not satisfied. He makes a move to search my inside jacket pockets, but my hands are up fast, push his well-manicured paws away. "Keep your hands to yourself, bucko. I said I'm not carrying and I meant it."

"That penknife could do some damage."

"Only if your boss tries to use it as a toothpick. Listen, Loreale sent me here to do business with your Señor Big Shot, and I'm not stupid enough to cross either of them. Are you?"

That stops him, though he's not happy about it. The graceful mouth tightens into a childish pucker, the dreamboat blue eyes narrow in a bully's defeat, but he nods that I can put my stuff away. As I start to walk out of the vestibule, he grabs my arm, taking one more shot at being the ape in charge. "Pants cuffs, lift 'em."

I do it with a smile, showing off that I don't have a gun strapped to my ankle or a shiv tucked into my sock.

It's a good thing there's no mirror in the vestibule; the way the guy's rubbery sneer uglies up his pretty face he'd probably faint. The idea strikes me so funny I have to squelch a laugh as I walk into the living room.

The living room's big, bright, with a couch and chairs covered in palm-frond-patterned upholstery and tropical lemony peach walls hung with decent Cuban landscape paintings. But the only thing grabbing my attention is the well-groomed middle-aged man eating breakfast at a white-cloth'd table near the open sliding door to the terrace, the gentle breeze barely disturbing his brown hair, well-trimmed and combed back. His cream colored suit is impeccably tailored, his powder-blue tie with a cream pinstripe knotted perfectly against a crisp white shirt. He's not a Cuban Señor Big Shot. He's an American New York Big Shot. He's not tall—he's actually rather short, which got him the nickname Little Man. But there's enough power and influence in that small package to make governments tremble. At least, the Cuban government does. And from time to time, so has Uncle Sam.

He sees me, waves me over to the table, greeting me with a disconcertingly impish smile, eyes crinkled, mouth curving into a V in a face right out of the Lower East Side. It's leathery and tough with bushy brows over almond shaped eyes alert to everything, curious about everyone, and with a glimmer of humor peeking through their ice-cold assessment of it all.

"Have some breakfast?" he says through that smile, sweeping his hand across the spread of fruit, eggs, toast, and a silver pot of coffee. He nods for me to take the chair opposite his.

I toss my hat on the couch on my way to the table. "No, thanks, I've had my breakfast," I say, sitting down. I've just said no to a legend, to the man who set up that mobster gathering in '46, the man who's the brains behind the takeover of every cash operation in Cuba. I've just said no to Meyer Lansky.

"So, Cantor—you don't mind if I call you Cantor?"

"Not at all, just as long as I can keep calling you Mr. Lansky."

His smile, less impish—though the humor's not altogether gone—is comfortably grateful, the smile of someone accustomed to respect, expects it, but isn't puffed up by it and is even appreciative of those who give it. Whatever power and danger are in the man— and there's plenty, as much or more as Sig's—the threat is blunted by the charm of that smile.

"Cantor," he says, as if examining the syllables. "Interesting name." He says it like he's inviting me to eat a slice of cake at his kid's Bar Mitzvah.

But after he takes a sip of coffee his smile fades. It doesn't go away, it just has less sparkle. It's the kind of smile that announces it's time to get down to business. "I believe you have something for me from our mutual friend in New York?"

I take the envelope from my jacket pocket, hand it across the table to Lansky. He opens it, takes a folded letter out, and as he reads, he purses his lips slightly, nods with what seems to be approval, then gives the whole thing a Lower East Side shrug, full of acceptance of life's fate.

He folds the letter back into the envelope and places it on the table. He's smiling again. I get the feeling he enjoys smiling. Well, I guess there's no law that says a big shot gangster can't have fun. They don't all have to be as cold as Sig.

"So, what brings you to Havana?" he says. "I'm sure you didn't come all this way just to deliver my mail."

I thought he'd never ask.

I take the photo of Sophie and me from my jacket pocket, look at it a moment, remember the morning it was taken when we were silly with love and lusty as wild animals after our first night together, before I turn the picture around and show it to Lansky. "The woman with me was nabbed off the street in New York in March of '48. She was forced onto a flesh boat, the *Belle Caribe*. I found out just yesterday that it sailed here. I'm looking for this woman."

Lansky takes the photo, his eyebrows subtly rising as he absorbs the relationship between Sophie and me. I'm not crazy about the picture being out of my hands, but I'm not about to tell the most powerful guy in Havana, a guy who has a bodyguard in the vestibule and two more lugs outside the door, to give it back or else. Sure, Lansky likes to smile a lot, even seems to be a personable guy, but getting on his bad side is a lousy idea. Just ask the ghost of Bugsy Siegel.

"You look happy in this photograph, Cantor. So does the woman," he says, handing the picture back to me. "You know, I've never understood your kind, how you can do what you do. The *faygeleh* boys, or the bulls like you. It makes no sense to me. I don't think it's"—he wrinkles his nose as if he's just smelled something rotten—"kosher. But who am I to judge?" he adds with a shrug, the look on his face easygoing again. "There are plenty of people who don't like me and my kind, either. When they couldn't send us back to the shtetl, they tried sending us to the ovens. But the hell with them, right?" The sparkle, the dangerous fun, is back in his eyes.

"Look, Mr. Lansky, I'll come right out with it. I'd like any help you can give me in finding Sophie. That's her name, Sophie de la Luna y Sol. You're the guy who knows everybody and everything in Havana."

He leans back in his chair, pours himself a fresh cup of coffee, takes a sip, then says, "You think she's still alive?"

It's the question I wish he hadn't asked. I've never dared touch that question, never let myself get anywhere near it. "I'm counting on it," is all I say.

Lansky keeps his eyes on me. "And you think she's still in one of the brothels?"

"Mm-hm," comes out more grunt than sound, my throat suddenly dry as dead wood.

He says, "You know, locating her might not be as easy for me as you obviously think, Cantor. Many of the cathouses here are either controlled by local Havana gangs or paid to protect them. And the gangs are currently at war with each other. Not just over women, either."

"Yeah, the island used to be a port in the bootleg liquor trade."

"Gun running, too. Still is, but instead of bootleg booze, now it's narcotics," he says. "These local boys are playing a big game. Getting the gangs to give up their secrets is no easy matter. And their shoot-'em-ups all over the streets are causing us all kinds of problems. All that violence scares the tourists away, which is bad for our current hotel and casino business and our future plans. On top of that, there's trouble brewing among certain disgruntled members of the population. I don't think it will amount to much," he adds with a nonchalant shrug and a dismissive smile, "and my friends in the government assure me the army has everything under control. But these rebels are getting guns from the gangs and making trouble all over Cuba. They hide in the hillsides like rats. I'm telling you,

Cantor, between the gangs and these radical troublemakers, poking around in the wrong places can be very dangerous."

"From what I hear, a little danger never stood in your way."

"I don't go out and meet it, either. Remember, I have a wife and children in New York. They would prefer that I do not die. But I tell you what. I'll make a deal with you. I hear from Mr. Loreale that you're in the art game. You move art from one place to another? One owner to another? It just so happens I want to acquire a painting."

"So buy one. I'm happy to advise you on a—"

"The painting I have in mind is not for sale. Not for any price."

"The owner doesn't want to sell? I'm sure you can, uh, convince him."

"Cantor, you've got me all wrong. I am not a violent man. Never liked violence," he says, crinkling his nose again and adding a shake of his head. "It brings unwanted attention, so I do my best to avoid it. And besides, if I use local talent to lift the painting, I'd have to pay them. But with you, well, we can do each other a favor. I look into your problem, you handle mine."

This time, his smile is full of the take-it-or-leave-it cheeriness of a man whose options always leave him with the winning hand. If I don't do his favor, for a few bucks he can line up a dozen local light-fingers who'd gladly take the job. Sure, he'd rather keep his money in his pocket, but he didn't get where he is by being stingy. He pays if he has to, trades deals if he can. Today, I'm the deal he can trade on.

So if stealing a painting is the price for his help in finding Sophie, I'll steal a painting. Hell, I'd steal a whole museum. "What am I looking for and where can I find it?"

He takes a pen and small pad from his jacket pocket, writes a few lines, tears off the sheet, and hands it to me.

What's written there is the name of a painting by a Cuban modernist I've admired, Carlos Enriquez. "You have good taste, but this painting is in the States," I say. "I saw it in a show of avant-garde Cuban stuff at the Museum of Modern Art back in '44, and now it's in a private collection of an anonymous buyer. I suppose I could get information on who—"

"That private collection is here in a villa in Havana," Lansky says with a dismissive wave of his hand. "The painting won't be hard to spot. It's in the owner's living room. Señor Estrada likes to show it off."

"Estrada? Pete Estrada?"

"You know him?"

"I wish I didn't."

CHAPTER THREE

Nilo Anaya, happily married father of three daughters, is one of the world's great middlemen. Deals between Those Who Have and Those Who Want slide through his fingers like water through a sieve for a clientele stretching from North America to South. He could easily afford a villa in the Vedado, but that isn't Nilo's style. He lives with his family in a tiny street in a tangled section of Old Havana, an alley, really, of modest pastel-painted stucco houses nearly hidden by the broad fronds of enormous palm trees, a street of shadows and secrets.

Ten years ago, the last time I was at Nilo's place, he was merely a father of one, Maricela, a sweet little girl four years old. Nilo's wife, the warm and charming Isabel, was pregnant with their second. Isabel, as wonderful a wife as anyone could wish for, was a terrible cook, but Nilo, as I recall, is a terrific cook, so the couple is very happy.

I've done business with Nilo during these past ten years, but it's been through intermediaries or, like last night, by telegram with coded information about something I want handled. But here I am at his doorstep, older, sadder, and when Nilo opens his door to my knock, we take our time before our hellos to survey the changes etched into our faces: a few new wrinkles on Nilo's, a bunch of new scars on mine. Soon, though, a big smile spreads across Nilo's face. With his full lips, deep set warm brown eyes that look at everyone as if he's known them for years, the square jaw of an aristocrat but the well-muscled neck and body of a street fighter, Nilo Anaya has the slightly aging good looks of a shady nightclub crooner. Too bad the guy can't carry a tune.

He finally spreads his arms in greeting, his shirt, a discreet pastel plaid, stretching across his chest. "Cantor," he says, his accented English slightly rolling the final *r*, "Welcome to my house. It has been too long!"

"How's everything, Nilo?" I say, taking off my hat and walking inside.

"Fine, fine. I am a happy man, Cantor, the father of three precious girls, the husband of a loving wife, and I make a lot of money."

"Some of it mine."

"Ah, sí, some of it yours. And with your money, Cantor, you will be happy to know I buy my wonderful Isabel the most beautiful jewels."

"I don't doubt the jewels are beautiful, Nilo, but I don't believe for a minute that you buy them."

With a shrug and a smile, he says, "But my Isabel looks beautiful in them anyway. And it is right that she should have them. She is from an old family, you know, very aristocratic. They say they have bloodlines all the way back to the native Taino before the Spanish arrived. But ah, all of this family business is not why you are here, Cantor. Please, come into my office. I have what you asked for in your telegram. And then we will go out to the veranda," he says as I follow him through the airy house. "I made coffee, and Isabel is setting out merenguitos I bought in the market this morning. Believe me, those merenguitos, it is like eating sweet clouds."

Nilo's office is the domain of a contented man. The furniture is comfortably upholstered in pastels, bright-colored rugs are scattered on the blue-and-white zigzag tile floor, and pictures of his wife and daughters share space on his desk with newspapers, sports magazines, and an overflowing ashtray. But for all of its easygoing style, the office is also the room of a careful man. The venetian blinds are angled to allow in a bit of the midday sunlight but prevent prying eyes, and all of the desk drawers need keys to open them.

Nilo pulls a ring of keys from his pocket, opens a drawer, and takes out a Smith & Wesson .38 and a shoulder rig, much like the gun and rig I left back in my apartment in New York. I could've tried bringing them in, or paid off a customs guy, but it's been a while since I've been back to Cuba. Old arrangements may have changed, and I wanted to slip into Havana without notice. I don't need any official curiosity following me around.

Nilo hands me the gun and rig. "Just as you asked," he says. I take five hundred bucks from my envelope of cash and hand it over in exchange for the gear. That's high line for a basic handgun, but a small price for a clean gun that can't be traced.

He also gives me a box of bullets, which I put into my trouser pocket after I load the gun's chambers and shoulder the rig.

I pull out an extra two hundred from my envelope. "Can you change this into local lucre? I'd rather not leave my face and signature at a bank."

He locks the gun drawer, unlocks a drawer below, and takes out a strongbox, also locked. Opening it, Nilo counts out a hefty handful of Cuban pesos. "A better rate than the bank," he says with a smile.

"Better for who, you old thief." But I chuckle when I say it. So does Nilo, taking care to lock the money box in the drawer before we leave the office.

Walking through the breezy living room on our way to the veranda, Nilo says, "You should compliment Isabel on her trees and flowers. It is a hobby she has taken up in the years since you were here, and she takes great pride in her plantings."

"I'll keep it in mind."

Isabel Anaya may be a terrible cook, but she's one helluva gardener. Colors bright as a carnival parade burst from clay pots and flower beds edging the veranda, their sweet floral scents perfuming the air. Bright green leaves curve like beckoning hands, tendrils coil like sleepy snakes. Fleshy petals of red, purple, pink, and yellow quiver as I walk by. I don't know the names of most of the flowers—my acquaintance with nature is generally confined to Central Park or a weedy vacant lot—though here and there I recognize the pale blue of a jacaranda and the red of a hibiscus.

Groups of big palms rise in all four corners of the veranda, their treetop fronds joining in a canopy lush as a jungle, keeping the tropical air cool, the midday sun soft, and conversation shielded from any neighborhood busybodies.

Isabel herself, still elegant as ever if a little earthier after ten years and two more pregnancies, is setting plates and coffee cups on the table, the china making a delicate clatter on the tile tabletop. Streaks of sunlight through the palms slide along her hair, a glistening rust-black pulled into a loose bun at her neck. Seeing me, her dark brown eyes, warm and cozy as a quiet evening in an intimate library of rare books, crinkle above her smile. She spreads her arms in greeting, her motherly body in her sleeveless floral dress as welcoming as a treasured memory. Nilo is a lucky man.

Isabel's "Cantor!" rolls like syrup off her tongue. "It is good to see you again," she says, sliding me into a hug, that soft kind that comes from a woman's happiness.

Oh yeah, Nilo is a *very* lucky man.

Still in Isabel's embrace, I say, "It's good to see you, too. And I see you've added gardening to your many talents." I slide Nilo a wink. "Your veranda is as luscious as the Garden of Eden."

Isabel releases me, but not all the way, taking my chin in her hand, her eyes roaming my face. "Well, I must do something with my time now that all three of my daughters spend their day at school. But look at you, querida. More scars. Too many. Cantor, your life is too dangerous."

"The price of prosperity," I tease.

"It is not a joke. You must be more careful, like my Nilo. But no more talk of danger. Come have coffee and merenguitos. They are especially sweet today. My daughters will be jealous they missed them." She leads me to the table, where the three of us take our places on bright aqua-painted wooden chairs, the seats covered with yellow cushions.

Isabel pours the coffee. After a sip of the rich brew, I take the photo of Sophie and me from my jacket pocket and show it to Nilo and Isabel. "This is why I've come to Havana. I'm looking for this woman. She was kidnapped in New York three and a half years ago, forced onto a flesh boat called the *Belle Caribe*. I learned just yesterday that it sailed here. I need names, Nilo, and addresses."

Isabel takes the picture from me, looks at it, then looks back at me. "You are in pain over this woman."

"Deep pain."

Nilo says, "This will be difficult, Cantor. If she is in an especially rough house, it will be hard to get anyone to talk. The street gangs are hired guns for many of the houses, and they are at war with each other at the moment. Bodies turn up every day. Everyone is very nervous. But I will see what I can find out. How is she called?"

"Her name is Sophie de—"

"No, no," Nilo says, "not her real name. She will have an el burdel name, a brothel name, you know, something alluring, like Dulce, or Lujuria—"

Isabel's hand goes to her husband's mouth, cutting him off after he gives me the Spanish for *sweet* and *lust*. "Stop it, Nilo. Cantor does not need more pain." Taking her hand from Nilo's lips and stroking my cheek instead, she says, "Where can we reach you?"

"The Plaza in Habana Vieja."

There's enough warmth in Isabel's eyes to melt even the steeliest soul. "We will do what we can, Cantor. I promise."

I'm no saint. I'm certainly no prude. I've been visiting cathouses—what the old-timers call notch joints back in the States—since I was a teenager and Sig owned a few houses back in our Coney Island days. The professional ladies of pleasure know what they're doing, and sometimes, on my loneliest nights in my dangerous life, when I miss Sophie so much I'm dizzy with longing, it takes a professional to do what needs doing. And I have a soft spot for the ladies. They and I have something in common: we make our living outside the Law, because the Law dealt both of us rigged hands. The Law says I'm a criminal just because I romance women.

And the Law says it's a crime for the ladies to decide what to do with their own flesh and bones.

I can't kid myself, though. I know that the life can be risky. It's not unusual for a lady of pleasure to have the pleasure beaten out of her by rough trade or a vicious pimp who gets his kicks by using her as a slave. The only freedom she can hope for is to grow old, discarded, and die. The idea that Sophie, my Sophie, is caught in such a life scares me to death.

And then there's the filthy horror that sends its stench through all those other horrors, a scenario twisting me up so bad I can barely breathe: the thought of Sophie pawed over by sweaty tourists and needy locals not only breaks my heart, it makes me sick.

Sure, add hypocrite to my list of sins.

I soothe myself a little by believing that whoever took her would realize Sophie is a class act and would stow her in one of the town's fancier, ultra-discreet joints catering to the island's secretive aristocrats and moneyed clientele, the kind of places where the women aren't batted around, are even protected from violent clients.

It's been a long time since I was last in Havana and availed myself of its erotic pleasures. Considering the current power shifts in the local underworld, and those gang wars Lansky and Nilo talked about, the who's who of the cathouses is probably not the same who's who I dealt with ten years ago. As far as I know, nobody in the fancier fleshpots owes me any favors, and without an invitation from a regular client or someone else well connected, I can't get into those joints, and I don't even know where they are. I can't get information about those places without Lansky's or Nilo's help. But until that help comes, I'm on my own, with nowhere to look but the back rooms of bars, the fleabag hotels, and the streets.

CHAPTER FOUR

Turn two corners from the Prado, Havana's tree-lined boulevard of flashy hotels, neon-bright high-hat casinos, well-dressed locals, and swanky tourists, onto Consulado and the accommodations and entertainment become a lot less high-hat or flashy, the locals a lot less fashionable, and the tourists are more interested in the kind of sleaze they can't get at three o'clock in the afternoon back home in Cornfield County. Make another turn at a corner with no name and you're in the Callejón de los Burdeles, the Alley of the Brothels, a narrow strip of Hell in the Colón Quarter's red-light district.

One step into the callejón and my face is smothered in a humid fog of cheap perfumes on sweaty flesh and the stench of stale sex. The aromas ooze into my nose and seep into my mouth, puckering my lips and tongue. Clashing music from radios and tinny phonographs rolls through the sticky air from saloons, cafés, and the open windows of flea-bitten brothels; conga drums and brasses collide with steamy crooners and sentimental strings. I'm tossed around by despair and desire at the sight of so much sex for sale by so many women of so many colors of flesh, some pale as linen, others dark as coal smoke, and all the lovely shades between. Women in fishnets and flashy spangles and not much else beckon with curling fingers, smeared smiles, and voices flirtatious and brittle in Spanish and English: *Ven aquí, chica. You want a good time?* Here and there, pretty boys give me the eye before they realize their mistake and look past me with a sly smile. I'm not their clientele, but we understand each other completely.

So many faces, so many swaying, desperate bodies, the young bodies still succulent, the older faces wise in the ways of staying alive for one more day. They all see me and figure me, know what I am and what I like. They call to me with the promise to provide it.

I want to see Sophie among these faces. I want to find her, take her home, leave Havana, get out from under Lansky's thumb, get back to New York, bathe Sophie clean in my arms.

I don't want to see Sophie here in this filthy street with its scabby bodies and destroyed lives. Not here. Not here…

"Cantor Gold?" My name comes up next to me through a woman's voice, an American voice, gravelly from too many cigarettes, too much booze, and probably too many years earning the rent on her back or her knees.

The voice is faintly familiar, but when I turn to look, the face—its high cheekboned, blue-eyed remnants of a once delicate beauty now puffy under bottle-brunette waves—brings the memory home. "Agnes Cain," I say. In her expensive light blue linen suit and matching little hat, the fishnet veil softening the life-smart lines of her face, she's a lot better dressed than she used to be. Her cathouse must be doing well.

Like all savvy working girls, and the madams who employ them, Agnes can read a face straight through to the thoughts in your head. "I'm down here shopping," she says, going right to the question that's evidently written all over me. "See if there's any fresh new trade I can buy off the street and put to work for me. But what about you, Cantor? I haven't seen you in Havana in years." She puts her hand on my chin, turns my face this way and that, examining. "You've bought yourself a few scars since I saw you—what?—ten years ago? Before the war, anyway. You know, those scars suit you, especially that knife-shaped number above your lip. Makes you look dashing. But what are you doing here? I never pegged you for the gutter trade." I'm about to answer her, even press her for information about Sophie, but she's not through with me. She puts her alligator clutch under her arm, slips her arm through mine, and walks with me along the street as if strutting me down the aisle. "You know," she says in the intimate manner of a bride, "I'm all done with my business here, so what do you say we go back to my place? I've moved up in the world since the last time you patronized my establishment. I run a top-of-the-line house now."

"From what I hear, the local gangs have a grip on the houses. How do you get by?"

"Same as I always have. Same as everybody. I pay whoever's in charge. It used to be the cops, now it's the gangs for protection," she says with a shrug. "Tell you the truth, the gangs are easier to deal with than the cops. Less greedy. So how about it, Cantor? I've got a lovely little sweetie at my place who's right up your alley. I know it's been a long time, but a good businesswoman never forgets a customer's tastes." The smile she gives me could eat right through my teeth.

I stop our walk. "Okay, Agnes, let's do business. What's an hour cost with that lovely little sweetie?"

A hand on her hip, and with the chummy attitude of a peddler trying to sell me a souvenir tablecloth, she says, "For you, a special price, Cantor, as a way of welcoming you back as a customer. So shall we say a hundred dollars American? But if you're paying in pesos—"

"Uncle Sam's burning a hole in my pocket." I take a hundred from my stash in my jacket and take out the photo of me and Sophie. I give Agnes the hundred but hold on to the photo. "We can do our business right here, Agnes. The hundred's for information. I'm looking for this woman," I say, showing her the photo. "She was kidnapped in New York and brought into the Havana flesh trade over three years ago. Ever see her?" My breath sticks in my chest while Agnes looks at the photo. Maybe my search can end here. Maybe Agnes recognizes Sophie, knows where she is. Maybe it's even Agnes who has her...

The veil of her hat sways as Agnes shakes her head.

My breath seeps out again.

But Agnes keeps looking at the photo a little longer before looking back up at me. That hat veil does nothing to soften the look in her eyes, filled with both pity and scorn. "You look like you could use a drink," she says.

I'd like to drown my disappointment in a whole bottle, but a friendly bit of alcohol with Agnes could loosen her lips, tell me who's the current who's who in Havana's sex racket. "I'll buy," I say.

She gives me a coquettish smile that wore out years ago and rips the photo of me and Sophie in half, right down the middle.

I don't hit women, and I've been known to exact a terrible price from guys who do, but right now it takes every ounce of my willpower not to swat Agnes across the face for her desecration. My jaw's so tight I'm afraid my teeth will crack by the time she gives back Sophie's half of the picture, and says, "If you're going to show this woman's picture around town and expect to get information from anyone"—she hands back the half of the picture with me—"never let them see your heart."

❖

After the rotten air and rotting bodies of the Callejón de los Burdeles, being back on the Prado feels almost as good as a shower and clean underwear.

Agnes leads me to the Hotel Sevilla Biltmore at the corner of Trocadero. Aside from the Sevilla's recent tower wing, the original architecture is less Havana Neon and more Moorish Spain, a curlicued confection of Islamic scalloped and trefoil windows, Classical Greco-Roman arches, and Spanish grillwork balconies, all of it wrapped up in bright tropical colors. The lobby is a headache of patterned tile, and I'm relieved when Agnes leads us out of it and into a pleasant Spanish courtyard where well-dressed ladies and gents are enjoying afternoon cocktails at pretty little tables. Quiet conversations, mostly in Spanish and English but here and there with a curl of French and a spike of German, float in the warm air, drift around through cigarette and cigar smoke.

Just like back in the States, the ladies and gents give me the slant eye as Agnes leads me to a table. But unlike the States, where some highfalutin prude would quietly complain to a maître d' or bell captain to have me removed from normal company, Havana is an anything goes kinda town, where the locals take anyone's money, and the tourists shed their prudish inhibitions and just enjoy the town's lust.

After a waiter takes our drink order—daiquiri for Agnes, Chivas neat for me—I say, "Okay, Agnes, my hundred cash American is going to buy me questions and answers. First question—since it's clear you're still in the trade, I assume you know who's operating the houses? The classier spots all the way to the dives."

She takes a pack of smokes from her alligator clutch, snaps the bag shut, and holds a cigarette between her fingers. Giving me that worn-out-but-still-trying-to-be-coquettish smile, she waits for me to light the smoke.

I'm willing to play the chivalry game if it softens Agnes's heart. I pull out my lighter and hold its flame to her cigarette. She glances up at me as she takes a drag of the smoke, looking at me as if she wants to buy my soul.

After lighting a cigarette for myself, I'm about to press Agnes to come across with the answer to my question when the waiter arrives with our drinks. Agnes, barely noticing the young man, says to him, "Please ask Señor Hidalgo to join us."

"Who's Hidalgo?" I ask when the waiter's gone.

"The hotel's chief concierge. We're old friends."

"Friendly enough to be my friend, too?"

"That depends on you, Cantor."

"Yeah, my money can be very friendly. Meantime, answer my question, Agnes. Do you know the operators or information brokers I need to talk to?"

Taking a deep pull on her cigarette, then exhaling as slowly as she can, letting the smoke coil around us while she enjoys stringing me along, she finally says, "But I've already answered it, Cantor."

Hidalgo.

He arrives at our table, elegant in pomaded splendor, his well-tailored brown linen suit generally succeeding in camouflaging his plump physique. "Agnes," he says, bending to kiss her offered cheek, his Spanish inflected pronunciation softening her hard-edged Yankee name.

Turning to me, he looks me over with his small eyes, two dots of passionless brown in his smooth face on a round, balding head. His eyes momentarily narrow and then recover after he's sized me up and figured me. Smiling, sort of, his very white teeth peeking between thin lips, he extends his hand. We shake our greeting. His hand is fleshy, soft, and expensively manicured. "Rudi Hidalgo," he says and sits down.

Agnes says, "Rudi, this is Cantor Gold, and she'd like to do a little business," getting right to the meat, adding, "She's good for it," meaning he can gouge me for cash.

I don't bother wasting time with pleasantries. "Since Agnes threw it on the table, let's get to business," I say. "The business I'm here to talk about is Havana's sex trade. And please don't act like you're offended," I say in response to his phony offended sniff. "Agnes wouldn't have brought me here if you weren't the man to see."

Agnes smiles and shrugs like the cat that let the canary fly away instead of eating it. Hidalgo smiles through an awkward clearing of his throat.

I pull out the photo of Sophie. The torn edge grazes her cheek and tears me up inside. "I'm looking for this woman," I say, pushing my emotions aside as I show the picture to Hidalgo. I keep my voice flat, give away nothing. "She was forced onto a flesh boat in New York and brought here. The boat's name is the *Belle Caribe*. Ever hear of it?"

Hidalgo looks at the photo, runs his finger along the torn edge as if trying to imagine what, or who, is missing. "Beautiful woman," he finally says. "However I have no memory of seeing her. But yes, I have heard of the *Belle Caribe*. She sails the world but is not now in our waters, so you are out of luck if you'd hoped to question her captain. But there are many such ships which supply Havana."

The way he says *supply*, like he's talking about a butcher shop delivery, turns my stomach.

But Hidalgo is still talking, and I have to hang on his every word despite my twisting guts, listen for even the smallest kernel of information that could help me find Sophie. "That does not mean this woman is not here in the city," he says, "only that I do not recall seeing her. Not here in my hotel, anyway." The invitation to pitch him a bribe could not have been clearer if he'd put his hand in my pocket.

"What will it take to refresh your memory?" I say.

He gives back the picture. The tight smile on his face is annoyingly close to a sneer. "Let me ask you something," he says. "Why do you want to find this woman?"

I keep looking at Hidalgo but see Agnes in the corner of my eye, her expression reminding me to keep my heart hidden and my own face blank. "She was stolen from me," is all I say.

Hidalgo's eyes narrow again, like he's trying to make out a speck in the distance and decide if that speck is friend, enemy, or just plain lost. "Stolen?" he says. "From your business?"

I don't like the line he's taking. I don't like lying about my feelings for Sophie, and I don't like Hidalgo's assumption that I'm her pimp. But I don't have to like any of those things. I just have to like Hidalgo's information, if he really has any, because I don't like being shaken down, either.

I pull two hundred in American bills from my stash, spread the bills on the table so Hidalgo can see the amount, but keep my hand on the cash, keep him from grabbing it. "Here's two hundred answers to your questions, Señor Hidalgo. That should buy me everything you know about who to see in the flesh trade in this town."

This time, Hidalgo's smile even has a little laugh behind it, the kind of snide chuckle you get from someone who thinks you're an idiot. "This is not real money," he says. "This is just the sit-down stake in my Friday night card game."

The guy's good. He's just played me into a tricky spot. If I let him shake me down for more cash, I'm a sucker who he can feed useless information while he pockets my dough. But if I don't fork over, he just says toodle-oo, gets up from the table, and keeps what he knows to himself. I'd be no closer to getting a lead on finding Sophie.

I've got only one way out of this corner: play to the guy's card playing tastes for a gamble. "Agnes," I say, "I never figured you for a chump."

"What?" It comes out through a snort of her daiquiri.

"You're a chump if you believe this guy's the big buck around here. Only little guys, the second-stringers, play the bluff. Makes them feel important. Do you feel important now, Señor Hidalgo?"

Hidalgo leans across the table, his smile now sharp, toothy, cold, his tiny brown eyes drilling straight through me. "Do *you?*"

"Compared to who?" I push back, hoping for a jackpot payoff.

Hidalgo leans back again, still smiling as he takes a deep breath and then lets it out slowly. Something's coming at the end of that breath. With any luck it's my jackpot payoff. "Compared to Meyer Lansky," he says.

It's hard work to keep the flat expression on my face.

"You Americans think we Cubanos are dull-witted children dancing in the sun to mambo music all day," he says. "Well, we are used to the sun, we are not blinded by its glare the way you Yanquis are. We see everything very clearly. And that mambo music? We hear every ripple in the tune, just the way I heard through the concierge brotherhood that Señor Lansky met with you this morning. Oh yes, everyone in the hotel business knows who is coming and going." My breath is barely moving. I hear Agnes suck hers in. Hidalgo just keeps smiling. "So keep your money, Gold. Your two hundred Yanqui dollars are nothing to me. If you want my help in finding this woman, it will cost you something more important than American cash."

I don't know which mistake is worse: underestimating the reach of Rudi Hidalgo or overestimating the power of Meyer Lansky, or if either idea is a mistake at all. For the moment, all my chips are with Hidalgo, who's just thrown down chips of his own.

I put the two hundred away. "All right, Señor Hidalgo. Suppose you tell me just what it will cost me to see what you're holding."

With the relaxed satisfaction of a piranha who's just chewed a particularly tasty prey to the bone, Hidalgo says, "Be at Agnes's establishment this evening at eight o'clock. Someone will come and give you a small package. I want you to take it to Lansky."

"Why don't you take it to him yourself?"

"It will be better if you take it," he says with a shrug. "You were his welcome guest this morning. He knows you, and he will see you."

"You don't know him?"

"Not as well as I would like. Not yet."

"You give me too much credit," I say. "This morning's meeting was arranged through a third party. Lansky might not see me just on my say-so."

"Of course he will see you. He is a good businessman, and a good businessman does not ignore unexpected details. He deals with them. Having you show up at his door so soon after your meeting is an unexpected detail he will deal with."

For a guy who's not a close associate of Lansky's, Hidalgo seems pretty sure of how Lansky thinks. The fact is, though, he's probably right. Taking care of details is the lifeblood of any business, even mine. But details can also be lethal. "How do I know your package isn't a bomb? The kind of bomb that goes off when the package is opened?"

"Please," Hidalgo says, with an offended sneer, "do not insult my honor. I have no wish to harm Señor Lansky. I want to do business with him. My gift can open his door a little wider. So, do we have a deal?"

"That's only half a deal," I say. "Your half. When do I get my half? When do I get information about Sophie?"

"Ah. That is the young lady's name? Sophie?"

"Yeah. Sophie de la Luna y Sol."

The way Hidalgo's eyes widen, like the eyes of a small boy getting a new bicycle for Christmas, you'd think I'd told him her name was Madre Maria. "She is a Cubana?"

"No, born in the States. Her folks hailed from Puerto Rico."

His interest shrivels. He says, with another shrug, "Sophie would not be her burdel name. Do you know it?"

"Nope. But you didn't answer my question, Hidalgo. When do you come through with my half of the deal?"

"That is a fair question," he says, getting up from the table. "After you've told me you've delivered my package, I will start making inquiries."

"Uh-huh. And how will I know you're making those inquiries?"

"I tell you what. I will give you something now, as a gesture of...good faith. Isn't that what you Americans call it? Good faith?"

"Yeah, that's what we call it. We also call it a down payment. And yours better be hefty, Hidalgo."

"I do not know this word, *hefty.* But what I am going to give you might be worth your while." He takes a pen and small pad from his inside pocket, writes something on the pad, tears off the sheet of paper, and hands it to me. He's written a name: Tomas Santiago.

"Who is he?" I say.

"The leader of Los Perros Enojados, the Angry Dogs. The biggest and most dangerous street gang in Havana. If your Sophie is in the hands of one of the gangs or in any of the brothels he deals with, he will know."

"And where can I find him?"

"First you do my favor"—he tut-tuts—"and then I will do yours. In the meantime, I advise you not to look for Santiago on your own. He will hear of it, and he will have you killed. And now, I bid you good afternoon. Agnes," he says, reaching for her hand and lightly kissing her fingertips, "you will see that our guest"—he nods at me—"is accommodated this evening?"

"Of course, Rudi."

"Very good. And do not worry about the bill for your drinks," he adds with a salesman's good cheer. "You are my guests!"

When he's gone, Agnes says, "Well, it looks like I'll get you to my place after all, Cantor."

"Looks like it. Give me the address."

She takes the paper Hidalgo gave me, and with a pen from her purse writes her address and gives the paper back to me. Smiling her best saleswoman smile, she says, "Are you sure I can't interest you in some afternoon sweets? It's only"—she reaches for my wrist and turns it to look at my watch—"a little past four thirty. You have plenty of time until Rudi's man comes tonight."

"Thanks anyway, Agnes," I say, getting up from the table. "I have to see a guy about a painting."

❖

Sig told me to deliver a letter. Lansky challenged me to deliver a painting. And Hidalgo wants me to deliver a package. I don't remember going into the delivery business, but here I am. Maybe I should get a uniform, save myself a lot of tailoring bills.

And in exchange for all this delivering? A whole lotta maybes: maybe Lansky can get a line on where Sophie was taken; maybe Hidalgo can find out if Sophie's in a fancy house or trapped in a dive; maybe this Tomas Santiago won't have me killed.

The only sure thing in all this is that I'll stay in Cuba until I find Sophie, that I'll do whatever it takes—deliver packages, steal paintings, beat someone bloody until they talk—because what's left of my broken heart can't break any more or it will crumble to dust.

CHAPTER FIVE

The rental desk at my hotel didn't have a Buick, my preferred automotive conveyance, so I wound up with a '51 Olds convertible, oxblood red with white interior and white sidewalls. It'll do.

It's a golden late afternoon, perfect for a drive along the Malecón with the convertible's top down, sunlight sliding along the car's curves, flashing on the chrome accents, catching sparkles from the sea. I've got my panama pulled down against the sea breeze as I drive, on my way to see my old pal, the murderous Pedro "Pete" Estrada.

I used to run into Pete now and then during his trips to New York, but it's been quite a while since he was stateside, and ten years since I've been to his Havana place, a Vedado villa a few blocks off the Malecón, about fifteen minutes west of the Hotel Nacional. When I arrive, I see that nothing's changed in those ten years: the same spike-topped iron fence surrounds the property with the same ornate iron gate guarding the old-world Spanish stone pile, creamy white in the sun. Tall palm trees, swaying in the breeze, throw spikey shadows along the villa's walls and poke at the windows. The only thing missing from the old days is the thug who used to guard the gate to keep people out or let them in on Pete's instructions. The thug has evidently been replaced by the telephone gizmo mounted on a pole near the gate, reachable from the window of my car. Lifting the receiver, I hear a couple of rings and then, "Sí?" in a rough voice, which unless Pete has laryngitis, or had his throat slashed since our last chat, isn't his. I guess the thug has moved inside.

"Cantor Gold aquí...uh...para Pete," I say in my labored Spanish.

I don't have to wait long, just the minute, more or less, that it takes for the guy to pass the word and get the okay from Pete to swing the gate open.

As I pull up to the house, a guy comes out to greet me, probably the guy at the other end of the telephone gizmo. He's outfitted like a house servant but built like a truck. There's a bulge under his white jacket near the waist. It's not a muscle, though I have no doubt he's got plenty of 'em.

"You follow me," he says, his English as rough as his voice.

When we're inside the vestibule, the guy reaches to pat me down, but I push his hands away. There's no chance I'll let this guy's paws touch me. "You want my gun?" I say. "All you have to do is ask." I put one hand up to tell him to hold his horses while I reach inside my suit jacket to take my gun from my rig. "Yeah, I know, I'll get it back when I leave."

"Sí, when you are leaving," he says, none too friendly, and puts my gun in his pocket. Now he has two guns, mine and the one under his jacket in the waistband of his pants. Great. He can kill me twice.

He waves me to follow him.

There's another gate beyond the vestibule, a fussy black iron grille filling an enormous arch nearly to the ceiling. I never did like this overdone grille. Looks like tarted up jail cell bars.

Pete's house servant thug takes a ring of keys from his pocket, uses a key to unlock the grille, swings a section of it open, and we walk through into a light-filled, whitewashed two-story courtyard. The courtyard hasn't changed at all since I last saw it, still that hacienda style with a blue tiled fountain in the middle of a pale blue tiled floor, brick-crowned arches, and big blue-and-white doors off a wooden balcony running around the second floor. I've never been up there. I used to wonder what goes on behind all those big blue-and-white doors. They could just be doors to guest rooms for all I know, but I've never been an overnight guest here, and

I don't want to be. It doesn't seem like a good idea to spend the dark of night under the same roof with a guy whose professional accomplishments include paid assassin.

Pete's man leads me across the courtyard to a heavily carved wooden door. He opens it, signals me to step through, but remains outside and closes the door behind me.

I'm in the living room, which is pretty much how I remember it: the same pale sea-green walls, the same fringed lamps, the same view through glass-paned French doors out to the greenery on the veranda. What's new is the painting in a carved wooden frame over the mantel, a wild horse fashioned in wildly curving lines and wild colors. It's the painting Lansky wants me to steal, a masterpiece by the Cuban Modernist Carlos Enriquez. It took my breath away when I saw it in New York. It looks even better in its home country, where all that passion Enriquez put into the painting wants to ignite the air in the room.

Getting up from a red leather couch is Pedro "Pete" Estrada. I remember him as taller, his hair less gray than the salt-and-pepper now crowning his leathery tough-guy face, which has gotten fleshier, but not kinder. His good taste in clothes hasn't changed, though. His cream suit is tailored to perfection, the collar of his pale blue shirt is crisply pointed, and the red chevrons on his brown tie are a nice touch. In all that good taste and tailoring, you'd never guess Pete has a hefty .45 under his jacket. At least he used to. Probably still does.

The other thing about Pete which hasn't changed are his eyes, gray, dead eyes that seem to lure you into sharing death with him.

He's smiling. It's not warm. "Cantor, this is a surprise. It's been a long time," he says, his flawless English acknowledging his lineage: American mother, daughter of a hit man for the Boston Mob; Cuban father, Havana gangster. "You honor my house with your visit. What brings you to Cuba?"

Since he's brought it up, I may as well take advantage of the situation. If Pete has any answers about Sophie, maybe I can ditch Lansky and Hidalgo and not be anyone's delivery service anymore. And anyway, I need to account for just dropping by, since I'm not about to walk out of here with a four foot tall painting under my arm. That's for another visit.

I take out the photo of Sophie. "I'm looking for this woman," I say. "She's in Havana, forced into the flesh trade. I'm tapping everyone I know to get a line on her. You were always in the local pipeline, Pete, so I figured you might know who runs the houses these days, who I should talk to."

Pete's eyes flicker with a spark of lust. Sophie is a beautiful woman. I just wish Pete didn't think so. I also wish I wasn't thinking the sickening thought that maybe Pete patronized whatever house Sophie's in, patronized *her*.

"Can't help you, Cantor, sorry," he says and hands back the picture.

"Too bad. It would save me a lot of trouble."

"It might also save your life. It's not like the old days. It was beautiful then, remember? We paid off the policías and the políticos, they came to our casinos and our whorehouses, and the money just kept going around Havana in a circle. Everyone had a good time, and nobody got hurt. At least, not very often." His sudden smile is nostalgic, remembering, I suppose, the people he was hired to turn into corpses. "But nowadays," he adds with a sigh and a shrug, his eyes going back to their unfeeling flatness, "Havana is overrun by local gangs."

"Yeah, so I've heard."

"Then you know these gangs are dangerous, Cantor. They slice you up if you don't pay for protection, or buy their narcotics or their guns or their women. And they slice you up if you ask too many questions. So I am sorry I can't help you find this woman. It's too dangerous. Dangerous for you, too. But enough of this unhappy talk. Let me offer you a drink, and we can catch up, yes? What's your pleasure?"

"Scotch, neat. Chivas if you've got it."

"Certainly," he says, sitting down on the couch again and motioning me to a matching club chair nearby. He presses a button under the side table next to the couch, and within seconds the house servant thug walks in. "Dos Chivas, Armando."

"Sí, Señor Estrada."

When Armando's gone, Pete says, "So, Cantor, what's new in New York? Are you still in the art game?"

"I am." I wasn't planning on giving away my interest in his painting, but now that he's opened that door, the right conversation might give me an idea of what kind of security he's got protecting it.

I give the painting a nonchalant glance, say, "So why didn't you ask me to get that nice Carlos Enriquez for you, Pete?"

"Oh, I got it legal. No strings."

"It's a terrific painting, but I never figured you for the art type."

"I'm not. I mean, this picture is very nice, but that's not why I bought it."

"Investment, then? It should bring you a pretty dollar over time. Enriquez is going places. After his showing at the Modern, the New York art money is taking notice."

Armando comes back with our drinks before Pete answers, but after he's gone again, Pete says, "How long has it been since you were in Havana, Cantor?"

"Spring of '42."

"Well, a lot's changed. The local street gangs are pretty much the only native Cubans still in the game. They've pushed out—or killed—the old-time Cuban operators, you know, the traditional big shots who had class, or at least wanted it. The Americans are filling that void now, taking over the big operations, even picking which politicians to run the government. The Americans are starting to run it all. But look, I don't mind all that. I'm half Yanqui, after all. But I'm also half Cubano, so I'm getting squeezed between the two to pick a side."

"So which side are you picking?"

"Let's just say there are people I want to succeed, and people I want to…well, fail." I get the impression that the word fail was a last minute substitute for the word *die*. "This painting was my way of testing some American waters," he says. "Once I heard who was interested in it, I had to have it. You know who that was, Cantor? Meyer Lansky, the brainy boy himself. I didn't care if took every centavo I had, I was going to outbid him and get this painting. And

I was right. He's been tickling my ass about the painting ever since. He wants to lord it over me, the last Cubano from the old days, make a big show of the new American power. Now I wait and see how far he'll go. Let's see what he'll give me for it, maybe in money, maybe a spot in his organization. So far, what he's offered for the painting isn't good enough. Chicken feed that won't supply me with good meals or good women. And I'm not interested in his money anyway."

"Has he been here to see it?"

"Nah. I won't let him anywhere near it. I don't trust the little bastard."

"What's he gonna do?" I say with a chummy laugh I hope seduces information from Pete. "Walk out of here with it under his coat?"

With a laugh of his own, the kind that flaunts petty power, like the laugh of a kid pulling the wings off flies, he says, "Couldn't if he tried. I got an electric button behind the painting. If you take it off the wall, that button pops out and alarms go off. Armando would be on him in seconds, with the cops not far behind."

Bingo.

"Well, Pete," I say as I get up after a last swig of my scotch, "if you change your mind about selling the painting, give me a call. I have collectors who'd—"

"Nope. I ain't selling," he says, pressing the button under the side table before getting up from the couch. "The buyer could be a Lansky proxy. Let me tell you, Cantor, that little New York piece of pastrami will *never* get his hands on it. Not as long as I'm alive." If there was any more cold hate in his eyes, they'd ice over.

"Suit yourself," I say with a shrug. "Look, I'm at the Plaza in Habana Vieja. If you hear anything that could lead me to the woman in the photo, get in touch with me, yeah? I'll make it worth your while, Pete. You know I'm good for the dough."

He claps me on the back like we're the best of friends. "Sure, sure," he says as Armando comes through the door. "We go back a long ways, Cantor. I know you're good for it. But I gotta tell you, those gang boys play it pretty close. Not sure how much I can help.

Meantime, don't be a stranger while you're in Havana." Then he claps me on the back again, saying, "Armando will show you out," the smile gone.

Armando walks behind me, making sure I don't get nosy and wander off into forbidden parts of the house. But I'm nosy anyhow, in a professional way. I memorize the living room windows, the placement of the French doors to the veranda, have a glance at the lock on the living room door as we walk through, figuring how to pick it if I need to, or if it's wired. Crossing the courtyard, I note the number and location of windows, count how many steps from the living room, and make a quick study of the lock on the courtyard's iron grille. It's definitely not wired, not unless Pete's planning on electrocuting Armando if he fumbles his key or spills Pete's drink on the iron bars.

When we reach the vestibule, Armando, unsmiling, without any shred of courtesy expected of a house servant, takes my .38 from his pocket and gives it back to me. Then he opens the front door.

I'm sure if I hadn't walked through he'd have pushed me out.

❖

A slow drive around Pete's block refreshes my memory of the setup of the fence and palm trees around his villa. Since Pete's gone modern with his electric entry gate and the alarm behind the Enriquez painting, I'm especially interested in spotting any wires or those newfangled radar detection boxes that are the rage in fancy burglar alarms back home. Not that I can't get around them, I just like to be prepared.

I don't see any electrical equipment, no wires, no detection boxes, just the ugly spikes topping that iron fence. Putting that information together with my observations inside the house, I run various plans through my mind as I drive back to my hotel. Traffic slows to a crawl along the Malecón—the six o'clock snarl of tourist-occupied taxis on their way to and from hotels, city buses with restaurant and casino workers on their way to the night shift, private cars with office workers and limos with big shots all going home for dinner—the slow pace gives me time to carefully think things over, walk it through. By the time I'm back at the Plaza, I know the stuff I'll need for the job and where to get it.

Up in my room, I call room service for a bottle of Chivas and a light dinner of chicken and rice with an ensalada des frutas of fresh mangoes, melon, and pineapple. The concierge says it will be about thirty minutes. I fill the time with a leisurely shower, and a phone call to Nilo Anaya.

CHAPTER SIX

Agnes wasn't kidding when she said she's got herself a top-of-the-line establishment. Her jewel box of a two-story house on a quiet, palm shrouded street is a far cry from the raucous ramshackle joint I used to visit in the Colón. But what that old brothel lacked in fancy charm it more than made up for in services. Agnes understood that a client who feels welcome and at ease, and isn't nickeled and dimed for every sip of whiskey and every minute of erotic pleasure, is a loyal client.

And, oh yeah, Agnes had great taste in women. That old place might've been down at the heel, but that didn't stop Agnes from stocking it with the classiest females she could find. And her taste in men was also right on the mark. Young and pretty ones, sure, but older pros, too, guys whose gigolo days were over but who still knew how to satisfy a lonely woman or an equally lonely man. Agnes's slummy old dive catered to every type of client with every type of taste, all preferences provided for. The Havana cops and other believers in machismo didn't like the idea of male trade, but Agnes paid plenty for the privilege of turning their eyeballs the other way. And anyway, it was Havana, whose sultry, perfumed nights still melt prudish morality into a sidewalk puddle.

I push those pleasant old memories aside as I get out of the Oldsmobile and walk up the shadowy, flower-lined path to the front door of Agnes's fancy new joint.

It's about seven forty-five, already dark, and in the raking glow of streetlamps the peach colored house and its polished Caribbean rosewood door are fleshy invitations to enjoy the flesh within. But I'm not here to satisfy my lust. I'm here to repair my heart, get a line—*any* line, no matter how thin or tangled—to finding Sophie. There's a twist in my gut telling me I could be very near yet very far from her, and it's killing me not to know which is which. Killing me, too, is an image eating at my mind: someone just like me, or not like me, or meaner than I am, or needier, walking up a similar path to a similar establishment with money in hand to buy Sophie's body and attentions. I hate that nameless, faceless person.

Yeah, sure, my own hypocrisy bites me in the face again, shoving its cold question down my throat: how many mothers and fathers of women of pleasure, how many worried husbands, sons, daughters, lovers, have hated *me*?

I ring the doorbell, my hat in hand, my gut twisting tighter. My mouth is dry.

The melody and rhythm of a lovely Cuban danzón flows softly from inside the house when Agnes opens the door. She's all decked out in a gold lamé gown that reminds me of a getup I saw in an Ava Gardner picture, except Ava Gardner is svelte and beautiful and Agnes is puffy. But there's beauty in Agnes tonight. Maybe it's the classy Cuban music behind her with its strains of elegant romance, or maybe it's her no-nonsense gutter wisdom at ease with her hard-won luxuries, like the expensive lamé gown and the gold and ruby rings on her fingers. Here at the door of her stylish temple of pleasure for profit, built by perseverance and brains in a hard game, the up-from-the-Havana-gutter New England spinster Agnes Cain is beautiful.

"Come in and have a drink, Cantor," she says, leading me inside. "Chivas, neat, yes?"

I nod assent, impressed that Agnes, ever the good businesswoman, might have remembered my preferences from all those years ago. Or more likely but just as astute, that she paid attention this afternoon in the courtyard café of the Sevilla Biltmore. Either way, it's clear that Agnes still knows how to treat a guest in her establishment.

She gives my drink order and an order of a champagne cocktail for herself to a knockout redhead in a chic black low cut number as we make our way through a crowded, tropically decorated living room that smells of exotic flowers. The aroma's a seductive accompaniment to the danzón playing in the background. The people in the room could pass as guests at an up-to-date cocktail party, not customers for the flesh serving them drinks and making conversation. The men appear to be a mix of well-heeled locals and the classier variety of tourists. Agnes's working girls aren't all Cuban, or even Latin American. They seem to be from all over the place, of every race, and with languages and accents as far flung as Paris, France, and Paris, Texas. But they are all drop-dead gorgeous, and done up in evening wear that would be right at home on the world's better boulevards. Bodies slither in long, slinky gowns, or brightly colored, pencil thin cocktail dresses ending just below the knees of fabulously shapely legs. But the gowns and dresses all have one thing in common: the décolletage is cut low enough to make sure conversation is steamy, even if the chatterers are talking about the Yankees winning last year's World Series or the goings-on of the angry laborers arming themselves in the Cuban hills.

I see, though, that Agnes still caters to an assortment of tastes. Not every couple is the mix-and-match variety. Some are matched sets. Across the room, three young men, two in pale linen suits, the third in a white dinner jacket which shimmers, gather in the softly golden light of a tall, amber-shaded lamp. I can't tell who's working and who's paying, but that threesome is going to be expensive. And standing in a corner, leaning against a wall of bookshelves, is a conservatively dressed matchstick of a woman who's trying her best to resist the onset of age. She's extending her adventuresome youth, at least for tonight, with the companionship of a stunning brunette whose fiery red lipstick and hoop earrings are meant to accentuate a tourist's fantasy of Cuban womanhood. Miss—Mrs. on the sly?— Matchstick is eating it up. And frankly, so am I.

Until it starts to claw at me. Is this what Sophie is being forced to do? Be a caricature, a Sophie de la Luna y Sol posed to satisfy someone's Latin Lovely fantasy? And it's clawing at me twice as bad because, once again, Havana is throwing my own hypocrisy in my face: I'd be lying if I didn't admit it was once part of my fantasy, too. One night I playfully told Sophie how beautiful she'd look with a mantilla. She curtly reminded me she was born and raised in New Jersey. Put in my place, but bowled over by her pushback spirit and fierce pride, I fell in love with her all over again.

I have to find her. I have to love her even better.

"It's almost eight," I say to escape the pain of memory and bring myself back to business as Agnes and I take seats in a couple of club chairs. The chairs are well upholstered in a deep purple that caters to whatever you're wearing. It looks swell against my light gray linen suit. And the little blond wood table between us, where I put down my panama, sets off the purple upholstery nicely, too. I'm not surprised that Agnes's new money allows her to buy herself a lot of swank, and I suppose I'm not surprised that her good taste in girls and boys extends to good taste in decor.

I say, "Listen, Agnes, I hope Hidalgo's delivery boy arrives on time," looking around for someone who might fill the bill.

"I'm sure he will, Cantor. Believe me, Rudi is a man of his word. But what's your hurry?" she says with a raised brow and a sly smile, her eyes twinkling with mischief and business. "Are you really planning to deliver the package to Lansky tonight? He probably has better things to do, like squeezing more money from Cuba."

"You sound like you don't approve of the guy," I say. "I figured you like people who make money."

"Of course, I do," she says as if I should know better. "And I've got nothing against Lansky. I just hope that when he and his mobster friends finally take over the whole island they remember who made things easier for them."

"I take it you're greasing his wheels."

"Let's just say I'm not gumming up the gears."

The sensational redhead who took our drink order returns with my Chivas and Agnes's champagne cocktail. When the redhead sets my glass down on the table, she bends low enough to make sure I have a good view of the goods and a whiff of her musky perfume. Her black dress is a marvel of peekaboo engineering, providing a view all the way down from cleavage to belly button, and a bit of shadow below. "Is there something else I can help you with?" she says, her voice silky as hosiery sliding off a leg and with an accent hovering somewhere west of New York but east of California.

Agnes says, "We'll let you know, Veronica, dear," slightly tossing her head for Veronica to get lost, but not too far lost.

The scotch helps settle me, until a pair of legs in fishnet stockings appear at my side. Above the legs is a sweet little gift from the Far East in a lacy black outfit with a tray of cigarettes at her waist. "I have American cigarettes," she says in a lilting Chinese accent, figuring me out right away. I have to hand it to Agnes—she not only hires the most beautiful, she hires the smartest.

I already have a pack of smokes in my pocket, but I'm not about to turn this cutie down, or deny Agnes a profit, so I ask for a pack of Chesterfields. She gives me the fifteen cent pack, and I give her an American buck. She keeps the change without even asking.

Yeah, Agnes hires the smartest.

I'm lighting a smoke and offering one to Agnes, who ignores it and waves someone over instead. "Hola, Basilio," she says to the muscular guy with the dark-skinned saddlebag face and badly fitting sharkskin suit. He arrives carrying a small package, maybe four inches square, wrapped in brown paper and string.

"Hola, Señorita Agnes," he says through a phlegmy whisper. He passes Hidalgo's package to Agnes, who puts it on the table.

Agnes lifts the hem of her gown, takes a Cuban note from a wad in her garter, and gives Basilio the money. "Gracias, Basilio. Buenas noches," she says and waves him away.

His mouth droops in disappointment, his hopes of being invited to hang around the moneyed crowd, maybe enjoy the pleasures of a pretty woman, dashed with the wave of the boss lady's jeweled hand. As he lumbers away, he's like the proverbial dog slinking away with his tail between his legs. I feel sorry for the guy, but not much.

I stub out my smoke in the ashtray on the table and reach for the package. "I'll be on my way, then. What do I owe you for the drink?"

But Agnes's hand comes down on mine, one of her rings hard against my knuckle. "The whiskey's on the house tonight. Let's just say it's my gift to you. So why the rush, Cantor? I doubt Lansky's expecting a package delivery tonight. You can bring it to him in the morning. Meantime, why not enjoy yourself?" She motions for Veronica to join us again, then bends toward me, says in an intimate whisper, "Like I told you today, you were a good customer in my early days, so let me welcome you back with a good time at a good rate." She loads every word with the promise of pleasure.

Veronica's behind me, her musky scent drifting around me, its seductive appeal mingling with the music in the room. Her hands slide onto my shoulders, her midriff is against the back of my head, as her hands now slide down the front of me. It feels good, better than I want it to. And then she stops, suddenly, when she feels the gun under my jacket. She bends to me, her breast against my shoulder, her lips against my ear as she whispers, "I promise to keep your weapon safe."

It's not easy to pull away from the too tempting Veronica, and I don't quite make it all the way, even as I say, "This is not what I had in mind tonight, Agnes."

"You have something better to do?"

Actually, yes. I have a painting to steal.

But Veronica's breath in my ear, her hands on my body, and her warm lips and flick of her tongue on my neck are making escape difficult.

Her hands move between my legs. Escape is now impossible.

❖

The exact moment when my resisting mind caved in to what my body wanted is a blur, but here in a second floor bedroom equipped with toys for every taste, it doesn't matter. Nothing matters except the fire inside me, a need, a craving, for all that Veronica knows how to do, lets me do. She's figured me out fast, who I am and what I am, and she accommodates all of it.

All of it.

❖

I wake up to Veronica sitting next to me in a swirl of rumpled bedsheets. Cigarette smoke catches lamplight as it curls along her face, her red hair tousled, her body flushed and lovely. Not a bad way to wake up.

She puts her cigarette to my lips, and after a satisfying pull and exhale, I say, "How long have I been out?"

"Not long," she says in that silky voice. "Maybe twenty minutes. I thought you'd be out longer. We were at it over two hours."

Two wild hours I hadn't planned on and should probably regret, but the sanctimony would strangle me.

It's a crummy thing to admit, but I'm just now really looking at Veronica's face for the first time. The lamplight is kind to her, not that she needs any special arrangements. She's beautiful, maybe twenty-three, twenty-four years old, and with something more than just gorgeous blue eyes, cheekbones that the Classical sculptors would've loved to get their hands on, and lips molded to lust-fulfilling perfection. There's also a remnant of sweetness in her eyes. But just a remnant. Hundreds of nights like this one, servicing a thousand needs and enduring a thousand fucks, have shredded the girlish sweetness which might have been natural to her. Behind its ragged remnant is…I don't know. It's too deeply hidden, where Veronica can keep it alive. Maybe it keeps her from feeling dead.

"Is Veronica your real name?" I say, just to make conversation and block the misery of imagining Sophie suffering Veronica's fate.

"Does it matter?" she says with a shrug.

"Probably not. Just curious." With conversation going nowhere, and with a painting waiting for me to steal to make Lansky happy enough to use his clout on my behalf, I slip the remainder of the cigarette from Veronica's fingers, take a last drag as I get up, stub it out in the ashtray on the night table, and get ready to leave. Two hours, even at Agnes's good rate, is going to cost me.

"Elspeth."

"What?" I say, still sitting at the edge of the bed.

"Elspeth. Elspeth Beattie. From Galena, Ohio. Not that it's any of your business."

"Actually, it might be my business. Just not in the way you might think. Listen, lovely Elspeth Beattie"—that gets a small, reluctant smile from her—"how long have you been in Havana?"

"Three years almost."

"And before that? Something tells me you didn't come to Havana straight from Galena, Ohio."

Laughing, she says, "They probably never even heard of Havana in Galena, Ohio! No, I left little ol' Galena for the bright lights of Chicago. I figured I'd make it big there, maybe get a spot dancing in a nightclub. I was always a good dancer. Leggy, y'know?"

Yeah, I just had two hours' worth of dancing lessons.

Her easygoing reminiscence slides into a sneer so mournful it's like someone died. "Things…didn't work out," she says. "Next thing I know, I'm walking the streets just to keep a roof over my head and food on the table. But those Chicago winters nearly killed me, and when I heard some of the boys—"

"Mob guys?"

"Yeah, probably. Anyway, when I heard them talk about the action in Havana, I said that's for me, and I got the hell outta Chicago. Been here ever since."

"How'd you know to come to Agnes?"

"I didn't. I started out in that awful alley in the Colón."

"The Callejón de los Burdeles?"

"Yeah, that place." She folds her arms around herself as if trying to keep her flesh from bleeding with the lousy memory. "Agnes found me there. She shops the alley, you know, finds young girls she thinks might do okay in her house, buys them from the pimps who run the alley. Believe me, I'm grateful. Agnes runs a good setup.

Takes care of her girls." Her chitchat suddenly dries up, replaced by a nervous, frowning suspicion. "What's any of this to you?"

"I want to show you something," I say and grab my suit jacket from a nearby chair, take out the photograph of Sophie. "Have you ever seen this woman here in Havana?"

She looks at the picture, looks up at me, gives me a half smile that says she's got my number. "You have good taste, Cantor Gold. She's beautiful. At least, if she still looks like this."

"What do you mean, if she still looks like this? Why wouldn't she?" I know the terrible answer before the words are even out of my mouth.

But it's Elspeth "Veronica" Beattie who makes the horror real. "Because I think she's got it rough."

"Then you've seen her?"

"Yeah, I think so. About a year ago."

"*Where?*" I say it so hard, the woman shrinks from me. But I come back with, "Please," with as much tenderness as I can muster.

Maybe it's that remnant of sweetness that brings her hand to my face to stroke my cheek. "Honey, I'll tell you, but it's going to send you down a dark tunnel."

"Tell me."

She nods as if it's a waste of time to feel sorry for me, then says, "I think I saw your girl—She is your girl, right? You're crazy about her?"

"Crazy enough about her to slide into that dark tunnel to find her."

"Yeah, you're crazy. Okay, here's the lay of it. I'm pretty sure I saw her at a party for a big shot politician and his cronies. Agnes and some of the other houses supplied the girls. But there was something else going on there, something you're not going to like."

"I don't care if I like it. I have to know what happened to her."

"Suit yourself, but it's your funeral, or maybe—" She stops herself before she says the dreaded word *hers*, slides her eyes away from me for a second, then looks back at me and gives me an apologetic shrug. She follows that up with a deep breath, the kind that announces bad news. "There was an auction," she says. "Highest bidder won the girl of his choice. She was the choice."

First I didn't want to hear the word *hers*. Now my stomach knots at the word *his*.

I don't want to hear the details. Every word would skin me alive. I only need to know one thing. "Where is she?"

"I don't know where she is. But the guy who won her might. He took her out of there."

"Who is he? *What's his name?*"

"Tomas Santiago," she says.

I'm dressed and downstairs so fast my shirt's still only partly buttoned and my tie's still in my jacket pocket. I spot Agnes talking to a silver-haired gent in a fashionably lapelled dinner jacket who fancies himself aristocracy, or maybe he is aristocracy and he's not going to approve of my rude ways. But I don't care what he thinks as I push my way across the crowded room and grab Agnes by the arm. Without even an *excuse me* to the gent, I yank Agnes away from him.

Agnes's surprise at my rough behavior quickly becomes annoyance. "Let go of me, Cantor! What do you think you're—"

"Why did you lie to me, Agnes? Did Santiago pay you to lie? Or was it Hidalgo?"

"What the hell are you talking about?" She squirms in my grip, tries to escape. When she looks around the room and nods, I notice a couple of bruisers headed our way.

I don't want trouble, I want answers. I let go of Agnes's arm.

The bruisers slink back out of sight.

Agnes, rubbing her arm, says, "Is that any way to treat an old friend?"

"Yeah, some *old friend*," I say with a sneer so tight it barely lets the words through. "You lied to me, Agnes. You knew Sophie was taken by Tomas Santiago. You knew it even when Hidalgo dangled

Santiago's name today. I bet Hidalgo knew it, too. What's your game, Agnes? What are you and Hidalgo playing at? And where do I find this Santiago?"

"The only games I play are the ones I teach my girls, which, by the look of you," she says through a wisecrack leer, "you seem to have enjoyed. Now suppose you calm down and tell me what you're talking about."

"I'm talking about a party last year for some politician. You supplied the women."

"You mean that shindig for Álvarez? Cheche Álvarez? He's not a politician, he's a general. Wait a minute—you're telling me the woman you're looking for, the woman in that picture, was there?"

"Yeah, she was there. Veronica saw her. Didn't you?"

"How could I? I wasn't there. I sent over some of the goods and a couple of guys to keep an eye on them, make sure they didn't bolt, but that's all. A few other houses did, too. Maybe she came from one of those. I doubt Santiago would have sent any women to Cheche's party. He only pimps street trade."

Every word out of Agnes's mouth twists me up tighter. "He didn't send her," I say. "He *took* her. Won her in the night's flesh auction. He took her out of there."

Agnes gives me a look as close to pity as her hard business heart can offer. "If she's with Santiago—"

"Spare me the ugly details, Agnes. Just tell me where to find him. Or maybe this Álvarez character."

"You won't find Cheche Álvarez," she says, waving her hand as if swatting a fly. "He's dead. He took his soldiers into the hills to clean out a rebel nest. Instead, the revolucionarios sent home the general's uniform and his eyeballs, which was their way of telling his family he'll never see them again."

That's a new one. I don't think Sig Loreale or the other Mob guys in New York ever pulled off that nasty number. I wonder if Lansky might be underestimating the guys in the hills. "And Santiago? I want to talk to him."

Agnes guides me back to the area where we had our drink.

"You can't," she says. "Not without Rudi Hidalgo's help. And the only way he'll help you is if you do his favor." She takes the package from the table and gives it to me.

So I'm back to being a delivery service. I have to make Hidalgo happy by delivering his package to Lansky. And if I want to keep Lansky as an insurance policy, make sure I have his power behind me as I pick my way through this Havana tangle, I have to deliver his painting.

First I have to steal it.

CHAPTER SEVEN

I pull into a dark spot on an already dark street, quiet except for the nocturnal racket of tropical critters buzzing, clicking, and whining in the trees. I put the convertible top up, get out of the car, open the trunk, and take out the duffel of supplies I'd asked Nilo to put together and that I picked up on my way to Agnes's brothel. I didn't tell him why I needed the stuff or where I'd be using it, and he didn't ask.

Getting back in the car with the duffel, I pull out a knit pullover, a pair of pants, rubber gloves, and crepe soled shoes, everything black. Hidden by the night and the cramped quarters of the car, I change clothes, put my .38 in my trouser pocket, and drive away.

❖

It's a little past eleven o'clock when I arrive at Pete's place and park where the property's surrounding iron fence abuts a line of big palm trees. Moonlight between the palm fronds outlines the sharp spikes topping the fence, making them look like something cooked up for a horror movie.

The palm trees' deeply scalloped trunks will be useful though, giving me handles and toe holds when I climb Pete's fence, providing good balance when I step over the spikes. But that will have to wait. The lights are still on in the house.

Patience is a requirement in the burglary racket, patience and a bottle of booze. A fifth of Chivas is among the supplies in the duffel. I told Nilo not to bother with a glass.

By my third pull on the scotch, I'm settled comfortably, my head resting back against the driver's seat of the Olds while I wait for the lights in Pete's villa to go out, signaling that the household has gone to bed. It could be a long wait. I remember Pete as a night owl. But he's older now, grayer, and if today's conversation is any hint, less of a player than he used to be.

A fourth pull on the whiskey and a smoke from the pack I bought from that adorable cigarette girl at Agnes's shore up my patience. I open the window a crack, let the smoke curl out of the car. The silvery coils shred in the sultry breeze, tendrils drift into the Havana night. I stare at the smoke and get this crazy idea that I can put my thoughts onto one of those tendrils, let it drift across Havana to wherever Sophie is, let her know I'm here, I'm looking for her, I'm coming to take her home.

Home. The word has barely had any meaning since Sophie disappeared. Before that terrible night when my knock on her door was answered with just the chilling silence of an empty apartment, home was the dream I'd hoped to make real. Home was the place I'd planned to ask Sophie to make real with me, our own outlaw marriage, our own love nest where society's sneering disapproval couldn't touch us, a vicious beast locked outside, snarling its impotence.

I have to bring Sophie home.

But I have to find her first, and I can't do that without information. One of the requirements for that information is over that spiky fence guarding that villa whose lights are still on. The dashboard clock says it's now eleven twenty.

I rest my head back again, take another pull of the whiskey, serenaded by the clicks, chirps, buzzes, and hums of Havana's nocturnal critters. Frankly, I'd rather be listening to the snappy all-girl band at the Green Door Club back in New York, my favorite place to drown my misery over Sophie in whiskey and pretty women. But the clatter of Havana's creepers, crawlers, and flyers gives an edge to the night, keeps me awake and alert in case of a long wait.

I won't go over the fence and into the house until the lights have been off for at least a half hour, enough time for Pete—and Armando, assuming he's a live-in thug—to be tucked up and asleep. I use the time to go over my plans: the fence, the house, the living room, the wired painting. My nerves are charging up, poised like runners at a starting line. My fingers tingle.

The lights have gone out.

❖

Midnight. That sliver of now between yesterday and tomorrow, when plans made in the mind face the reality of flesh and bone. It's crime's personal moment. Crime owns midnight.

I put the black rubber gloves on. They're the smooth, tight-fitting type which leave no identifying pattern.

I leave the whiskey in the car but take the duffel.

❖

The palm trees along Pete's fence are the type whose swaying fronds make a noise like wood cracking. The sound isn't conducive to steadying my nerves. But one of the trees does the job I need it to do; its fronds hide me while its scalloped trunk provides good places to grip as I scale the fence and throw a leg over the spikes. The iron fence is slick in the humid night, and my crepe soled shoes slip on the crossbars, a spike coming too close to shanking me where I really don't want to be shanked, not if I want to keep enjoying one of life's great pleasures.

In a moment, though, I'm on the ground, crossing the lawn to the back of Pete's villa, the strap of the duffel over my shoulder. I feel the duffel's weight, feel the weave of the strap, the spongy ground under my feet, the cottony air against my face. I feel my own breath, my own skin. The excitement's kicking in, sharpening my feel for the world. Sharpening me.

I clear the low stone balustrade surrounding the veranda with an easy toss of my leg, and within a few steps—careful not to trip over the patio furniture in the darkness—I'm at the glass French doors to the living room.

It locks from the inside.

Don't believe the claptrap you see in the movies, where some smart aleck hero smashes a windowpane with his elbow, reaches inside for the doorknob, and opens the door. The reaching inside part is fine, but the smashing glass part is amateur stuff, unless, of course, you want to wake the inhabitants of the house and ask them to join you for a sherry while you're stealing the family silver.

A simple glass-cutter knife does the trick with a lot less hoopla, and I take one from the duffel of supplies. I cut a small circle just below the long, curvy door handle. The circle is big enough to slip a few fingers through, but small enough so that when I snap the glass and it falls to the living room's tile floor, the noise is minimal, just a little tinkling which won't wake anyone.

The rubber glove protects my fingers from the cut glass as I reach inside, find the knob for the lock, and turn it, then reach for the inside door handle and pull it down. The latch gives. I open the door.

Taking a flashlight from the duffel, I switch it on and walk inside.

Something is wrong.

A meat-and-latrine stench fills the living room. I put a hand to my nose and mouth to keep from gagging.

My flashlight searches the floor, runs up against the body of Pete Estrada. He's a bloody lump, his throat cut, his blood all over his shirt and in a puddle around his head on the tile floor. His pants are smeared brown where he voided his bowels, the source of violent death's inelegant bouquet.

Beyond Pete, half in–half out of the living room door, is the body of Armando, his chest a bowl of blood. The loyal thug must've died trying to protect his boss.

The assassin made quick work of death. A slash to Pete's throat, a stab to Armando's heart. A job done by an efficient killer who took care of the little details, like turning off the lights after the business was finished. No one calls the cops because a house goes dark in the middle of the night.

I wonder, for a nasty second, if I hadn't waited the half hour after the lights went out if I'd have seen the killer. I wonder if I'd have been able to stop the slaughter, or if I'd have joined Pete and Armando on the floor, another body in the bloody business.

But what *was* the business? If this was a robbery gone bad, they left behind the priciest thing in the room: the Enriquez painting. It's still on the wall.

So yeah, sure, too bad about Pete and Armando, but I won't shed a tear for either of them. Armando was a thug, and Pete was a hard guy who did his own share of murder in the old days, and maybe these days, too. He might have slowed up, but he was still working the game. I don't know who he annoyed, but a slit throat ain't no love note.

So good-bye Pedro "Pete" Estrada. Rest in peace, old pal, but I still have a job to do, a job whose completion could help me find my beloved Sophie, whose life means more to me than your death.

The job is suddenly made easier now that Pete and his thug aren't around to stop me from making off with the painting. I don't have to rush the work to avoid being discovered, don't have to tiptoe in silence, don't have to worry about making a sound and waking the household when I drag a chair to the mantel so I can reach the painting. All I need to worry about is not setting off the alarm.

I turn my flashlight off for the same reason the killer turned off the house lights. I don't need nosy neighbors sniffing around or calling the cops while I work.

I don't need light anyway. Pete described the alarm as the pressure-button type. It goes off when whatever's against it is removed, which pops the button and triggers the alarm. I've worked button jobs before. It's delicate work, but with that patience that's part of my racket I can manage. And there's just enough moonlight coming through the windows to keep the place from being pitch dark.

Standing on the chair, the first thing I do is touch the painting with a gentle pressure to see if the canvas is backed with a solid panel. The give in the canvas tells me it's not. So I run my fingers very lightly along the surface and find what I'm feeling for at the typical place for a painting this size, about four feet tall by three feet wide: the juncture of the horizontal and vertical stretcher bars at the center of the canvas. That's where the alarm button will be.

I pull a long, thin, flat piece of steel, about a yard long, from the duffel. If Nilo followed instructions, and I'm sure he did, the steel is an inch wide by a thirty-second of an inch thick, thin enough to slide between the center vertical stretcher bar and the wall, thick enough to keep it steady. Two inches above the bottom of the steel is a three inch wrapping of extra strong, extra sticky double-sided tape.

Holding the tape-free bottom of the steel between my rubber gloved fingers, I place it flat against the wall at the lower edge of the painting's fancy wooden frame. I take a deep, long breath, let it out very slowly, let it control my excitement to make it work for me, keep me sharp. I move my breathing into easy, shallow breaths that won't jar my body or my arm. Shallow breaths also keep the room's death stench from choking me.

Everything is all by feel now through my tight rubber gloves, feeling the steel find the center of the vertical stretcher bar, feeling it slide along the wood, slide up in a long, slow glide until I gently meet a slight resistance about two feet up. I've reached the bottom of the pressure point between the stretcher bars and the alarm button.

I stop, hold the steel very still, let my breathing even out again, ignoring the foul stench. The slightest twitch in my body could telegraph right up my arm, disturb the button. The shrieking alarm would wake the whole neighborhood, maybe even the two lumps of dead flesh on the floor.

With my breathing under control, I slide the steel—*fast*—between the button and the wood before the button can react, pressing the taped section hard against the wall at nearly the same time, keeping the steel in place against the button.

The button doesn't pop out. I've fooled the alarm. The room is silent. I let my breath out.

With the steel bar taped to the wall, it's usually good for a couple of hours until it loses traction, though in this humidity maybe less, but enough time for me to be long gone and leaving no fingerprints on the steel or anywhere else. With both hands free now to lift the painting from its mounting hooks, I take it down slowly, careful not to jar the steel, and settle the painting on the floor against the wall.

Getting down from the chair, I take the painting out of the heavy wooden frame. I don't need the extra weight and bulk when I climb back over that spiked fence. And besides, Lansky can afford to buy his own damned frame.

❖

I drive back to that same dark spot on that same dark street where I'd changed into my work clothes. What's left of my bottle of Chivas will be the nightcap leading to shut-eye. I'm not about to show up at Lansky's hotel at this late hour—it would be almost one o'clock in the morning by the time I got there—and going back to my own hotel isn't a wise move, either. Not with two bodies on Pete Estrada's floor. The policías will find them sooner or later, when the steel rod loses traction, the button pops, and the alarm goes off. The cops will see an empty spot where a painting should be, they'll assume that the thief is also the killer, and the hunt for the murdering thief will be on. So walking into my hotel lobby in the middle of the night with a stolen painting isn't a good idea.

But walking into Lansky's hotel in the morning will be a little less risky. I can pick up some gift wrap at a local store, wrap the painting like a present, and no one will be the wiser, even if Hidalgo's concierge brotherhood blabs it that I've gone to visit the Little Man in the big penthouse suite.

All of that is in the morning.

So for now I lay my head back against the Oldsmobile's driver's seat, drink myself into oblivion while I listen to the palm trees crackling and the night creatures whining and buzzing. Someone's playing a radio in the distance, a moody instrumental tune floats in the air. I hum along a little bit, supply it with a single drunken lyric, "Sophie," and then…nothing.

Chapter Eight

The same two tough-guy bookends who were outside Lansky's door yesterday are lined up again today. The smooth one, the guy who could pass for a politician's bodyguard, frowns and sneers at me at the same time. "Where do you think you're going with that stuff? And what's that you got under that fancy paper? It ain't nobody's birthday."

"They're for Lansky. One's a gift from a local friend," I say, nodding to Hidalgo's little paper-and-string wrapped box in my left hand. "And a painting's in the gift wrap."

"You're kidding. What would he want with a painting?"

"You'd have to ask him. He just wants me to deliver it, and that's what I'm going to do. So if you don't mind..." I tilt my head to tell the guy to open the door. I want this business over with fast. I want to hand over the painting and Hidalgo's box, secure Lansky's promise to use his clout to find Sophie, get back to my hotel, get out of my black duds, and have a hot shower and breakfast. Then I want to go see Hidalgo, tell him I delivered his package, and squeeze him to get me to Tomas Santiago, who'd better know where Sophie is, and who'd better not have hurt her, or he won't have any hands and arms left to hurt anyone ever again.

Meantime, the other guy at Lansky's door, the cold-eyed, leather-faced one who could be mistaken for the hotel's house dick, says, "He didn't tell us about any painting, or about you dropping by today."

"Suppose we let him decide if he wants to see me or not," I say. "That way, no one's in the doghouse. Not you, not me, everybody's happy." I give the boys the best palsy-walsy smile I can muster.

House Dick takes a second or two to think it over, squinting his eyes as he takes stock of my burglar's duds. He seems to finally get the picture—of course he does, he's probably done a little night work himself here and there—and then turns around and knocks on the door.

The door's opened by Lansky's inside man, Mr. Hollywood Handsome.

House Dick says, "Gold's back. Says she's got a painting for the boss."

Hollywood's smile spreads with the pleasure of someone who's just heard his worst enemy dropped dead of a heart attack. "Sure," he says, looking at me with a hearse driver's grin. "Bring it in."

Inside the vestibule, I save time and trouble by taking my .38 from my pocket and handing it to Hollywood.

"Go on in," he says. "They're waiting for you."

They?

The living room is as sunny as it was yesterday morning, the breakfast spread as bountiful, but my gut turns over when I see who's in my chair sharing Lansky's fruit and coffee: Rudi Hidalgo.

Well, well.

Forget about worrying over Hidalgo's concierge blabbermouths. I feel like the sap who stands at the curb with a wilting bunch of flowers while my date drives by with a better looking sucker. "Mr. Lansky," I say with more chutzpah than is good for my health and safety, "if I'd thought I'd be interrupting this exercise in Cuban-American relations, I wouldn't have rushed right over with your painting. I might've stopped for a cuppa coffee first. Or maybe a hand of pinochle at one of your casinos."

The way Lansky tosses his napkin on the table, with a sharp flick of his wrist and a tight purse of his lips, I figure he's not happy with me. Well, that's all right; I'm not happy with him, either.

"Cantor," he says, a hard edge taking the music out of his usual Lower East Side cadence with my name, "you've made a lot of trouble for Señor Hidalgo and me. We wanted Estrada humiliated. We wanted him to know he could be gotten to and licked. We did not want him dead."

I don't have to ask how he knows about Pete and Armando. A guy as connected as Lansky to the upper and lower reaches of Havana—the cops, the crooks, the government, every postman and milkman in town—probably knows when anyone in Havana takes a leak. Same probably goes for Hidalgo. Whoever found the bodies at Estrada's place—the postman, the milkman, the cop—passed it into an ear in the pay of Meyer Lansky or Rudi Hidalgo.

No wonder Hollywood Handsome looked happy to see me. He thinks I'm on my way to my doom. I sincerely hope he's wrong.

"Listen, Mr. Lansky, you ask me to steal a painting as a tit-for-tat favor, I steal a painting. And you, Hidalgo"—I hold up his little box—"you ask me to deliver a package in exchange for information, I deliver a package. But I didn't kill anybody. Those boys were dead when I got there. I had no beef with Estrada or his muscle-bound butler, but I have plenty of beef with people who skip on their promises. I held up my end. Here's your painting"—I look straight at Lansky and pull off the wrapping paper with dramatic flair; Enriquez's wildly colored horse catches sunlight—"and ding-dong, here's a special delivery package from Rudi Hidalgo to Meyer Lansky." I put the box on the coffee table. "Okay, fellas, your turn to pay up. And while you're at it, why don't you let me in on why you're sitting together at breakfast. I was under the impression you two barely know each other." It's Hidalgo I'm staring at now.

His shoulders rise in a desperately innocent shrug that practically swallows his round head, reducing it to a pimple. He starts to speak, but his mouth suddenly shuts tight, cutting off whatever else he'd planned to say as Lansky slowly and quietly gets up from the table and walks over to me. Never has so much power been expressed in such easy movements in such a small man's frame. And he wears it all with his charming, playful, V-shaped smile.

He takes the painting from me, lifts it for a better look. "Very nice picture, though it would have been fun to see Pete's face when he knew his prize possession was gone. He'd know I have it. He'd know it was my way of telling him he was finished in Havana. But what are you going to do?" he says with a New York shrug and puts the painting down against the coffee table. "Some things are not meant to be. You know what I mean, Cantor?"

"Yeah, sure." One minute he looks like he'd be happy to gut me, the next minute he talks to me like we're kin from the old neighborhood. Okay, if he really wants to play the kindred tribe game, he'll have to step up and play it. "A real shame about Pete," I say, "but a deal's a—"

"Rudi," he says, cutting me off while picking up Hidalgo's box and shaking it next to his ear. It doesn't make much of a noise, nothing rattling, just something sliding around. "Is this what I think it is?"

Hidalgo's head has emerged from his shoulders, his smile self-satisfied enough for him to feel good about what's coming, but discreet enough to keep him on the safe side of Lansky's pleasure.

Turning to me, Lansky says, "Would you like to see what's in this box, Cantor?"

"I guess so. I've been carrying it around long enough."

His manner, so charming a moment ago, becomes downright impish in anticipation of this special present. I find myself swallowing hard, trying to settle my stomach as Lansky unties the string. I keep remembering Agnes's story about the revolucionarios sending General Álvarez's eyeballs to his family. By the time Lansky unwraps the brown paper and opens the box, my mouth is dry as dust.

He lifts out a small bundle in a scrap of yellow oilcloth. When he opens the bundle, I finally get a glimpse of the cold, pitiless power which lives behind his charming smile and jaunty joy of life, because he didn't bat an eye or wrinkle his nose at the sight of a bloody tongue protruding from a torn and shriveled pair of lipstick-smeared lips. Instead, he playfully wags a finger at them. "Ah, Señorita Pilar, you were very naughty, and now your loud mouth is very quiet."

There's a lump in my chest hard as stone. It's the only thing keeping me from spewing my guts all over the floor when Lansky puts the gruesome bundle on the coffee table, next to the painting. A dribble of blood leaks against the edge of the canvas.

"You see, Cantor," Lansky says on his way back to the breakfast table, where he spears a piece of pineapple with his fork, "in a way, you're part of poor Pilar's demise."

"No, I don't see. And I don't want to see. I just want—"

"What you *want*, Cantor, and what is *necessary* are not the same things." He pauses to eat the pineapple. His eyes, crinkling with enjoyment, stay on me even as he chews the fruit and sits down at the table. "What you want is strictly in *your* interest," he says. "What is necessary is in *our* interest." He nods at Hidalgo, who's poured himself a cup of coffee and takes little sips of it. I wouldn't say Hidalgo is being subservient, but he's playing the quietly respectful Latin second banana to the hilt. The smile he gives Lansky is somewhere between gracious and reverent. The smiles he gave me yesterday were hardly reverent, were barely gracious. But I guess you'd have to have money and muscle in a bunch of casinos and have your hand in the government's pocket and at their throat to get a gracious smile from the likes of Rudi Hidalgo.

"Have a seat, Cantor," Lansky says. "Would you like some coffee? Maybe breakfast?"

"I'll pass, thanks." Even if coffee could get past that lump in my chest, it wouldn't stay put in my churning stomach, not after seeing that torn tongue and those mangled lips.

"Suit yourself, but have a seat. If you want to find that girl of yours, there are things you need to know. You see?" he adds, his charming smile back in its playful little V, which now sends tingles crawling like roaches up my spine. "I said I would help you, and now I am. Why would I not keep my word? My word means everything in our circles, Cantor." It's as if he's slapped me across the face and then handed me a glass of the finest champagne as a chaser.

Chastised and not liking it, I sit down in a nearby club chair. My heart's pounding so loud in my ears I have to take a deep breath to quiet it, keep it from drowning Lansky out while I hang on his every word.

"You see, Cantor," he says again, "that letter you brought me from our friend in New York, Mr. Loreale—that letter set this whole business in motion."

"Why am I not surprised," I say with a *tsk* and a snort. "Sig likes to play chess with people's lives. He's been trying to shove me around the board since I was a kid in Coney Island and he was muscling to checkmate Coney's old-time boss."

Lanksy's laugh is quiet, short, a rascal's grunt of pleasure. "We were all a lot younger then," he says, "a bunch of schlemiels out to prove how tough we were. Well," he adds with a shrug, "we won our battles. Sig, too, and now he's a major investor in our Havana operations. But he's not just a business associate, Cantor, he is also a friend, a friend I find it useful to keep up to date on how things are progressing in Havana. You know what I'm talking about, don't you."

"Everybody knows. And everybody wants their piece, like Señor Hidalgo here."

Hidalgo's coffee cup comes down so hard on the saucer I'm surprised the china doesn't break. "And why not?" he says. "I, too, am an investor. I am entitled to my profit. I am not a Communist."

I'm glad it's Hidalgo and not me under Lansky's smile, a tight V without a trace of humor or an ounce of trust. "Don't worry, Rudi. No one would ever mistake you for a Communist. Your suit is too well tailored."

Hidalgo's tense chuckle has the rasp of a guy who's just been told his wife's lover died in a car crash but it's okay because his cheating wife died in the crash, too.

Lansky turns his attention back to me. The cold smile is gone. There's no smile at all. Just those deceptively impish eyes toying with me the way a cat toys with a ball of wool. "Listen, Cantor, while I've been busy making business arrangements in Havana, Loreale's been assessing the problem of the local gang wars. These wars, these rivalries, with their random gun battles in the streets"—he says this with a disgusted wave of his hand, his voice and face tight with distaste not just for the violence but for the locals causing it—"create chaos. And chaos, as you know, Cantor, is bad for business. The question became what to do about it. Now, as you also know, Sig Loreale is a master at getting rid of chaos."

"You mean he kills it off."

Lansky gives that a *tsk* and a dismissive sneer. "I'm surprised at you, Cantor. I thought you knew him better than that."

"The boneyards around New York tell me all I need to know. Look," I say, getting up from the chair, my patience with all this conversation running thin, "whatever you and Sig are up to in Havana is your business, not mine. I'm sorry about Señorita Pilar. Maybe I'm even more than sorry, maybe I want to cry over her killing, but I didn't come to Havana to get mixed up in the local rackets. All I'm interested in is finding Sophie. So if you don't mind, Mr. Lansky, let's cut to the bone. Give me some information that will help me find her. And you, Señor Hidalgo, you promised to put me in touch with Tomas Santiago. Time to fork over."

Hidalgo, with the deep breath and sideways smile of someone who finally sees an opportunity to take back a shred of power, says, "I will be happy to tell you where to find Santiago, but if you go to him without the information Señor Lansky has been trying to give you, you will be dead at Santiago's doorstep." He takes another sip of coffee, enjoying it almost as much as he did putting me in my place.

"Hidalgo's right, Cantor," Lansky says. "If you want to stay alive while you look for your Sophie, you can't run around blind."

Now it's me who takes a deep breath, the kind that forces the mind to stop fighting and the body to submit to sitting back down.

With a nod, Lansky says, "Okay. Good. So, here's the picture. These gang wars are interfering with our progress in Havana. We want the wars to end. We could do it ourselves, we have the muscle, and we could bring in more from our associates in the States, but it wouldn't be good politics. The Americans can't be seen as conquerors of the Cuban streets. So Loreale looked into the relative strength and position of the gangs, and he came up with a plan. We'll throw our influence and money behind one of the gangs, let them emerge as the winner, let them take over all the street action, all the profits. We'll pay them to keep the streets quiet, and they'll stay out of our operations."

Yeah, that has Sig's mind all over it, always the smart move.

After another swallow of coffee, Lansky says, "We're backing Tomas Santiago."

CHAPTER NINE

That's why Señorita Pilar is dead," Lansky says with no more emotion than if he was explaining why bread goes stale. After a last sip of coffee, he gets up from the table and takes a look out the terrace doors to the view of the sea. It wouldn't surprise me if he's figuring which deity he'd have to muscle to get control of the waters, make the waves roll in on the Mob's timetable and strictly for the Mob's profit.

Finally turning away from the sea view, he says, "My partners and I—"

"Loreale, you mean," I say.

"Among others," he says with a sly smile, his way of indicating the businessmen with guns without mentioning their names. "We had to get Santiago's attention, and then get him to trust us, so I arranged to take care of a little problem for him, a leakage problem you might call it. Señorita Pilar was one of Santiago's stable of whores, but it seems she was playing both sides of the street. She was crazy about some guy in a rival gang, the Animas Boys, and she'd tip him off whenever Santiago was making a move into a neighborhood. It was Rudi here"—Lansky puts his hand on Hidalgo's shoulder, which Hidalgo accepts with a nervous nod—"who alerted me. Isn't that right, Rudi?"

"Sí, that is so."

"And you have a relationship with Santiago you thought might interest me. Well, you were right, Rudi. Which is why I entrusted you with the job."

Hidalgo throws me a smile so self-satisfied it actually puffs up his face, like a balloon ready to fly away. "And lucky for me, Gold," he says, "you walked right into the plan."

Yeah, lucky for him. I was the accidental delivery service Hidalgo knew could get through Lansky's door.

I'm about to ask Hidalgo if he did Señorita Pilar's cut job himself or if he contracted the killing to a local assassin, but that's a side of Hidalgo's business I'm better off not knowing. Too much intimacy with murderers is dangerous. All I say is, "So I guess Santiago has the rest of poor Pilar? A gift to him, like Pilar's mouth is a gift to Meyer Lansky?"

And all I get for an answer is a smile from Hidalgo and a shrug from Lansky.

Lansky's nonchalance doesn't last long, replaced by a hard frown, deep with annoyance. "Pete Estrada's killing throws a monkey wrench into the business," he says. "Estrada was backing the Animas Boys, and they'll be on the warpath. My sources tell me they're already stirring. They'll probably figure Santiago ordered the hit on Pete, but I doubt he'd be that stupid. But a confrontation is coming. There will be more blood in the streets, which is *exactly* what we wanted to avoid. Scares away the tourists."

"Oh I don't know," I say. "If the flowered shirt and straw hat crowd I saw yesterday in the Callejón de los Burdeles is anything to go by, Henry Hayseed likes a bit of spice and banditry now and again."

I guess Lansky doesn't like my joke. He gives me a *tsk* so sharp it's like a knife to my throat. "If you want to find...this *girlfriend* of yours, Cantor, you'd better be prepared for the sewer you're walking into. I said I'd help you, and I will. I'll make inquiries all over my end of Havana—the policía, the politicians, everybody. And I believe you even have a separate deal with Señor Hidalgo. Am I right, Rudi?"

"Sí. As payment for delivering the remains of Pilar, I am to get her to Tomas Santiago. Are you available today, Cantor?"

"Sure, I'm available," I say. "The sooner the better."

Hidalgo, all business, says, "There is a hat shop at the corner of Calle Neptuno and Águila. Be there at twelve noon."

❖

I like Calle Neptuno, always did. It's a real place catering to real people, not tourists looking for more maracas and "Babalú" spectacle. The street hasn't changed much in ten years. It's still jammed with locals patronizing the discount jewelry stores, hock shops, gift joints, beauty parlors, barber shops, clothing stores, and the occasional saloon. Knots of Habaneros clog the narrow sidewalks, men and women shopping, gossiping, flirting, shopkeepers talk a little business, while cars, mostly American models dating from dull prewar styles to the latest colorful two-tone and chrome jobs, crawl through traffic, horns honking. Between the honking cars and zesty crowds, I'd almost swear I was back in New York, except for the neon store signs in Cubano Spanish and the craziness of noonday heat in January.

I'm tempted to take my suit jacket off, but exposing my holstered gun isn't a good idea. So I just wipe my neck and face with my handkerchief and make the best of the sweaty tropics.

I find the hat shop at the corner of Águila, walk in.

The shop is stuffed with all kinds of straw hats on sagging wooden shelves along pale orange walls, which could use a paint job. The slowly turning ceiling fan barely moves the hot, thick air. There's a counter along the back wall, tended by a bored señorita whose boredom is jolted when she sees me, gets my drift, and looks at me as if I'm a contamination oozing through her shop. Pity. Someone whose brown eyes are that pretty shouldn't fill them with so much disgust.

I tip the brim of my panama—I'm always polite to women, even if they give me the stink eye—and trot out my flimsy Spanish, keeping things businesslike. "Hablas inglés, señorita?"

"Sí, little. But it is no matter," she says, her eyes sliding to barely look at me in that way that means she really wants to look at me, wants to stare in horrified curiosity. "They tell me you come. They tell me look for woman who is not woman."

I've been called a lot of things in my life—some of it made me angry, some made me laugh. This one, a new line of insult, is the laugh sort. I counter it with a little smutty fun of my own. "Yeah, well, they didn't give you the real story. Wanna see?" I put my hand to my fly as if to unzip.

"No!" Her hands rush to her face as if warding off an attack of disease-carrying mosquitos. Tossing her head, she says, "You go there now. In there!" and waves me to a door behind her. "Go through la puerta—ahh…"

"Door."

"Sí, door. *Go.*"

She's adorable, despite her loathing of me, so on my way to *la puerta*, I give in to my inner scoundrel, put my hand to my fly again and give her a wink.

She makes a sound I can't quite identify, but it has a lot of sneer in it.

I'm in a windowless hallway when I go through the door. Two thugs appear in the flickering greenish light of an overhead fluorescent bulb. One thug needs a shave, the other needs a shave and a bath. If these two are typical of Santiago's Angry Dogs gang, a better name for the outfit would be the Dirty Dogs. The guy who needs a shave is a skinny fella but carries a big, thick .45 pistol. Typical. I'd laugh, but the gun's barrel aimed at my gut changes my mind.

The other guy, the smelly one whose unwashed shirt stinks of tobacco and week-old sweat, holds a rifle, the repeater type, the type John Wayne twirls in cowboy pictures, except Smelly Guy bears a stronger resemblance to beefy Ernest Borgnine than rugged John Wayne. The skinny guy with the .45 moves the barrel to my temple, which he seems to enjoy doing, if his ratlike grin is any indication. Smelly Guy puts down his rifle, leans it against the wall, reaches inside my jacket, and takes my gun from the rig. Either from neglect or stupidity, he doesn't bother to search the rest of me, completely missing the wad of cash in my jacket. It's not my entire bankroll, just enough to pay off Santiago if I have to. Smelly puts my .38 in his pants pocket, takes out a length of cord from his other pocket, walks behind me to grab my arms, and ties my hands behind my back. Picking up his rifle, he walks back around to face me, gives me his gap-toothed Ernest Borgnine smile, and crooks his finger to tell me to follow him. Skinny Guy with the .45 slides behind me and puts his big gun against my back.

If this is Tomas Santiago's idea of hospitality, he'd be the only guy to go broke in Havana's booming hotel business.

About ten feet down the hall, Smelly Guy puts his hand to the wall and a narrow section swings open into a shadowy staircase. The rotting wood creaks as our little convoy walks downstairs. If I could, I'd tip my hat to Santiago for not repairing these stairs; the creaking wood is a handy warning of intruders.

We arrive in a basement where hot, salty air scratches my face and burns my nostrils. A rusty light fixture with a single bulb hangs from the ceiling. Its pink glass shade is cracked, throwing jagged lines of shadows, like giant broken spiderwebs, onto the moldy and peeling flowered wallpaper. The only furniture in the place is a rickety chair against one of the two thick wooden posts supporting the ceiling.

There's no one else in the room except me and my escort thugs. "Where's Santiago?" I say. My escort thugs say nothing. They don't smile, they don't sneer, they just point their guns at me. "No knack for conversation, huh? Well, don't blame me if you're not invited to the better soirees." Not even a snicker.

I could use a drink, and I'd love a cigarette to help pass the time, but with my hands tied behind me, I can't reach into my jacket to grab my pack of smokes.

Oh well, the hot and heavy air is burning me up anyway, the cord around my wrists is cutting into my flesh, and those spiderweb shadows are annoying. But I'll put up with all of it if it means getting me one step closer to finding Sophie.

I'm thinking, *Where the hell is Santiago*, when Skinny Guy suddenly swats me across the head with the butt of his big .45 and I go down like an empty pillowcase collapsing to the floor. There's a fire in my head and a white blaze behind my eyes for just a second, and then—

❖

Something wet and sour splashes all over my face, seeps into my mouth, and by the time I realize that the lousy taste is dirty water I'm gasping for air, my mind clawing back from the dreamless black of nowhere. The fire's in my head again, only now it's more like hot embers than a burning blaze. I can't move. My hands are still tied behind my back, I'm tied to the chair, and the chair is tied to the post behind me.

My eyes burn from the foul water, makes it tough to see, blurs what I think are two people standing in front of me, their faces and shoulders lined with those spidery shadows from the broken light fixture. One appears to be a guy in what I can just make out are brown trousers and a yellow shirt; the other's a woman in purple. I know it's a woman by the shape of the purple and the soft contour of her short blond hair. She seems to be welded to the side of the guy.

My hearing's coming back to life, though, and I hear the guy say, "The American is awake," in a rough-voiced Spanish accent. Two other guys laugh, one a guttural chuckle, the other a stupid giggle.

My eyes are starting to focus. The laughers are Smelly Guy and Skinny Guy on either side of the room, their guns out. The guy in front of me, the one in brown trousers and yellow shirt, his sleeves rolled up to the elbows, has his arm around the waist of the woman in purple. She slinks along his side. Lucky fella. Even in those horror-movie shadows, she's more beautiful than the señorita upstairs, and less bored, if I'm reading those green eyes correctly, sharp and slanted like a snake's eyes, and looking at me as if I'm an intrusive creature she'd like to poison. I guess I've ruined whatever plans she had for her day.

The guy in the yellow shirt says, "I am told you want to talk to me. I am Tomas Santiago, leader of Los Perros Enojados." His

Cuban accented English comes through that rough voice, like he's been punched in the throat too often, or maybe cut.

My vision's just about clear now, and I get a good look at him: thirty or so, wavy black hair that flops a little over his forehead, deep-set soft-as-a-kitten's dark eyes, and a smile so pretty I bet he uses it to sweep women off their feet, or weld them to his side, like the blonde in purple.

Did he use that smile on Sophie? I suddenly hate this guy. I want to kill him. I want to tear him limb from limb, rip his smiling lips off and put them in the box to spend eternity with Señorita Pilar's torn mouth. If I ever get out of this chair, maybe I will.

But I'm still in this chair, and I still need information only he can give me, so I force down the anger that scrapes like a bone in my throat. "Yeah, I want to talk to you. I'm looking for someone, and I think you know where to find her."

Santiago's smile twists into a sneer as he keeps his eyes on me. He turns toward the woman and says, "You know, Zamira, this American was sent here by Rudi Hidalgo. And I thought Rudi was my friend. So why does he send me this...this—What is she?" This last rides on a snide laugh, a brutal sound through his broken throat.

Zamira slides away from Santiago, bends toward me, and puts her hand under my chin. Her fingers are warm and damp in the humid air of this basement hotbox. "I think she is a little bit gringo and a little bit gringa, sí?" There's a hiss in her voice to match her snake's eyes, which stare at me with vicious amusement. "But most of all, I think that she is enamorada. Lovesick."

"There's a photograph in my inside pocket," I say, nodding toward it. "If you take it out you'll see who I'm enamorada about. She's the woman I'm looking for." I silently congratulate myself for putting Sophie's picture in a different pocket from my cash.

Unlike the señorita upstairs, who'd sooner cut her hand off than touch me, snake-eyed Zamira is game. She reaches inside my jacket, not bothering to avoid brushing her fingers against my chest, and takes out the picture of Sophie. I didn't mind her fingers against my chest, hell, even liked it, but her fingers touching Sophie's picture turns my stomach.

"Beautiful," she says, looking at the photograph.

"Yeah, very beautiful," I say. "Now show the picture to Santiago."

My guts turns over again when Santiago's fingers grab Sophie's picture. "Ahh, sí," he says, flashing me a smirk. "I remember her. She gave me a lot of trouble. I paid good money for her and she did not do as she was told."

I could cheer. I want to cheer my brave Sophie. But I don't dare do anything to annoy Santiago before he tells me what I need to know. All I say is, "Where is she, Santiago?"

"First, I will tell you a story," he says, his smirk sliding back through his rough growl and turning into his pretty smile, almost angelic now if it wasn't for that nasty web of shadows across his face and the cruelty in his eyes. "You see, one night this beautiful chica comes up for sale at a party given by a friend. Sad to say, my friend is…" Santiago bows his head in mock mourning. "He is no longer with us. Taken by God in heaven, with a little help from los revolucionarios. They are my compañeros. I trained with them in the mountains. Anyway, my friend was a very big man in the army, General Cheche Álvarez, maybe you have heard of him?"

"His name came my way. Along with your name, and that party."

"Ah, well, poor Cheche. He did not do as he was told either, and he had to pay. But at least his family got his eyes back, something to remember him by. But how to make this beautiful but disobedient chica pay?"

My insides twist with fury, my saliva tastes like bile. It's tough to keep the rage under wraps. I try, because letting Santiago get the better of me would play right into his sick game, but I can't stop a question from blurting out, "Did you hurt her, Santiago?"

"Certainly no! What do you think I am? Un bruto? No. I am a businessman."

"A businessman with an army, or so I hear."

I can't tell if he's flattered or just amused, but his smile is a little less pretty, a little more savage. "There are many armies in Cuba," he says. "Listen, I did not hurt this chica. She was valuable *property.* I cannot make a profit from someone who has a broken face. No buyer would have such a woman."

My relief that Sophie wasn't roughed up is as deep as my anger that Santiago treated her like chattel. Trying not to gag on it, I say, "You *sold* her? To *who*?"

Zamira cuts in, "Un momento, Tomas! Do not give something for nothing."

"But this American has nothing I want."

That's the third time he's called me an American, spitting the word like it's poison on his tongue.

"She has information," Zamira says. "She can tell you about Pedro Estrada's killing. Why did you do it?" she says to me. "Did somebody hire you to make trouble for us? Was it that American big shot, Lansky? He has told Tomas that he wants to help our Perros Enojados, but I do not trust him."

Her *our* Perros Enojados hits me like a sudden flash of light. Makes me see a glimmer of another outline: Santiago might be the public muscle of his gangland outfit, but Zamira just might be the behind-the-man brains.

Santiago says, "Killing Estrada makes big trouble for us, sí. He did business with my enemies, Los Chicos Animas, and they will be plenty mad. They will think I ordered it, and they will want revenge. So now I will have to fight a war I do not want. It is not yet the right time, and it will cost a lot of my—"

"I didn't kill Estrada," I butt in, but I say it to Zamira. "He was dead when I got there. Who told you I killed him?"

Santiago's lips open as if to answer but a *hssst* from Zamira closes his mouth again. Zamira doesn't say anything, either, just narrows those snake eyes and stares at me through the spidery shadows across her face. She's gorgeous, and terrifying. Whatever angle she's figuring, she takes her time about it, one hand on her hip, the other balled up at her side.

I stare back at her. I can't tell if our stares are building a wall between us or an understanding. The woman is hard to figure, but then women generally are. It usually makes my life interesting.

Zamira's interesting, all right, if you find the possibility of getting your throat cut interesting.

In the meantime, I have more urgent figuring to do, like who told this outfit I murdered Estrada. I come up with four players for the honor of framing me, two of them a double act. The double act is Loreale and Lansky: Loreale because I've been a thorn in his side for years, pestering him to make good on his promise to help find Sophie; and Lansky, because if Sig wants me out of the way, Lansky, as the Mob's man in Havana, could make it happen. He'd be off the hook for doing me any favors in return for getting him the Enriquez painting. Still, it's a stretch, considering that Lansky thought I'd killed Estrada.

I can't rule out Rudi Hidalgo, though, chummy and helpful one minute, happy to feed me to the dogs the next, just like he fed me to these Angry Dogs. But that scenario doesn't sit well, either. I can't quite see the fussy Hidalgo setting up a messy gang war.

Someone else is suddenly lurking in the back of my mind, someone with no name—yet—the one who might really be the killer of Pete Estrada and his man Armando. Who else is a player in this game?

Zamira is still looking at me, and I'm still looking at her. The expression on her face has changed from devious to thoughtful. I'm pretty sure the expression on my face has changed, too, from defiant to determined. The truth is I couldn't care less about Estrada and Armando, don't give a damn that they're dead, but whoever set me up had the frame cut right to my size. Someone doesn't like me poking around Havana. I wonder if that same someone doesn't like me looking for Sophie.

"Listen, you two," I say, "it sounds like we're all being yanked around. Someone wanted Estrada dead, and I was the convenient patsy to pin it on. While everyone's looking at me, the real killer is sitting back watching you go to war while the American Mob spends time and money trying to stop any blood in the streets from scaring the tourists away. Someone's getting ready to have the last laugh, and you're playing right into it."

Zamira says, "How do we know it is not you who is doing the yanking around?"

"Because of the picture in your boyfriend's hand," I say. "The woman in that photo is the only reason I'm in Havana. Tell me where I can find her, and she and I are gone from this island. After that, if you and your Angry Dogs want to wipe out the Animas Boys, if you even want to put a bullet into Lansky, I don't care. I have no horse in this race."

"But you do," comes the growl from Santiago. "You are a friend of Señor Lansky."

"I've only met the guy twice. We're not friends."

"And yet Rudi Hidalgo tells me that you have stolen a Cuban painting for Señor Lansky. You are like all Americans who come here and steal from Cuba. You are even stealing our government."

"Listen, Santiago," I say. "Keep your politics. I'm not interested. The only thing I want to steal from Cuba is the woman who was stolen from me in the first place. I want to steal her away from whatever hell you sold her into. Now tell me where she is."

He growls, "Tell me where Lansky has the painting you stole for him."

"What's it to you? Suddenly you're an art lover? You want a painting of your own to hang on these elegant walls? Cut me loose and I'll get one for you. Hell, I'll get two, if you want."

"Do not laugh!" Santiago's shout bursts like rocks crashing through his throat. Assaulting as that is, it's nothing compared to the wallop he gives me across my face, his knuckles smashing into my cheekbone. I've barely recovered from Skinny Guy banging his gun against my head, and now this. I'll have a headache from here to Sunday, made worse by Santiago's continuing rant. "The paintings of Carlos Enriquez are part of the soul of the Cuban people! I should give you to the revolucionarios. They—"

"Stop it, Tomas!" Zamira cuts him off. "You are talking nonsense. It is getting us nowhere. You do nothing but shout, and it makes it impossible for me to think."

My face burns, my head aches, but Zamira's given me an

opening and I grab it. "With these ropes around me, it's impossible for me to help you."

Zamira and Santiago each shoot me suspicious looks, though Zamira's has something more behind it. "How do you help us?"

"By getting out of Havana and out of your way."

She makes a sound like *phssssh,* and waves her hand as if shooing a fly. "That is nothing," she says. "If we kill you, you are out of our way." A grunt and a chuckle come from Smelly and Skinny, as if I didn't already have enough of a headache.

I have one more card to play. It's not a card I want to give them, but with my hands tied behind me, my body tied to this chair, and Smelly and Skinny pointing guns at me, it's the only play I've got left. "If you kill me, I can't find whoever killed Estrada. Whoever did it is your real enemy, because while you're knocking yourself out with a bloody war, could be they'll make their move on your operations—the narcotics, the street walkers, the gunrunning, all of it. And Lansky won't save you. He'll just deal with the new street boss."

Her hand back on her hip, jutting her jaw like a doubtful diva, Zamira says, "What do you care what happens to us?"

"Okay, so I don't care. But I care about finding whoever framed me for the Estrada killing."

Santiago blurts a laugh, says, "Do not trouble yourself! We will find Pedro's killer."

"Not as quietly as I can," I say. "Everyone in Havana knows you, maybe they even know about the hat shop upstairs. And believe me, the American Mob is watching you, and your army, too."

Zamira takes a deep, thoughtful breath that does wonderful things to her purple dress, especially the upper part. She lets the breath out slowly. I enjoy that, too. "No, they will not see our army. Tomas trained them to be las guerrillas, you know, silent fighters, like he learned in the mountains. But you are right, Cantor Gold. You can be useful. Tomas, let her go."

There's something deeply satisfying in watching a man obey a woman, no matter how reluctantly. Santiago's pretty face is gnarled with reluctance, even as he cocks his head to Skinny Guy and tells them to cut me loose.

Seeing Skinny approach me with his big pistol in one hand and a knife he takes from his pocket in the other is not a comforting sight. For all I know, the savage slash across his mouth that passes for a smile is his way of telling me he's going to cut my throat. But he slips his knife behind me, cuts my ropes. I'm free.

"Okay, Santiago," I say and grab Sophie's photo from his hand, which gets me a small but malicious smile from Zamira, "where is Sophie?"

"Well, it has been a long time since I have seen her," he says. "A year, yes? So I am not sure if she is still in the burdel of the man who bought her. But he is a countryman of yours. Another of your gangsters who comes to steal from us."

"His name?"

"He is Señor Ossatura, Charlie Ossatura."

Now there's a name I haven't heard in a long time. Never figured he'd leave New York for Havana. Tell you the truth, I figured he was dead.

"You look surprised," Santiago says.

"Never mind how I look. Just tell me where I can find him."

"He runs his women through his nightclub, the Rumba Room."

"Okay. Now give me back my gun."

CHAPTER TEN

My cheek's swollen and black-and-blue where Santiago walloped me, and there's a lump on the side of my head where Skinny Guy slammed me with his .45. But I made it out of the basement alive and got back to my hotel room about an hour ago. I'm cleaned up and in my eggshell linen suit that I had the hotel sponge and press. I've got a new lead on Sophie's whereabouts, and I've got her picture safely back in my hands.

I look at the picture for a long time, slide my finger along the curve of Sophie's cheek, and remember. I remember the first time I saw her, September of '47, at a little restaurant down in Greenwich Village, one of those shadowy, old-timey Italian places that have been serving good food, cheap wine, and great coffee for generations. I was at a table with a guy who tried to convince me he had access to a lost etching of the English countryside by Rembrandt. I told him Rembrandt never laid eyes on the English countryside. When I'd had enough of his small-change ramblings and got up to leave, I saw a vision that stopped me where I stood. The woman sitting alone in a booth, sipping coffee and reading the evening newspaper, brought time to a halt. One look at her, and I felt like she'd known me all my life and for several lifetimes before this one. She was reading the paper by the light of the candle on the table, giving her face the soft glow of a Renaissance painting. When she looked up and saw me, her deep brown eyes catching candlelight, I blurted like a tongue-tied teenager, "Sorry, I didn't mean to—"

"Stare?" There was a small smile in back of her creamy voice, a very small smile, just enough to say that she forgave me but wasn't ready to trust me.

I didn't know where this was going, except I knew it wasn't going out the door, because she didn't sneer at me in fear or disgust. She might not trust me, but she wasn't afraid of the staring butch in the black silk suit holding my cap so tight I nearly ripped the tweed.

I was the one who was afraid. I was afraid I'd never forget her, never get over it if she'd say no when I asked, "May I buy you a cup or two or three or a forever supply of coffee?"

She didn't say no. But she did laugh.

That laugh—kind and sexy at the same time—and all the laughs and tears and nights and days that came after it are why I'm here in Havana, why I'll take wallops from sniveling gunmen, humiliating lectures from big shots like Loreale and Lansky, sneers and threats from little shots like Hidalgo.

I slide the picture back into my jacket, slip my gun into my shoulder rig, put extra rounds into my trouser pocket, and get the hell out of my hotel room and out of the painful grip of memory.

It's nearly four o'clock in the still hot afternoon when I arrive at the Rumba Room, too early for the nighttime revelers, but open for business, anyway. The place is somewhat out of the way, past the Vedado and on the road to the Havana suburbs. It's a big place, a long two-story mishmash of Cuban-Spanish Baroque and twentieth century sleek. It shares the street with palm trees but no other buildings, just a parking lot surrounding the club. Most of the cars in the lot are low-end American models, two-tone Chevys and Dodges and that ilk, with a few midpriced jobs and here and there something in the luxury range, a Lincoln or a Caddy.

The whole story tells me the place isn't a tourist joint. It's what the Mob calls a rug room: low rent but good enough to have carpeting, a cut above the gutter casinos and cathouses with nothing but sawdust on the floor.

I've got a chunk of my bankroll with me in case I have to pay off Ossatura in exchange for Sophie. And if he says no, I'll put a bullet in his arm or leg, one knee and the other, toe after toe, places that hurt until he gives her up.

I'm dizzy with the hope of finally finding her, so I need a deep breath to steady myself when I get out of the car. Keeping my mind focused and my nerves on a leash, I walk into the Rumba Room. Inside, the main room of the club is a wide open space whose decor is somewhere between ornate and dingy. The air is a cigarette-and-cigar-smoke haze, tinted red from the red oilcloth tablecloths, heavy drapes, and the stained red carpet. The clatter of a casino filters in from another room and mixes with the murmurs and sloppy laughs of the men and women drinking at the tables. Cheap prints of pinup girls hang between the arches along the white stucco walls, the pictures probably a good indication of the tastes and desires of the Rumba Room's patrons. The men at the tables are a mixed crowd, some well-dressed in suits, some in the colorful short sleeved shirts popular in the tropics. The fellas are a range of ages, from geezers to peach-fuzz young. The women sharing their drinks aren't the men's wives or girlfriends, not in those expose-it-all outfits and pasted-on smiles. So yeah, this ain't no tourist joint. There are joints like this in every town in America, too, and all over the world, the place where locals come for a respite from the deadening routine of their lives, the dull familiarity of their marriage bed, and where the more awkward young men are sent by their fathers to finally pop their cork.

Sophie's not among the women working the room. I wish she was. It would mean she's not upstairs in a bedroom, not servicing the demands of some guy's paws.

I have to stop my stomach from heaving.

A pinch-faced guy in a white dinner jacket and black tie formal wear, all of it trying too hard to be classy, looks me over like maybe I've wandered into the wrong place, but then changes his mind with a shrug, figuring a paying customer is a paying customer, and the girls will do as they're told.

In its way, I guess the Rumba Room is as worldly as Agnes Cain's joint.

I say, "Sí, Señor Ossatura, por favor," the words all tangled around my tongue.

My lousy sounding Spanish gave me up, because the guy says, "You have a meeting?"

"You mean an appointment? I don't need an appointment. I have friends," I say, pushing my luck. And considering I've never met Charlie Ossatura, only heard stories along the Brooklyn docks about his rise and fall, I'll need plenty of luck to pull this play off. "*American* friends," I say, letting the insinuation do its work. "Señor Ossatura is an American, so he'll understand." I give the guy my best You Don't Want To Cross Me smile.

His own smile, which starts out as a doubting scrunch of his lips and ends in a sideways sneer, makes it clear he's not impressed. "Señor Ossatura is a busy man. He will want the names of your *friends*."

"Just tell him—" I wonder how far I can take this without the guy catching my play. "Just tell him I'm a friend of the Little Man."

"I do not know this Little Man."

"But I bet Ossatura does." I put a little extra into my Don't Cross Me smile.

The guy's face folds. "You will wait here, please."

"I will not wait here, please. I will go with you to see Ossatura. But first," I say, taking Sophie's photo from my pocket, hanging on a chance that maybe I can bypass Ossatura altogether, "do you recognize this woman? Is she here?"

I fight off that dizzy feeling again as I watch the guy's face, try to figure if he's playing dumb when he looks at the picture and says, "I do not discuss these things. For this, you must talk to Señor Ossatura." He's not playing dumb. He's just scared stiff.

"Then let's go."

He leads me across the room toward the clatter of the casino. I get a few stares along the way, but nothing much. The men are more interested in the women they're paying for and the women are too busy earning their pesos.

The casino is just as shabby as the main room but brighter, busy with the same sort of male clientele and barely dressed women at their side, stroking them to play another hand of cards, take another spin of the roulette wheel, roll another round of dice, throw down more cash. I search the faces of all the women in the room. Sophie's not here.

I'm led to a door at the far end of the casino. My escort gives it a gentle knock, opens it carefully, and puts his head inside. "I am sorry to disturb you, Señor Ossatura—"

"But I'm not," I say, pushing past him into a small office with blacked out windows, chipped brown walls, a battered wooden desk, and an overhead light fixture with a green metal shade that seems to have a bullet hole in it, sending a streak of light past my ear. Its single bulb throws a sharp glare onto the beefy guy in white shirtsleeves and floral-pattern tie loose at the knot. He's seated at the desk, smoking a cigar, his clumped salt-and-pepper hair looking like gravel tumbling from his head onto his lumpy face. Cigar smoke hangs in the air, surrounds his face like a shroud. There's a half empty bottle of Cuban rum on the desk, no glass. Next to the bottle is a .45.

"Who the hell are you?" he says through cigar stained teeth, his Brooklyn dockside accent turning the question into *Whooduh hella you?* It's accompanied by a look I know well; it starts out puzzled, moves along to amused, and ends up disgusted.

I've taught myself to ignore it if the look stays at disgusted and doesn't progress to threatening, which Ossatura's doesn't. He just keeps smoking his cigar, flicking ashes on the floor. I close the door behind me, leaving my escort outside. "My name's Cantor Gold," I say, "and I'm not here to waste your time. I'm here to do a little business. The kind of business where I get what I want and you get a bundle of cash."

His chair creaks as he leans back, cigar between his teeth, and folds his hands behind his boulder-like head, exposing yellow sweat stains in the armpits of his shirt. "Izzat so? And to what do I owe the privilege of doin' business with—what you say your name was?"

"Cantor Gold."

"Oh yeah," he says, stretching words out. "I heard about you. You're the busybody who's becomin' the talk of the town." He's staring at my face, gives me a smile I hope to forget. "Looks like somebody worked you over, gave your face a wallop."

"Never mind my face. Where'd you hear about me?"

"Word gets around," he says, grinning around the now juicy cigar.

"And word gets around about Charlie Ossatura, too. They used to call you Break Bones Ossatura when you were muscle for the Brooklyn Mob—what, five years ago? You're a long way from the Red Hook docks, Charlie."

"What's it to you?"

"Nothing," I say with a shrug. "I just didn't know you're in Havana." I stop myself from adding *and running a cut-rate cathouse*, because I'm here to get Sophie, and insulting the guy who might have her is probably not the right move.

"Hurry up, state your business," he says, chomping on his cigar. "I thought you didn't wanna waste my time."

"Right," I say, sliding my hand into my jacket, but Ossatura's gun is in his hand and pointed at me before I can retrieve the photo of Sophie. "Whoa, slow down," I say, raising my palms. "I've got a picture in my pocket I want to show you. That's all. The woman in the picture, she's the business."

Through wet lips expelling cigar smoke, he says, "Just take that picture out slow," his gun staying on me.

He must've caught sight of my gun under my arm when I slide the picture from my jacket because he gives me a smirk that says it doesn't matter if I've got a whole army in my jacket, he's still the one with the big gun pointed at me.

I show him the picture of Sophie. I fight to keep my nerves steady and my voice even, because what I'm about to say could end my long misery of living without her. "I was told you have this woman. I'm prepared to buy her from you." It makes me sick to say those words, to talk about Sophie like she's meat for sale. I fight to keep that hidden from Ossatura, too.

He puts the gun down and takes the cigar out of his mouth, rests it on the edge of the desk, and lets the ashes fall to the floor, some by way of his lap. And he smiles. A big, grotesque smile, eyes crinkling in his lumpy face. "Oh yeah," he says, drawing it out, "Mariposa."

"Mariposa?"

"That's what Santiago said her name was when he sold her to me. I guess it was her workin' name, if you get my drift. She was quite a little handful."

"What do you mean, *was*?" If I was breathing any harder, my lungs would burst from my chest.

"I *mean*," he says, picking up his cigar again and putting it between his teeth, still smiling while he lets his eyes follow Sophie's picture as I put it back in my pocket, "she was fiery, obstinate. I had to teach her a lesson." His smile grows even more grotesque. "She learned."

My guts are twisting so bad they threaten to squeeze all sense out of me, urging me to pounce on the guy, rip his tongue out. But I'd be dead before my hand ever reaches those thick lips, because he'd put a bullet in me with his .45. And Sophie would still be a flesh slave.

So with every ounce of self-control I can dredge up, I revert to being the underworld operator come to do business. It's not easy. I try to keep my voice level, not give away that I'll tear this place apart bedroom by bedroom to find her. "How much do you want for her?"

"How bad you want her?"

I hear, "Bad enough to kill you to get her, Charlie," from a voice that surprises the hell out of me coming through the door. "And I would not stand in her way."

It's the Little Man. Lansky.

CHAPTER ELEVEN

The two sharp-dressed goons who usually guard Lansky's hotel door walk in with him, until he tells them to wait outside.

"Really, Charlie," he says when the boys have closed the door, using his fedora to wave away the haze of cigar smoke, "you need to get some fresh air in here. The place is like an incinerator."

"Don't need no fresh air," Ossatura says. "If I want fresh air I'll go sit under a palm tree. A lotta palm trees here in Havana. So what brings you around, Mr. Lansky? I ain't missed no payments."

"I'm here for the same reason Cantor's here, Charlie, but it seems she beat me to it." Turning his most charming smile on me, he says, "What? You still don't believe I would help you? A deal's a deal, and we made a deal. So I made some calls. Those calls led me here." He's looking at me as if finally really seeing me, seeing my bruised face for the first time since he walked in. Then he shrugs, dismisses whatever he feels about the beating I obviously took, and talks to Ossatura instead. "Okay, Charlie, where is she? Where's this woman Cantor's looking high and low for? Have her come down here and hand her over so we can get back to the business of making money in peace and quiet. I assume Cantor offered to pay you?"

"Whatever it takes," I say.

"She can offer me all the money in the world, but she ain't gettin' Mariposa, or whatever her name is." He says all this to Lansky, as if I'm not even here.

But I am here, and I let him know it. "Now listen, you disgusting bag of cigar juice, even that big gun of yours won't stop me from tearing you and this place apart if you don't hand her over. And her name is Sophie."

Ossatura lumbers up from his desk, pulls his cigar from his mouth, and points it at me, the burning tip too damn close for comfort. "Look, I don't know who the hell you are," he says, "and whatever deal you made with Lansky cuts no ice with me, but you ain't gettin' that woman. An' you know why?" He's positively grinning now.

"I'm not looking to play games, Ossatura. I'm looking for answers. Fork over."

He sticks his cigar back in his mouth even as his grin gets wider, his eyes narrowing into slits glassy with contempt. "You ain't gettin' her because she ain't here no more."

Never mind that my guts just sank like jagged stones. Never mind that explosions are going off in my head. My hands, with a will of their own, grab Ossatura by the collar. Words shoot like spikes from my mouth. "*Where. Is. She?*"

My grip is so tight around Ossatura's collar his face is turning red. I keep squeezing, keep saying, "Where is she? Where is she?" over and over until Lansky finally pulls me off.

"He can't tell you where she is if you choke him to death, Cantor."

I have to force my fingers open, force myself to let this sack of pus go. Ossatura falls back into his chair, nearly knocking over the bottle of rum on the desk, but when he reaches for his gun, it's not there.

It's in Lansky's hands. He must've grabbed it when Ossatura fooled around with me and took his attention away from the desk. "Charlie," Lansky says as if speaking to a naughty schoolboy, "you know I don't go in for violence. Now, do yourself—and me—a favor and answer Cantor's question, you understand? Where is this woman?"

I'm having a tough time believing that the sweat stained lump in the chair was once a feared enforcer for the Mob, the guy who scattered skeletons and earned his Break Bones moniker. He's so cowed, he even needs a swig of rum before he can talk. "I don't know," he says, then takes another pull on the rum. "She...she skipped."

"Got away? Right out from under your nose?" I say, teetering between smashing the guy's face with my fist or laughing in his face instead. The laughter wins, a small, bitter, miserable laugh with no joy in it, except for the thrill of letting it dig deeper into Ossatura's humiliation. He must be the only brothel owner to let a woman get away. "When?"

"Coupla months ago," he says, "November. Yeah, November. Jeez, they ain't got no seasons here. Can't tell summer from winter."

"Well, Cantor," Lansky says, "maybe she's found her way back to New York. You should go home, look there. You have connections there who can help you."

"You mean Loreale? He'd sooner help me into a coffin."

"You misjudge him, Cantor. Loreale is much too careful with his money to waste it on a coffin."

Very funny. But I'm not laughing anymore. I'm thinking scary thoughts, thinking about why I haven't heard from Sophie if she really got away from Ossatura. If she'd made it back to New York, she'd have phoned, or even showed up at my door. If she'd made it back to New York... "She must still be in Havana," I say.

"Mebbe," Ossatura says with a shrug, "but if I was you, I'd get off this island."

"Not until I find her," I say.

He shrugs again, says, "It's your funeral," and takes another swig of rum. "People are lookin' all over for you. Like I told you, word gets around."

"Word gets around about what?"

"About that Estrada business."

"If word's going around that I killed him, then everyone's got the word wrong. Where'd you hear it, Ossatura?"

Lansky says, "I'd like to know that, too, Charlie."

Ossatura's jutting out his jaw, trying too hard to be the tough guy he once was. But I guess he hopes we won't notice he's holding his cigar so tight between his teeth he almost chews it in half before he says, "You know, around. I heard it around."

Lansky, calm as an undertaker, puts his hat down on Ossatura's desk, the move a cunning signal that Lansky will use his considerable power to move in and take over Ossatura's turf if he doesn't cooperate.

Ossatura's jaw gets back where it belongs, his teeth loosen up on the cigar. He gets the message. "I heard it—"

A commotion at the door stops Ossatura from talking, but it doesn't stop him from bleeding where a knife thuds into his chest.

❖

One of Lansky's goons, the well-dressed one who could pass as a politician's bodyguard, has his arm around the knife thrower's neck. Blood drips from the goon's hand because the other goon, the one who could pass as a hotel's house dick, is dead in the doorway, his throat cut. People are screaming in the casino, scrambling to get out.

The knife thrower, a tall skinny guy in a cheap powder-blue suit, his eyes bugging out from the press of the arm around his neck, tries to talk but can only sputter, "Perros Amer-i-canos!"

I'm pretty sure he's trying to call us all American dogs.

"Hold him," Lanksy tells his thug, "but let go of his throat."

The guy gulps air when his throat's free, his arms pulled behind his back by Lansky's man.

Lansky's still calm, but there's no charm in his smile now. The little V is sharp and hard. "Listen, my friend, who sent you to kill Charlie?" The sight of short Lansky looking up to the tall killer would be funny if it weren't for the cool, menacing power that flows through the Little Man as easily as breath.

The guy's answer is to spit in Lansky's face.

Lansky barely flinches. He just takes out his handkerchief and wipes the spittle away.

Sure, you don't get to be the Mob King of Havana by rolling over just because an assassin spit in your eye. "Perhaps he doesn't speak English," he says.

"Oh, he savvies English, all right," Lansky's thug says. "He jabbered plenty outside, tellin' me and Barney to get outta the way. I was tellin' him to get lost when he pulled that knife and slit Barney. He almost slit me, too, but I grabbed him. The sonovabitch jabbed my hand, otherwise he wouldna made it through this door." He sounds a little desperate. Failing Meyer Lansky is probably not a good career move.

"Well, then," Lansky says to the assassin, "let's try again. Everyone deserves a second chance, right? After all, it's the American way. Listen, things will go better for you if you tell me who wants Charlie Ossatura dead, and why."

The guy looks from Lansky to me to dead Charlie Ossatura and back to Lansky. "You Americanos, *every* Cubano wants you dead."

"No," Lansky says, looking at the guy like he's no more than a mote of dust to be swept aside, "not every Cubano." He turns away from the assassin, takes his hat from Ossatura's desk. "I have no more time to waste on this schlemiel, and we won't get anything from him, anyway. Either he's so far down the pecking order he doesn't know which higher-up ordered the hit, or he's a true believer ready to die for his capitán. Either way, he's useless. You know what to do," he tells his thug. "After it's done, call the hotel, tell the boys to send someone over to help you clean this mess up. I'll keep this," he says, pocketing Ossatura's gun. Putting his hat on, he smiles at the assassin. "Good-bye, my friend."

❖

The parking lot, empty except for my rented Olds and Lansky's big blue Lincoln, shimmers in the late afternoon heat. "Sorry about your man," I say. "A slit throat is a helluva way to die."

"A risk of the game," is all Lansky says, sending a chill through my bones even in the Havana heat.

"One of us has been ratted," I say, lighting a smoke. "But by who? And which one of us was the mark?"

"I wouldn't put it past Hidalgo," Lansky says. "He's a *pisher*. And a sneak. Can't trust his handshake. He'd just as soon pick my pocket as do business with me. And he knows I had a connection to

Ossatura. Charlie and I go back a long way. He used to be a good soldier in the New York outfit in the old days."

"So I've heard," I say.

"All Five Families trusted him. Poor schmuck lost it to the bottle."

"Too bad," I say with no feeling and a *Who cares?* shrug. "You and I both know better than to depend on brainless muscle. And Ossatura struck me as brainless. Maybe he was stupid enough to be in cahoots with Hidalgo, or side with the Animas Boys against Santiago, or maybe he was in bed with Santiago after all. Could be it was Santiago who ratted *me*. He sent me here in the first place."

"Was it Santiago who roughed you up?"

"He let one of his goons try to rearrange my face with the butt of his gun, but I guess Santiago didn't like the result and he tried his own talents as a bone sculptor. Fists and a big mouth may be all he's good for. The real brains in Santiago's outfit seems to be a dame named Zamira. She may have her own reasons for hating Ossatura. You know who I'm talking about?"

Lansky shakes his head, a slow, single back and forth that makes it clear he's never heard of Zamira, but I bet it won't be long until he knows everything about her, right down to her birth certificate.

I'm a little surprised, even amused, that Lansky and Sig Loreale had no idea about Zamira when they decided to throw their gangland support to Santiago's Angry Dogs. I suppose even the biggest big shots miss a trick sometimes, or maybe Santiago's reputation as a tough guy was enough to convince them he's the boss and the brains. They'd never guess there's woman in the picture. Men never do.

Either way, it's not a point I'm going to press. I just stick to business. "Maybe Ossatura's killing is tangled up with the Estrada killing and the gang war. Did Charlie take sides?"

"Not if he was smart, but who the hell knows?" A glint of humor is back in Lansky's eyes, the pleasure of someone who enjoys a puzzle because he controls the board and can smash the rules to solve it. "Whoever sent that knife thrower will wonder why he hasn't reported the job done. There'll be trouble over this, Cantor. Maybe more blood in the streets. Well," he adds with a smile and a shrug, "it won't be the first time I have to deal with trouble. Comes with the business, right?" The twinkle in his eyes is chillingly bright. "Listen, come back with me to my hotel. We'll have a drink, see if we can figure out who might be after one of us."

"Thanks, but no. I've got things I need to look into, people I need to see."

"About your lady friend?"

"It's the only reason I'm here."

"You're playing a dangerous game, Cantor. More dangerous now that you're tied up in this Estrada business."

"I'm not tied up in that. I just stubbed my toe over it while doing a favor for you, in case you've forgotten." I should be sorry for saying that the minute it falls out of my mouth, sorry for poking the eye of the most dangerous guy in town, but I'm not. I've had it up to the neck with guys who want something from me: Lansky wanting the Enriquez painting; Hidalgo wanting a path to Lansky; Santiago—and oh yeah, the beautiful Zamira—wanting me to find out who killed Pete Estrada. I don't give a damn who killed Pete Estrada. From here on, all I do is look for Sophie. If I stumble over Estrada's killer, I'll tell Lansky and Santiago. Otherwise, I really don't care.

But Lansky does. There's no charming little V-shaped smile on his face, no twinkle now in his eyes. "Be careful of going your own way, Cantor," he says. "The world operates on favors. Don't be stupid enough to step on favors, not the ones people do for you, and not the ones *you* do, either. It turns friends into enemies."

"Which are you, Mr. Lansky?"

His smile is back, a tight V, but no twinkle.

An adorable little girl of maybe seven or eight in a blue school pinafore opens the Anayas' door. She has Isabel's warm eyes and silky dark hair but Nilo's solid build. "Well, hola," I say, politely taking off my hat. "Me llamo Cantor Gold. Está tu padre en casa?"

Eyes wide, she hurries into the house, calling, "Papi!"

It's only a minute until Nilo's at the door with his little daughter in tow, her small hand in his big one. This tableau of innocence turns my experience of Havana inside out. Love and tenderness in place of brothels and murder.

"Cantor," Nilo says in a warm proud-papa greeting. "Come in. I see you have met my youngest, Ezmeralda."

"Hola, Ezmeralda," I say, smiling, taking a bit of joy in the little girl's trusting eyes.

"Ezmeralda," Nilo says, "Saluda a Cantor."

"Hola, Cantor," she says in that angelic voice of a well-loved child.

Having done her obedient child's duty, Ezmeralda skips away into the house. Nilo, still beaming with a father's pride, calls after her, "Go upstairs to your sisters and study your English! Ah," he says to me, "she is a treasure, Cantor. And smart. Smarter, even, than her older sisters. I think it will be Ezmeralda who will take over my business when Isabel and I are too old."

So much for innocence.

"Isabel is preparing afternoon coffee," Nilo says as we walk through the house. "I baked pastelitos today. Perfecto!" he says, bringing his fingertips to his lips for a kiss. "The pastry is like air, the guava inside is sweet. You are just in time." Passing the kitchen on our way to the veranda, he calls out, "Isabel, mi amor, bring another cup and plate. Cantor is here!"

The table on the veranda is already set with two cups, plates, cheerful yellow napkins, and a tray of the pastelitos. By the time Nilo and I are seated at the table, Isabel joins us on the veranda, carrying a tray with a coffeepot and an extra place setting and napkin for me.

Standing at the table, she's about to pour me a cup of coffee but puts the pot down, puts her hand under my chin, and lifts my bruised face instead. "You have walked into danger, Cantor. Didn't I tell you yesterday you must be careful?"

"I'll be fine, Isabel," I say, taking her hand from my face and giving her palm a light kiss. "Nothing Nilo's pastelitos and your tender concern can't fix."

"It is no joke," she says, pouring coffee all around and sitting down at the table. "You are dealing with dangerous people. They will not be afraid to kill you to protect their secrets."

"Which brings me to the reason I'm here," I say. "It seems I've been bumping into a lot of people's secrets, none of which I'm interested in. The only secrets I care about are ones concerning Sophie. Have you found out anything else about what might have happened to her? Any lead on where she is?"

Nilo says, "I have heard nothing, and the Estrada killing complicates things."

"You know about that?"

"Cantor, please," he says, taking a sip of coffee, "this is a city on an island. Information has nowhere to go but around in circles, hitting everyone in the ear."

"Yeah, well, I seem to be running around in circles, too. And everywhere I go, someone gets killed. First Estrada and his thug of a butler, then an old-time gangster down on his luck. Charlie Ossatura. You've heard of him?"

"Sí," Nilo says, "I think they called him Break Bones, yes? Used to be a strongman for the American Mob? I understand he has been in Havana."

"Yeah, that's him. Runs a casino and bordello, the Rumba Room. Or rather, he ran it until a knife found its way into his chest. And, oh yeah, the guy who threw the knife is probably dead now, too."

"On whose orders?"

"Meyer Lansky's."

"More coffee, please, mi amor," Nilo says to Isabel. "And Cantor, have a pastelito. You will think you are in heaven."

No pastry is going to take me out of the hell I'm trapped in until I find Sophie, but one of Nilo's pastelitos might take the bitter taste of Havana's disappointments out of my mouth. I came here to find the woman I love, but all I've found so far is blood and betrayal.

The coffee and pastry are going down well enough, but a stiff dollop of Cuban rum would make them go down better, soothe

the ache where Santiago and Skinny Guy clobbered me, quiet my painful worry about Sophie. "She's still in Havana," I say idly.

Nilo says, "You speak of your lady?"

"She's been passed from pillar to post, sold off from one brothel to another," I say, nearly choking on it. "The last one was Ossatura's Rumba Room. But she got free of it."

Nilo's looking at me as if he suddenly doesn't understand English. "But that is impossible—I mean, I have never heard of a woman escaping el burdel. Your lady must be very brave, and very smart."

All I can do is nod, because if I speak, I'll break down and cry. I can cry later, when I've found Sophie and we cry in each other's arms. Until then, no tears, just carry on according to the tough lessons I learned on the streets of New York and the Coney Island neighborhood of my lawless youth, lessons that have kept me stealthy, and alive.

Nilo says, "And you are sure she is still here?"

I nod again, swallow hard, find my voice. "If she'd made it back to America, she'd have gotten in touch with me. So she must still be here in Cuba. Listen, Nilo, I'm going to keep searching, but I'm in people's gun sights, so I have to play things quiet. I need you to be another set of eyes and ears, listen for whispers, listen for anything."

Nilo takes a sip of coffee, frowning in deep thought. Carefully putting down his cup, the china making a delicate tap on the saucer, Nilo says, "Who have you spoken to so far?"

"It started with Meyer Lansky, who put me on to Estrada," I say.

"People are saying you have killed Estrada."

"I didn't kill anyone. I talked to Pete earlier in the day, asked him if he still had the contacts he used to have, maybe help me find Sophie. I was also there to case the place. Yeah," I say in answer to the curiosity on Nilo's and Isabel's faces, "I was figuring how to steal a painting he had on his wall. It was a deal I made with Lansky: steal the painting in exchange for Lansky's help in finding

Sophie. When I went back that night to do the job, Pete and his man Armando were already dead, knifed. But they hadn't been dead long. The blood was still fresh."

Isabel, looking like a worried mother, says, "You are lucky the killer did not see you, Cantor. You could have been killed, too. Did you see who did it?"

"Uh-uh. They were gone when I got there, but I figure the killer must've been known to either Pete or Armando, because Pete's security alarm didn't off go in all the time I waited outside for those guys to go to bed and kill the lights. The killer had to be let in, and after the murder was done, the killer put out the lights and just calmly left by the front door. The alarm wouldn't sound from the inside."

Nilo, shaking his head, sips more coffee, while Isabel, worry still on her face, leaves the table to attend some of the veranda's potted plants.

Nilo says, "Who else did you talk to?"

"I ran into Agnes Cain—remember her?—who set me up with Rudi Hidalgo. Hidalgo sent me to Tomas Santiago, and Santiago sent me to Charlie Ossatura."

My litany of Havana's criminal names gets a stunned silence from Nilo, the quiet broken by the scrape of a large potted palm Isabel drags from one place to another on the veranda. I've always figured Isabel is a formidable woman, but I had no idea how formidable until I see her manhandling the big palm in the heavy pot. First time I've smiled with pleasure all day.

Catching sight of me watching her, she gives me a grin, says, "Do I surprise you, Cantor?"

"A little," I say.

"You should not be surprised," she says, sitting down again at the table and pouring herself a cup of coffee. "I have given birth to three children, and then carried them around. A mother is strong inside and out!" She delivers it with a hearty laugh.

I'm reminded again just how lucky Nilo is.

He says, "So, Cantor, what is your next move?"

"Dig deeper," I say. "Get deep down where the secrets are buried."

Isabel leans over to me, puts her hand to my cheek. "Please be careful," she says, her whisper full of tender concern and warm warning. "Take care not to pull the wrong secrets out of the ground, querida, or they will pull you back down into the ground with them."

CHAPTER TWELVE

Even at this near dusk hour, the Havana air is still heavy with heat and the sweet perfume of flowers lining the walkway to Agnes's place.

I ring the doorbell. A minute later, Agnes opens the door. Seeing me, she looks surprised, the result, I suspect, of the battered state of my face. She's already dressed for the evening trade, wearing a green and silver gown with an abstract pattern of circles that just misses being gaudy. Her gold and ruby rings catch the dusk light. Her bottle-brunette hair is tightly styled, her blue eyes heavy with mascara, her lipstick red as blood.

Her surprise gives way to greeting me with a sales pitch smile. "Back so soon, Cantor? Will you want Veronica again? I'll tell her you're—"

"Not Veronica," I say, walking in. "You. I'm here for you, Agnes."

"Well, I—I'm flattered," she says with a pathetically pleased smile, "but I thought you knew I no longer practice the physical side of the trade. I'm strictly a business operator now."

"I'm not here for your flesh, Agnes. I'm here for your talk."

The pleased smile hardens into a protective grin, a wall of teeth guarding her humiliated pride.

"But I can respect the business angle," I say, lightening things up, working to keep Agnes friendly and talkative. "I'm willing to pay for your time." I pull a C-note from my stash, say, "This oughta do it," and tenderly slide the bill into the low-cut bodice of her dress. "Easiest hundred American you've ever made, Agnes."

"I doubt it," she says under her breath. Then, "Let's go to my office."

I follow her across the living room where last night's glamour girls and pretty boys seduced not-so-pretty men and women into bedrooms and out of their clothes and cash. I was one of them. Now, though, the living room is only sparsely populated with elegantly dressed working girls and tuxedoed professional Romeos attending to the early evening customers. Give the place a few hours, and the room will be stuffed with well-heeled locals and fat-walleted tourists living their champagne-and-sex fueled dreams.

Elspeth, aka Veronica, gives me a wave from across the room. I nod back at her, even give her a smile, but keep walking.

Agnes's office is down the hall from the living room. Even in the pale early evening light coming through the louvered window, I can see that the office is nicely furnished in what might be called Cuban Modern, the sleek look gaining popularity since the end of the War but given an island flavor with upholstery in colorful fabrics, mostly reds, pinks, and pastel greens. The room keeps the tropical feel with walls of warm pale yellow, the color of Havana's winter sun. The window looks out into a walled garden, a darkening green in the approaching dusk. But despite the office's cozy decor, the room testifies to a cold life. Except for a selection of liquor bottles and glasses on a credenza behind the desk, and fancy cut-glass ashtrays on the desk and coffee table, there's nothing personal in the room, nothing decorating the walls, nothing on Agnes's desk except a blotter, a black marble-and-brass desk set, and a telephone—no photos of loved ones, no snapshots of pals, not even a picture postcard from some wild weekend she might want to remember. I don't know whether to feel sorry for Agnes or put on a coat against the chill suddenly seeping into this corner of Havana.

Agnes says, "Drink?"

"I wouldn't mind," I say, taking a seat on the couch. "Scotch. Chiv—"

"Chivas, neat. I know. Don't you remember, Cantor? I told you I know every client's taste, even going back years. Good business."

"And it's evidently paid off," I say.

Handing me my Chivas, Agnes pours herself two fingers of rum, takes a sip, puts it on the desk, and walks over to a closet door. "Listen, since you're here, there's something I want to show you." What she pulls from the closet causes my breath to stop dead in my chest: the Enriquez painting. Even in the fading light, those wild colors zing through the room.

Agnes keeps an eyebrow cocked as she looks at the painting. "A gift from Rudi Hidalgo. He came by with it this afternoon, a present to spruce up my office, he said. Give it some personality. For chrissake, Cantor, I don't need personality in my office. I just need a place to tally the cash. But Rudi…well, he thinks of himself as a man of taste," she says in a mocking tone, "but I don't know about this picture. I mean, sure, it's colorful, but what the hell has a horse got to do with my business? And why is there a drip of blood on the edge? You're the art expert, Cantor. What do you think?" Finally looking at me, her eyes wide, she says, "Hey, you okay? Why are you gagging on your scotch? It's your favorite label."

I manage to swallow the scotch, then say, "Did Hidalgo mention where he got it from?"

"No, and I didn't ask. Didn't your mother ever tell you it's not polite to ask where a gift comes from? And anyway, it's never a good idea to ask too much about Rudi Hidalgo. He and I do a bit of flesh trading, but I never fish around in his pockets. He has dangerous pockets, and even more dangerous friends."

"You don't know how dangerous," I say. "I know where this painting came from, Agnes. It's passed through the hands of a couple of Havana's most dangerous guys. One of them is dead, and the other has more power than General Electric. Sit down, Agnes, we're going to start that talk now, and you're going to earn every dime of that hundred I gave you."

But Agnes doesn't sit down. She picks up her glass of rum from the desk and takes the hundred from the bodice of her dress as she walks over to the couch and holds the cash out to me. "No amount of dough is worth my life, Cantor. And I got a feeling you want the kind of information that trades on my life."

"Keep the money," I say, standing up and putting the C-note back into her cleavage. "Add it to your stack of get-outta-town-fast cash. You might need it someday, whether you talk to me or not."

"That woman you're looking for," she says, "she's at the center of all this, right?"

"She's at the center of it for me, but on the fringe of it for everyone else," I say, sitting down again. "That fringe is turning out to be full of razor sharp knives, but it's where I have to go if I want to find Sophie."

Drink in hand, Agnes sits down in a chair opposite the couch, the silver circles in her gown catching the last of the evening light through the louvered window, leaving her face in shadow. "I don't know what you expect me to do, Cantor," she says, her annoyance coming through the darkness. "I already told you, I've never laid eyes on her. I don't know who she is, so I don't know where she is."

"But you know people who do, or at least might. From what I can tell," I say, waving my hand around the expensive furnishings, "you're doing all right, Agnes. And you wouldn't be doing this good if you didn't know the right people, the sort of people who can find things out in places high and low. You might have found your girls and boys in the alleys, but I bet a lot of your clients have mansions on the boulevards."

"And those people wouldn't hesitate to carve me up if I opened my mouth, just like what happened to poor Pilar Estevez."

"So you heard about that."

"Everyone in the flesh racket knows about it—well, knows that she's been cut up." A slight quiver in her voice gives away her horror of the butchered Pilar, her fear of what happens to people who talk too much and into the wrong ears, but after a hard pull on the rum, she settles again, if uneasy. "I don't know who cut Pilar," she says, "and I don't ask. There's a war brewing in Havana, Cantor, and I'm not stupid enough to get in the middle of it."

"You mean the gang war for control of the streets."

"Sure. Yeah." She says it like there's more, much more she's too scared to tell. Another swig of rum provides her a momentary hiding place.

I calmly take my own pull on my scotch, put it down on the coffee table, then light a smoke. The flame of my lighter lets me catch sight of Agnes as her fear sinks deep into her bones. I count on that fear being acid enough to soften those bones, maybe even tempt her to make a play to win my protection.

After a long, lazy drag of my smoke, I offer Agnes one from my pack. She takes it, I light it for her, watching her eyes in the flame light. "You have two choices, Agnes," I say. "You can be scared to death about things you only half know, or scared about things you should know. If I were you, I'd go for the second one. At least you'll be prepared in case bad trouble comes your way. You might even recognize who's bringing it."

"And I suppose you're the one to fill me in?"

"As much as I can. Maybe together we can fill in the blanks. I'm hoping that somewhere in those blanks is where I'll find Sophie." Finishing my drink, I get up from the couch, fetch the bottle of Chivas and the bottle of rum, and turn on a lamp, throwing soft light through the darkening room. "We're gonna need these," I say, refreshing our drinks.

I sit down again, set the bottles on the coffee table, and start talking. I tell Agnes about Lansky, about how he brought me into his plan to humiliate Pete Estrada by having me steal the Enriquez painting off Estrada's wall in exchange for Lansky using his clout to get information about Sophie. "But I still haven't gotten anything useful from Lansky, and Pete Estrada's dead."

Agnes says, "Yeah, so I heard. Bad business." She takes a drag on her smoke and says through an exhale that clouds her face, "But Pete wasn't the big man he used to be." The smoke can't hide a snide edge to her voice.

"And he bet on the wrong side of the war between the gangs," I say. "Threw his lot with the Animas Boys instead of Santiago's outfit. Santiago's got the American Mob behind him."

Agnes says, "Yeah, but Pete never liked Lansky, been rivals for a long time, even back in the States, or that's the word. Look, whoever wins the war for control of Havana is aces with me. I'll just keep on doing business, pay off whichever side still has a hand left to grease. But where are you going with this, Cantor?"

"Tell you the truth, Agnes, I don't know where all this is going yet, but where I've been is a doozy, because after Lansky, there was Hidalgo, who I met through you, by the way."

"I thought he could help. I was trying to help you, Cantor, for all the thanks I'll get."

"My money's been thanking you plenty, Agnes, two nights in a row," I say as a reminder about last night's big bill for Veronica's talents, while I wave a hand at her cleavage, tonight's repository for my hundred cash. "And the only person Rudi Hidalgo wants to help is Rudi Hidalgo. Just like he helped himself to that painting. He thought he was doing me a favor when he sent me to Tomas Santiago, but all I got from Santiago was a working over and insults from his brainy girlfriend, Zamira. You know her?"

Agnes gives me a shrug, says, "I may have heard the name," then takes a pull on her drink.

I file away Agnes's noncommittal reaction to Zamira's name, and the possible lie behind it, and go on with my tale. "Yeah, well, all I got from Santiago was a slam to my head and face, and a dead-end chase to Charlie Ossatura's joint, only to be there when Charlie wound up with a knife in his chest."

Agnes takes another drag on her cigarette, but even the thick cloud of exhaled smoke can't hide the spooked look suddenly in Agnes's eyes. The Ossatura killing is news to her, terrifying news. "Cantor," she says, my name sounding like it's been scraped through gravel, "there's something else I need to show you." She snuffs her cigarette in the ashtray on the coffee table, gets up, walks over to her desk, and opens a drawer.

Well, I certainly never saw this coming, never figured Agnes Cain, an old pal from our old carefree days, would pull a gun on me. It's not much of a gun, just a quiet little derringer. But deadly at this range just the same.

"I guess it's official," I say. "*Everyone* in Havana hates me."

"It's your own fault, Cantor. You're stirring up a hornet's nest.

Everywhere you go, you ask questions and someone gets killed. And now you're here asking questions. Do you want to get me killed, too?"

"C'mon, Agnes. We go back a long way. I never wish death to my friends. So how about we stay friends?"

"Making jokes won't help you, Cantor. The only way you can help yourself is by getting the hell outta here."

"Okay, I'll go," I say, walking to the desk, my palms up, friendly as a puppy, "but not until I show you something, too."

"There's nothing you can show me that will change my mind. Either get lost, or so help me, old friends or not, I'll kill you. Believe me, everyone in Havana will thank me for getting rid of the pest who's poking her nose in places she shouldn't, and then we can all just get back to business."

"Consider it my last wish, then, if I'm going to die. So don't shoot, Agnes, until I show you what I've got. It's that photo of Sophie. I want you to see it again, maybe refresh your memory. And don't let your trigger finger get nervous, because—see?—I'm just reaching into my jacket pocket for it—" But my hand whips out my .38, pointing it right at Agnes's face.

I don't think I've ever seen a woman look so stunned.

"Agnes, you run a helluva good house, but you're a lousy gunsel."

If she was breathing any heavier, my hundred would pop out of her cleavage. But her heavy breathing is dangerous. It makes her hand shake, makes her trigger finger wobbly. It could make that dainty little derringer go off and send a dainty little bullet right into my gut.

"Cantor, please, I don't want to shoot you. But I will."

"I don't want to shoot you, either. So what are we going to do about it?"

"Don't test me, Cantor." Her eyes narrowing, her mouth folding into a tight line, Agnes raises the derringer—

But I swat her hand aside fast with the weight of my .38, grab her wrist with my free hand. My grip's tight as I shake the derringer loose. When it falls to the desk, I let go of Agnes's hand and scoop up the little gun. "A lady's gun for a daring lady," I say. "You've got spine, Agnes. I'll give you that."

"Not enough, it seems," she says, rubbing her wrist where I'd grabbed it. "You know, I really was going to pull the trigger, Cantor."

"I know you were. But we're both alive, and we could both use a drink."

"Why? So it will loosen my tongue?"

"If the booze doesn't, I will. Don't look so surprised. You were ready to kill me. I don't owe you kid glove treatment."

She sits down in her desk chair, practically falls into it. "Make that drink a stiff one," she says.

"Keep your hands on the desk while you get up from the chair, Agnes."

"What?"

"You heard me. You wouldn't be the first person to have a buzzer under the desk, alerting a goon or two to come in and work me over. So keep those hands on the top of the desk, stand up, and walk back to the chair by the couch." I raise my .38 to her eye level to make the point.

The smirk she gives me tells me I've pegged her play, but she does as she's told and walks back to the chair. When she's seated, I pour a hefty rum for her and a scotch for me, but keep my .38 in the open. "To our health," I say.

"Very funny."

After both of us swallow a deep and badly needed swig of our drinks, I say, "Okay, Agnes, I've told you my story. It's time for you to talk and tell me what I need to know. Start with Hidalgo. What's his action? I figure he's running something through the Sevilla Biltmore. Gambling? Women?"

"He can't touch gambling. He'd get his hand slapped until it was a bloody stump. Gambling in the hotels is strictly run by Lansky's Americans. They don't make room for competition. But yeah, Rudi runs women through the Sevilla. He keeps his own stable, sends them up to the hotel's wealthier guests. I hear he gives his girls a good cut, though."

"Nice of him," I say. "Is that it? He pimps through the hotel?

That's a good racket, but the money's not reliable. Sometimes a hotel has a guest book full of deep pockets, sometimes it's just cheap junketeers and their wives from Poughkeepsie. Hidalgo likes to live high. He needs steady money, and lots of it. The hotel flesh racket wouldn't cover it. So what aren't you telling me, Agnes?"

She throws me a look that buffaloes me, like I'm a wet behind the ears kid she's never seen before and just met for the first time. "Are you kiddin' me, Cantor? You've been around the whorehouses long enough to figure the money flow. Or have I figured you wrong? Well, I'll be damned," she says through a cold, slowly spreading smile. "You're just like all the other suckers who think they'll find an hour of honest romance between the rented sheets." And then she laughs.

I get laughed at a lot, usually before a woman turns me down for a date or a dance back in New York at the Green Door Club, or before some gangster's bruiser or snarly cop wants to teach me a lesson with his fists. But I've never been laughed at by a sex peddler. I guess there's a first time for everything.

And then I get it. I guess I always did but never thought about it. I guess I am what Agnes says I am, another romantic sucker who doesn't see past the pleasure I pay for, doesn't see the fate of the women providing the pleasure. "He sells the women," I finally say, each word dropping like lead. "He sells them off, just like Santiago sold Sophie to Ossatura. And just like you do, too, Agnes." I take a deep pull on my scotch, swallow it hard, hoping the whiskey might burn through all my lousy feelings. It doesn't.

Agnes isn't laughing now. "You were there when Charlie Ossatura was knifed? You saw who did it?"

"A tall skinny guy," I say, relieved to be talking of murder and not the sale of women, the sale of Sophie. "Lansky tried to get him to talk, say who sent him, but—"

That sits her up. "Lansky was *there*? He usually sends his boys to collect the skim. Never heard of him making the rounds himself. What the hell was he doing at Ossatura's place?"

Now it's my turn to smirk, but it's not at Agnes, it's at the memory of Meyer Lansky walking through Charlie Ossatura's low-rent door. "Believe it or not, he was there to help me get information about Sophie."

She gives that a snort so heavy it hammers right down to my bones. "That's his story, huh? Listen, Cantor, remember that war I mentioned?"

"You mean the one you tried not to talk about?"

"Okay, yeah," she says, squirming like a rat caught in a searchlight, "that one. You thought it was just rival gangs, but there's a lot more at stake than just the streets."

"So I hear. Look, I don't give a damn about any of it. It's not my fight, and I don't care who wins. I'm in Havana for one reason."

"You just don't get it, do you. You've walked into a battleground."

"You seem to be surviving it all right, Agnes."

"Because I play it smart. I don't poke my nose where it don't belong. Listen, Havana's a boomtown. Everything's for sale—flesh, gambling, and yeah, even death—and too many people want a piece of it all. Sure, the gangs figure it's their turf because they're native Habaneros. But they're not in it alone. Money and guns are going back and forth between the gangs and those troublemakers in the hills, those guys who want to throw out the Americans along with the Cuban government the American dollar is paying for. And then there's the money and guns flowing *to* the gangs from Lansky and the rest of the American Mob to try to stop the local boys from taking up with the rebels. And then there's the money and guns going *both* ways from the politicians and the police who talk out of both sides of their mouths and shoot whoever pays them more that week. And now here *you* are. You say you need to run around the fringe of all this, but you're actually running around in the middle of it, trying to find one woman who's probably been passed through all the hands in all those armies and ended up with Charlie Ossatura, one of Lansky's lackeys."

I hate everything that just came out of Agnes's mouth. I hate the words, I hate their truth. All I have is a weak but hopeful, "She escaped from Ossatura's joint. Two months ago, November."

"Well, good for her. On her own, no money, no protection, on the run from Ossatura for two months, no one's seen her since. You know what, Cantor? My money says she's dead."

"No. I don't believe that. I can't." Too bad I'd turned the lamp on. The light's making it tough for me to hide my shakes from Agnes.

She swallows the last of her drink, says, "Your loneliness is showing, Cantor. It'll get you killed."

CHAPTER THIRTEEN

A couple of tourists—him in an off-the-rack dinner jacket, her in a pink satin coat that wasn't bought on Fifth Avenue—are taking up Rudi Hidalgo's time at the Sevilla Biltmore's concierge station in the headache pattern lobby. Noticing me, he answers the last of the tourists' questions—"What's the name of that place where Hemingway hangs around?"—and sends them on their way to the Floridita bar.

Hidalgo is not happy to see me. He stiffens in his suit, a white linen double-breasted number that surrounds his plump body like a plaster cast.

"What's the matter, Rudi? Maybe you thought I was dead?"

"Why would I think such a thing?"

"You knew, didn't you, that I'd get a working over from Santiago. That's why you sent me there. I bet you figured a thug like Santiago would finish me off, get me out of your hair and out of your business, and you'd never even get one finger of your own manicured hands bloody. Wasn't that the idea?"

"Shhh! Keep your voice down. We are in a fine hotel."

"Yeah, so I saw with Mr. and Mrs. Package Tour. Listen, Hidalgo, we can talk here or we can find a booth in the bar."

"No. Not the bar. We can talk in my office." Hidalgo signals with a flourishing hand to a clerk at the reception desk to take over here. He then waves me along to follow him to a door behind the concierge station.

Inside his office, Hidalgo turns on a desk lamp but he doesn't sit down at his desk. Not that there'd be much room. His office is the opposite of Agnes's. Where her desk was sparse, his is a mess of papers, menus, cigarette and cigar packs, matchbooks, a telephone, and a half-empty bottle of rum. I guess all his fussy grooming is just false advertising. The guy's a slob, which fits my current opinion of his soul.

"Why are you here, Gold?"

"I'm here because you're a louse, Hidalgo. The worst kind of creep. But you're a louse with contacts in places I need to be to find the woman I'm looking for. Did you know Santiago sold her to Charlie Ossatura? And did you know Ossatura is dead?"

Even in the shadowy light of the desk lamp, I can see Hidalgo's face go pale. He finally sits down in his chair, which creaks. "I have never met this Ossatura." He says it like he'd rather bite through his tongue than say the guy's name.

"But you know who he is, or was. Used to be a big shot in the Mob, but fell out of favor and wound up in Havana as just another of Meyer Lansky's lackeys. Poor guy took a shiv to the chest, right in front of my eyes. Right in front of Lansky's eyes, too."

Hidalgo waves my words away, says, "That is nothing to me," with a bravery he can't quite pull off.

"Uh-huh. Speaking of our mutual friend Lansky, how did you get hold of the Enriquez painting I purloined for him?"

He sits up a little straighter for this one. "Not that it is any of your business," he says, getting a better grip on himself, "but Señor Lansky gave it to me as a present. He said he did not have any more use for it now that Estrada is dead and out of his way. How did you know…? Oh, you have been to see Agnes, sí? Yes, I gave the painting to her. I did not like it myself, and Agnes's office could use some, how do you say, *sprucing up*? I considered it a business gift, but I am sorry to say that peasant of a woman did not appreciate it."

"Very generous of you, giving away a work of art worth thousands."

So the cultivated man of taste Agnes mocked turns out to have no taste at all, knew nothing of the painting, or of his admired Cuban compatriot who painted it. Hidalgo's suddenly gone pale again, feeling thousands of American dollars slip through his fingers.

I hate smiling at Hidalgo, but it's the best I can do instead of laughing at him. "Well, much as I'd like to talk art and culture with you, Rudi, I'm here on more gutter matters."

"That woman in the photograph," he says. "You are trying to find that woman. Why do you still think I would help you?"

"Because, like I said, you're a louse, the kind of louse I wouldn't hesitate to beat to a pulp, or even outright kill you, but as long as you're alive, you can be a useful louse."

"I do not understand. Why do you call me this name, this *louse*? Why so much hate for me?"

"You sell women, Rudi. You sell them like so much meat off the shelf. For all I know, you found Sophie after she skipped out on Ossatura, and you sold her."

"Listen to me, you stupid American. I do not know this woman, this Sophie—"

"Then that's lucky for you. I won't kill you tonight, unless you don't play ball, in which case"—I pull out my .38, aim it at him—"I'll blast your head to pulp."

If he was pale before, he's now gone as white as his suit. "That will not be necessary," he says quietly but bitterly.

"Glad to hear it," I say and slip my gun back into my rig.

He lights a cigarette from an open pack on his desk, strikes a match. Even the light of the flame can't warm the icy blue of his small, nervous eyes.

"You've got your ear to the gutter, Hidalgo. Have you heard any whispers about a woman who escaped from Charlie Ossatura's bordello?"

The way he looks at me, you'd think I told him the moon fell out of the sky. "Women do not escape such places," he says.

"Yeah, that's what everyone keeps telling me. But Sophie escaped. Ossatura told me himself."

Hidalgo takes a long pull on his smoke, sits back in his chair. A thin smile, toothy and wolflike, spreads across his face.

"What's so funny, Hidalgo?" I say, getting a twisty feeling in my belly.

"It is true I have never met this Ossatura," he says through that sneery smile, "but I have heard of him. He fell a long way, as you say, from a man of respect to a lackey running a cheap house and a small-peso casino. In such a place, a disappointed man like Ossatura would never let a girl get away from him." He pauses for another pull on his smoke, then lazily exhales through that sneering smile while every muscle in my body tightens. "Do you understand what I am saying, Gold?"

I understand, but I don't dare believe.

"I think he has told you a fantasia, a story to send you away on the wild goose chase, or maybe just not kill him, though it did not do him any good," he adds with a shrug.

My jaw's clenched so tight, I have to force the words, "He. Did. *Not.* Kill her."

With another shrug, Hidalgo says, "Maybe he did, maybe he didn't. But I have never heard of a girl just leaving el burdel. The troublesome ones are either sold off—or gotten rid of some other way."

There's a frenzy inside me screaming loud, spinning fast, so I surprise myself by how slow and quiet I say, "Is that what you do, Hidalgo? Is that what happens to your troublesome *girls*?"

Hidalgo, his round face now hard as a smooth stone, stamps out his smoke and stands up from his chair. His pride, the confidence that comes from being on one's own turf, challenges the rage that threatens to weaken me. "Do not inquire into my business, Gold. You are not on your New York streets. You are in my Havana. I know its secrets. You do not. Do not be beguiled by our perfumed breezes and pretty sunshine. Havana's secrets go very deep and they can be very dark."

He's right. If I want to stop running around in circles, I need a map through Havana's sweet scented labyrinth. Hidalgo can provide that map, so I'd better settle down, respect his turf, no matter how much it eats me alive. "Then tell me those secrets, Hidalgo," I say. "Let's start with the secrets of the streets. Where would someone hide from a pimp?"

"You still think your Sophie is alive?"

"I will think that until I die."

"Then you are rushing your death. But never mind," he says with a flourish of his hand, sitting down again in the creaky chair. "As a Habanero, I am simpatico to romantic fools. So, you want to know where a girl in trouble would hide. She would have to leave the city, but the chances of her getting out of Havana are very small. If she really did escape from Ossatura, then he would make sure that people were looking for her. Once they found her, either they would return her to Ossatura, and he would—"

"Don't say it."

"As you wish. Or she would be sold, which would be the better business choice. Maybe the chance for profit saved her life."

"Who would he sell her to?"

"Not to the hotels or more high-class establishments, or I would have heard of such a sale. I suppose Agnes has not heard of such a sale, either?"

I shake my head.

"Well then, you must look in the low places."

"Give me names, Hidalgo. I don't want to have to knock on every door in the Callejón de los Burdeles."

"I can only give you one name: Zamira. I understand you and she have met." I could do without the smarmy pleasure he's taking now that the conversation is in the comfort of his turf.

"Yeah," I say, "we've met. She wears purple well."

"She is beautiful enough to wear a cigar wrapper well. But I am sure you have noticed." He seems to enjoy saying that. I don't know why. If he's trying to be chummy, he's wasting his time. Or maybe it's just because he's a Havana flesh peddler, in a town where anything goes, no judgments made, just take the cash. "And I am sure you have also noticed that she is very smart," he says. "Without her, Santiago and his Perros Enojados would still be eating garbage from the streets. But Zamira will not talk to you unless you make it worth her time."

"A handful of American dollars should open her mouth."

Hidalgo's *tsk* drips with ridicule. "You Americans. Everything with you is money. Zamira would not want your money. She would want you to keep your promise."

"My—?" Oh yeah. Estrada. I gave her that song and dance about looking into the Estrada murder.

Well, well. So Hidalgo knew I wasn't dead in the hat shop basement after all. I wonder how soon after I'd been freed Zamira let him know she'd set me loose, and why.

I grab the bottle of rum from Hidalgo's desk. The so-called man of taste didn't even have the taste to offer me a drink. Not seeing any glasses, I take a swig from the bottle, let the sharp booze fill my mouth and burn through me. "You have any ideas who might've killed Estrada? I guess his man Armando just got in the way."

Hidalgo says, "Yes, poor Armando. Loyal fool. But about Pedro Estrada, at first I thought it might be one of Santiago's people, since Pedro was stupid enough to side against him with the Animas Boys. But our friend Lansky would have known about that, and he did not. So it must be someone in the shadows."

"And Havana has lots of shadows."

"Maybe you will find your Sophie in one of them."

"But first I have to know where those shadows are. Where will I find Zamira at this hour?" I say, checking my watch. It's nearly eight thirty. "I doubt she's still in that hat shop basement."

"You simply do not just walk in on Santiago and Zamira, Gold."

"I do if you want to stay alive," I say, bringing out my gun again. "Where is she?"

"Please, just a moment. There is no need for violence." He picks up the phone, dials a number. When someone gets on the line, he starts babbling in Spanish. I catch enough to figure he's talking to Santiago, tells him I need to meet with him and Zamira. "Sí. Pedro. Sí."

Hanging up, he gives me an address.

❖

Sí. Pedro. Sí. Hidalgo's last words on the phone. The sonovabitch just set me up again. I'm sure he told Santiago I have something to say about Pete Estrada's death.

It's nearly nine thirty when I find a parking spot down the street from the address Hidalgo gave me. It's a bustling thoroughfare of small cafés and nightclubs a couple of blocks off the Prado. The clientele on the street looks local, the joints lively but not the flashy sort on Mr. and Mrs. Package Tour's itinerary.

The address I'm looking for turns out to be a supper club called Café La Dulce Noche, the Sweet Night Café.

Let's hope so.

Inside, it's a pretty place, a white tableclothed spot with potted palms around the room, cigar and cigarette smoke curling through the shadowy lighting and swirling around the men and women in fashionable evening clothes. A three piece combo of trumpet, guitar, and conga drum is playing easy salsa on a small stage, while light-footed waiters bustle around tables, taking orders, serving drinks.

Quite a change from a sweaty basement of a cheap hat shop.

The maître d', a silver haired gent in a perfectly tailored white dinner jacket, eyes me up and down, approving of my linen suit but not the person wearing it. He looks at me as if to say, *Sorry, we're fully booked*, even though there's an empty table here and there.

I have enough Spanish to ask to see Zamira, but instead I say "Hablas inglés?" just to give the snooty maître d' a little of his own back.

"Yes, of course," he says with more dignity than the question warrants. "But we are fully—"

"Please tell Zamira, Cantor Gold is here. I'm expected."

That changes things. I don't know if Zamira and Santiago own the joint, or if their gang of Angry Dogs simply has the squeeze on the owner, but whatever the connection, it sure gets me a lot more cooperation from the maître d'.

He snaps his fingers and a waiter appears. He's told to take me to tabla número tres, table number three.

I follow the guy through the club, get the usual stares and glances from ladies and gents as I pass their tables, though this crowd seems to be less sneery than the sneerers back in the States. Just a quick look, maybe a tittering laugh, then it's back to their good times and mojitos. No one here is going to throw a punch.

Table three is near the stage. The waiter removes the *Reservado* sign and takes my order for a Chivas, neat, as I sit down. A tall, leggy number takes my panama, gives me a claim ticket, then walks away with a sashay I enjoy watching. Too bad I lose sight of her as the lights in the room dim. A spotlight opens on the stage, the little salsa combo changes tempo to something bluesier in a Latin sort of way, and the woman who comes out on stage and into the spotlight is an absolute knockout in a gown of yellow and pale pink that fits like a second skin and sets off her blond hair and green eyes. Snake's eyes.

Zamira.

The waiter brings my drink. I need it.

Zamira nods at the combo, and as they riff her an intro, she looks over at me, gives me a smile through lips painted dark red and so full of rotten intentions she should probably be arrested just for thinking. Then she starts to sing. Her rich, dusky voice and slow Spanish rendition of the familiar lyrics certainly put an interesting slant on a Broadway tune of a few years back, "Old Devil Moon."

Any other night I might appreciate the entertainment. I'm a sucker for female torch singers. But I'm in no mood for songs, especially not from the throat of a woman who'd just as soon cut mine. All I want coming up from that chanteuse's throat is information about Havana's shadows and who's in them.

A heavily accented, growling whisper is suddenly in my ear: "Do not think you can play us for fools." It's Santiago, all cleaned up and tango-dancer handsome in a white dinner jacket which can't quite hide his street thug attitude. He puts his bottle of beer on the table and sits down.

"You know," I say under the music, "Zamira has a lovely voice. Does she sing to you, Señor Santiago, when you two…? Well, you know." My grin is the type my mother would have washed out with soap.

"Do your women sing to you?" he shoots back, his own smile even more skin crawly than mine.

We stop grinning at each other. He drinks his beer. I drink my scotch. Zamira oozes her way through "Old Devil Moon."

When she's done, she takes her bow to warm applause, steps down from the stage, and joins me and Santiago at our table. The salsa combo plays some local tunes.

"Querida," Santiago says, pulling out a chair for her.

"Mi amor," she says, sitting down.

"Hello, Zamira," I say. "Nice racket you two have here. You own the joint?"

"Does it surprise you?" she says.

"Nothing you do surprises me, Zamira. Not even that you can wrap your sexy voice around a song. I enjoyed your performance, by the way."

"Gracias, but let's—" She stops talking when a waiter comes by and puts a mojito in front of her on the table.

So the waiter's just a waiter, a regular employee, not privy to Zamira's and Santiago's secrets, maybe not even a member of their Angry Dogs. I now know a little more than I did when I walked in. Café La Dulce Noche is legit, but the money in back of it isn't. The place is a washing machine: dirty money in, clean money out. I look around, wonder how many of the patrons enjoying their drinks, their cigars, their laughter, and the entertainment have the slightest idea that their pleasure is financed by the human misery of the sex, dope, and gun rackets.

After the waiter is gone and Zamira takes a sip of her mojito, she says, "So you have information for us about Pedro Estrada's death? Something we can use?"

"Not so fast," I say, playing an angle, and playing for time. "Santiago, you're a businessman, or so you bragged today before you slammed my face. And wasn't it you, Zamira, who told Tomas not to give something for nothing? Well, I'm not giving something for nothing, either." A pull on my scotch helps warm me into my bluff. Then I light a smoke, another prop in my act. I offer one to Zamira.

"Not when I am singing," she says, her hand to her throat, diva-like.

"How about you, Santiago? American cigarette?"

He swats it away as if shooing an insect. "I do not need your American tobacco," he says. "It cannot compare to a Cuban cigar." He takes one from his pocket, makes a ritual of unwrapping it, removing the colorful band, and hailing a waiter who snips the ends, hands it back to Santiago, and lights his cigar. Tomas Santiago, gang lord of the manor.

Zamira says, "What do you want, Cantor Gold? We do not have all night."

"Oh, will you be singing again? I look forward to it."

Zamira studies me like she's trying to decide what to do with me, which, I see in her narrowing eyes, clearly includes killing me if I try any more of her patience. "Do not play games with me. You will not win."

"In which case, neither will you if I'm dead. So let's talk about shadows instead."

"Did you not hear me?" she says. "Do not play—"

"I heard you, and I'm not playing games. Look, Zamira, the answer to both our problems will probably be found in the shadows."

I have her attention now, Santiago's, too.

I polish off my drink. I need it to fortify my spine if I'm going to pull off convincing these two killers that I know what the hell I'm talking about. "As far as you know, no one connected to your Angry Dogs knocked off Estrada, even though your enemies might assume you did, since he threw his weight behind the Animas Boys. That makes it a safe bet that the Animas Boys didn't kill him, either. And we know Lansky didn't order it. He wanted Estrada humiliated, finished off as a player in Havana, but he didn't want him dead. Once Estrada was knocked down, Lansky could use him, and Lansky isn't a man to waste possible resources."

Santiago says, "Sí, Señor Lansky is an excellent businessman."

"Right," I say, feigning admiration for Santiago's astuteness, which he laps up with a smile and a pull on his cigar. So I keep going. "I thought maybe it was Hidalgo, but that didn't wash. He's trying to get into Lansky's good graces, so he wouldn't make a move on anyone without Lansky's say-so, and Lansky didn't want Estrada dead. And then there's Charlie Ossatura's killing. You heard about that, yes?"

Santiago smirks at the name.

"Yeah, well, no one will mourn him, but his murder throws another monkey wrench into things."

Santiago says, "He was one of Señor Lansky's people, yes?"

"Uh-huh."

"Then it must have been one of the Animas Boys, in revenge for the Estrada killing, or maybe one of the revolucionarios," Santiago says. "They hate you American bullies as much as I do. And Señor Ossatura was a bully."

"Okay, yeah, I can't argue with that. But I needed Ossatura for a little longer. You see, the woman I'm looking for, the woman you sold to Ossatura"—I can't keep the bitterness out of my voice— "actually managed to escape his joint. He might've been able to get me a lead on where she might have gone, but some tall skinny guy with a knife and a mouthful of curses for Yanquis stopped Ossatura from telling me a thing."

Santiago, cigar in his teeth, says, "Well, that is too bad."

"Isn't it," I say, my deadpan doing its best to smother my annoyance. "One thing puzzles me, though. Pilar. The murder of Pilar Estevez."

Santiago leans back in his chair, distancing himself a bit from me. Zamira doesn't move a muscle, except to say, "Do you think we killed her?"

"You didn't kill her," I say. "Lansky ordered it, as a favor to you. But none of your Angry Dogs did the job. I put it on Hidalgo, or rather someone he paid to do it. That fussy little snoot wouldn't dirty up his manicure. But Lansky knew Hidalgo wanted to cozy up to him, so I figure he tossed Hidalgo the contract for the blood work. In the end, everybody gets a favor all the way around: you two, Hidalgo, and Meyer Lansky. Pretty cute."

Zamira puts down her mojito, picks up a napkin from the table, and delicately dabs her lips, leaving a dark red impression of her mouth on the square of white. Even her movements are snakelike—graceful, seductive, and terrifying. "I do not care about any of this," she says as she puts the napkin down. "But what you say about the shadows interests me. I think you are right. I think someone is moving around behind all of us, sending us in circles to point guns and knives at each other. This person is very smart."

"This person is probably responsible for the death of Pete Estrada, and Armando, too," I say, "whether they actually wielded the knife themselves."

Zamira says, "Do you think this person has the woman you are looking for?"

I'm tempted to snap back, *You mean the woman you and Santiago sold?* but insulting Zamira isn't going to get me what I want, so I swallow it and just say, "It's possible, but I don't see where the two are connected. At least not yet, or maybe not at all. But this is why I wanted to talk to you, Zamira. We can help each other."

This finally gets a laugh from her, or a hiss that tries to pass for one. "I am not interested in helping you. I am only interested in finding this person in the shadows, the person who killed Pedro and made all this trouble, which you promised to do in exchange for your life."

"And I thought you were smart as well as beautiful," I say. "You're still beautiful, though."

Santiago leans in to me, grabs the lapel of my suit jacket, the he-man protecting his woman from the likes of me.

Zamira pulls him back. "Not here, mi amor."

"I told you, Zamira," I say, straightening my jacket. "I don't give something for nothing. You want to kill me? I'd like to see you try. I've survived all kinds of attacks on my life, from thugs tougher than you two. Even from the Law. But who knows? Maybe you two can finally pull it off. And then you'll have to find Estrada's killer and survive the gang war and Lansky's schemes all on your own, but you and your Angry Dogs will be too exposed to do it. By myself, I can move through the shadows, I've done it all my life. But first I have to know where those shadows are. That's where you come in. You *know*. You know where Havana's shadows are, the kind of shadows desperate people hide in. I'm counting on finding Sophie in one of them. And I'll bet you ten to one that Estrada's killer is in one of them, too."

Now it's Zamira who leans in to me, her glistening green eyes looking at me like I'm prey. To my surprise, she strokes my face. It feels like a slither. "I will send you to where you can learn about the shadows, Cantor Gold."

CHAPTER FOURTEEN

I have a name and address in my pocket, written by Zamira on the same napkin she used to wipe her mouth. She wrote it across the lipstick stain, smearing the impression of her lips.

This end of Calle Luz doesn't live up to its name, Light Street. The narrow street of down at the heel one- and two-story Spanish Colonials is dingy as a slum hallway. But it's not a dead street. A few hard shafts of light from the neighborhood's waterfront saloons cut into the street through slatted windows or when guys heading for hangovers stumble out through the doors, sometimes with equally stumbling women.

I get a sick feeling when I look at the women's faces, my soul squeezed between relief and disappointment that none of them are Sophie.

I spot the address Zamira wrote on the napkin. A sign above the door reads *Taberna Escorpión*, the Scorpion Tavern. I'm not crazy about the moniker with its implied deadly sting. I can do without more threats tangling up my search for Sophie. On the other hand, maybe they just pour strong booze.

I'm supposed to ask for a woman named Mirana. She evidently owns the joint.

Inside, the thick cigar and cigarette smoke makes everyone look like ghosts. But the rough crowd is very much alive, despite the sting of Taberna Escorpión's booze. And unlike the refined ladies and gents back at La Dulce Noche, someone here could very well throw a punch.

I start getting the business on my way to the bar: hard stares, sharp sneers, and phlegmy Spanish that's too street inflected for me to catch, but I get the gist. This crowd doesn't like outsiders, especially fancy-suited outsiders like me.

I'm not in the sophisticated precincts of the Prado or the Vedado anymore. I'm in the part of town where life is rough and attitudes rougher.

A big guy puts himself in front of me just before I reach the bar. The guy's brown chinos and threadbare red-and-white striped pullover are sweat stained, and he needs a shave. Could use a good tooth-brushing, too. But no amount of hygiene is ever going to make this lug a gentleman. Not with that snarl on his lips and a mean, drunken stare in his bloodshot eyes. I get the message. He wants me to get out of here.

I want to say, *Listen, big guy, I'm not here to make trouble*, but I don't have enough Spanish for it. Best I can do is "Mirana está aquí?"

"Hey!" comes from a woman's throaty, tobacco deep voice at the far end of the bar. "You Americano with the ugly Spanish! Who is asking?"

I step around the big guy. He tries to block me, but the woman says, "Siéntese, Raoul." The guy does as he's told, wanders back to his table and sits down. The crowd settles back into the business of getting stinking drunk as I make my way down the bar.

The woman with the throaty voice has seen better days, but what's left of her looks tells me those better days were probably spectacular. Under steel-gray wavy hair that has traces of its original black is a face still carved fine as a church Madonna but a lot lustier, even through her leathery skin. Plenty of curve remains in her lips and plenty of life in dark brown eyes that look me over with the efficiency of a she-wolf eyeing her prey. Her body might have gone fleshy but shows shapely remnants of youth. Years ago, that shape must have filled out gowns that draped around her like a goddess's chiton, but she's now more comfortable in her belted brown dress. I bet there's quite a story behind what brought her from the glamour queen she might've been to the dowager of this dockside dive.

"You Mirana?" I say. "Zamira told me to look you up."

"And why would she do that, chica?"

"Because you serve the best drinks in town?"

Her guttural laugh is sly and bitter, but with just enough pleasure in it to let me know that she enjoys my ice-breaking humor. "Sí, I am Mirana," she says. "Who are you?"

"My name is Cantor Gold. And I'm looking for someone. Zamira thought maybe you could help. She says you know the whereabouts of every shadow in Havana."

"Did she. And what do I get for this help?"

I glance around the room, take in the peeling mustard colored paint on the walls, the cracked and crooked venetian blinds. "A hundred American," I say. "That should get you a few gallons of new paint and some spiffy new window blinds."

"Show me," she says in her deep near-growl.

I pull a hundred from my stash, fold the bills into her fingers.

"Ah, but my windows are an unusual size," she says. "The blinds will have to be a custom order."

She's got me and she knows it. I pull out another hundred. It better do the trick. I can't eat up too much of my stash in case I'll need it to ransom Sophie.

I say, "Is there somewhere more private where we can talk?"

"The Escorpión is my taberna, this bar is my office," she says, putting the two hundred into a pocket of her dress. "We talk here. But first you drink."

"Sure. Chivas. Neat."

This time her laugh isn't so appreciative. It's just blunt and short. "Go back to Zamira's fancy club if you want fancy whiskey. I will give you rum, and you will give me…dos pesos."

Pretty steep price for the cheap rum she probably stocks. I give her the cash. She pours me a shot of dark poison.

It tastes like crankcase oil and bites like battery acid. I have to cough it down, which amuses Mirana. I get the feeling I've just failed her first test.

She takes a cigar from under the bar, chops the ends with a knife, puts the cigar between her lips, and reaches for matches on the bar. But I'm quick with my lighter, put the flame to the tip.

Keeping the cigar between her teeth, she gives me a smile which seems to suggest I've made up for my past failure and might even pass the class.

"So, American, who are you looking for?"

I take Sophie's photo and my pack of smokes from my jacket pocket. "This woman did the impossible," I say, lighting a smoke. "She escaped a bordello."

"You are right," Mirana says. "That is impossible, unless she is very clever or very lucky, or maybe just very dead."

"No," I say, the word coming out of my mouth like a punch. "Not dead. She's got to be somewhere in Havana. Where would she go to hide or be safe from getting picked up again?"

"Without money? Nowhere. She would be living on the streets. And there are even places..." The way her voice trails off, it sounds like there's bad news at the end of it.

"Tell me," I say.

"Is she Cubana or gringa?" The word *gringa* is extra harsh through the rumble of her throat. "If she is gringa, she will have a harder time if she does not speak Spanish."

"She's American," I say, "but speaks Spanish. The family has roots in Puerto Rico."

"Mmm, sí," she says, looking at Sophie's picture, "I see the Puertorriqueña in her. It is the eyes. Such eyes have power. I can see why you are in love with her."

"Yeah," I say, more mutter than speech. My love for Sophie must be too obvious to hide, though it's probably not helpful, not if I hope to survive the dangerous places I'll have to go to find her. But there's nothing I can do about it. It's all over me like thick syrup.

I put Sophie's photo back in my pocket. "Those places you mentioned," I say, "what kind of places? Where are they?"

The tip of Mirana's cigar glows as she puffs on it, the glow coming through the smoke billowing around her face as she squints at me through the miasma. "Chica," she finally says, taking the cigar from her mouth and leaning toward me, "if she is in any such a place, you do not want to know."

I do a little leaning in of my own. "Where are they, Mirana?" After a minute of eyeballing each other, Mirana puts the cigar back between her teeth and stands back again. "So Zamira says I know Havana's shadows, eh? She is right. I know which shadows are too dark even for the murderous Zamira and her gangster lover with that pretty face. But you and I have made a business," she says, patting her pocket, "so I will tell you where those shadows are, but there is, ah, la complicación."

"What kind of complication? You mean the war between Santiago's Angry Dogs and the Animas Boys?"

She waves that away with a snort. "They are just the soldiers. They are nothing. No, it is the murder that is causing trouble. There has been a murder of a much loved Habanero, and even the rats and cockroaches in the shadows are running around, looking for even darker places to do business. You have heard of this Habanero's death, I am sure, the murder of Pedro Estrada."

Havana, its perfumed air, soft nights, pink sea, and swaying palm trees, its gangsters, tourists, good-time places, easy money, and easy flesh all just came together and grabbed me by the throat.

"Ah," Mirana says, seeing the surprise I can't hide, "yes, you have heard of Pedro's death. You even knew him, they say."

"Yeah," I say, "I knew him. Any idea who did it?"

"There was some talk. It seems a painting of his was stolen, so maybe Pedro and his man Armando walked in and were killed by the thief. But some say no, it was ordered by the American gangsters. And some say it was Santiago's Perros Enojados. And some say it was you, Cantor Gold." Her Cheshire cat grin burns through the cigar smoke.

"I've been hearing that story all over town, and it's not any more true in your neighborhood than it is in Zamira's. And anyway, Zamira seems to think someone else is back of it, maybe someone in those shadows I want to find."

"Someone new?" she says, considering it with another shot of rum. "It is possible, yes. There was something too quiet, too elegant in Pedro's death to be just a bumbling thief, or even the American gangsters. They are brutes."

I never thought of myself as bumbling. "Anyway, Estrada's gone," I say, "and I'm not sure what he's got to do with where I might find Sophie."

"That is her name, Sophie? Pretty name," she says. "Maybe Pedro had everything to do with it, or maybe nothing. His murder is upsetting many people. Many people high as well as low."

"I thought he was washed up."

Mirana gets back to her cigar. "He was not the big man he used to be, that is true," she says, puffing smoke. "At least not out in the light. You know those shadows you want to find? Pedro had business there. Very bad business."

"Mirana," I say, my mind racing, trying to remember every twitch of Pete's eyes, every purse of his lips when I showed him Sophie's picture, "would Estrada have known who is in those shadows?"

"Do you mean, would he have recognized the woman in the photograph? Your Sophie?"

"Yeah, that's what I mean."

"Maybe," she says with a shrug, "but there are many such women in those places, and he would not know all of them. But don't say I did not warn you, chica, when you go where I am sending you. It is not just flesh you will find there, but every kind of...pleasure, and every kind of death."

CHAPTER FIFTEEN

Sometimes shadows aren't dark. Sometimes they're in plain sight, even bright, the glare hiding the rottenness inside them.

I'm standing in front of a small theater whose neon sign is bathing me in pink light—El Teatro de Arte, in Central Havana. The pink glow also picks out the Spanish Baroque gewgaws carved into the building's facade, giving the place an eerie personality of dangerous past and sleazy present. The theater, next to a pharmacy on one side and separated from a neighborhood saloon by an narrow alley on the other, is in the center of a street noisy with horn-honking automobile traffic and peppy with people walking by or hanging around on the narrow sidewalks. Customers are coming and going from a cigar shop on the corner, the camera and film shop next to it, the fluorescent lit pharmacy spilling its greenish light onto the sidewalk, and all the other businesses staying open all night to cater to the local trade and the touristas at the small, budget-price hotel across the street. But according to Mirana, El Teatro de Arte is the entrance to a rabbit hole darker than a nightmare and more depraved than Hell.

The ticket booth clerk, a worn-out woman with a tired face and equally exhausted red hair, doesn't even bother to look at me when I buy a ticket for the midnight show, which starts in a few minutes. Maybe she's grown numb to all the characters who patronize this place, or maybe she doesn't want to remember any of the people who come here. In any event, she just takes my pesos, slips my ticket under the glass, and goes back to reading a Spanish language movie magazine with Lana Turner and a fancy Hollywood mansion on the cover. I guess everyone in the world loves the American Dream, at least until it moves into town and takes over.

The ticket gets me into the main theater, which Mirana said is the easy part. Gaining entry into the theater's well-guarded secrets is going to be a tougher business, the clientele strictly controlled. But if I can work my way into the rabbit hole, I'd better be prepared for what I find there. *Every kind of pleasure, and every kind of death.*

The idea of Sophie forced to satisfy every pleasure and survive every kind of death threatens to tear me apart, but I push that terror deep down inside me, let it stoke the fire burning in my bones, the fire that feeds my rage and stiffens my determination to fight my way through whatever hell infests this place and find Sophie.

Inside, beyond a small lobby that's dimly lit by old-fashioned brass wall sconces on blood-red walls, the theater is an old movie house. It's much smaller than the grand old palaces of the 1920s but probably built around the same time by the look of it, with its own red walls covered in fussy carvings and shadowed with deeply cut niches. The room's hazy with cigar and cigarette smoke as patrons light up while waiting for the night's entertainment. The curtain hasn't gone up yet on whatever the midnight show has to offer, which is evidently going to be racy, if the fleshy naked ladies painted on the red velvet curtain are any indication.

The audience is an odd mix of tourists anxious for the start of the next exotic experience on their junket holiday, local young couples here to put an erotic charge into their romance, well-dressed sophisticates indulging in a bit of the wild side from the safety of theater seats, and the usual gaggle of guys who come to shows like this and keep their hands in their pants.

I take a seat toward the back on the left aisle. I'm not here for the show, but the seat is a good spot to scan a niche tucked into the left wall just inside the theater. Mirana says the niche has a door which leads to basement rooms but is obscured by the web of curlicue decoration.

I wait for the lights to go down, and when they do, I make my move. In the protective shadow of the niche, I find the door, fumble in the dark for the doorknob just as the curtain goes up on a half dozen naked females and one well-endowed naked guy in a tricorn hat. None of the females, to my relief and equal disappointment, are Sophie, but two of them are disturbingly young, nearly children, their faces expressionless except for a haunted look in their eyes. Mirana's words eat away at me.

Everyone's in a rowboat in an obscene tableau vivant of what appears to be "Washington Crossing the Delaware." Either the set designer's never been to America, or I've missed the forest of palm trees in New Jersey. And the presence of the girl children makes me want to wring the neck of whoever owns this joint.

The niche door's locked. There's a keyhole below the doorknob. I guess that's how they control who gets in: only select clientele have a key, which probably costs plenty. With my lockpicks back in New York, and the blade of my penknife too thick for the job—and I'm not the type who wears hairpins, though maybe I should make a habit of keeping some in my pocket—the locked door might as well be a brick wall.

Shooting the lock open is no good, either. It would scare everyone on stage and in the audience, cause a panic, and probably alert a couple goons to haul me out and work me over.

I could wait until the show's over and go backstage, get into the guts of the building from there, but I don't want to waste the time. If Sophie is here, I want to find her and get her out fast. I don't know what goes on in this place. I don't dare let my imagination wander around in my worst thoughts, because if I did, the fire in my bones would explode into an inferno and I'd tear this place apart, which would bring me nothing but those same goons to haul me out of here.

So I have to play it smart and careful, but I can't just dally in this theater while I figure things out, because if the shadows here are too dark even for Zamira, and the action here is as bloodcurdling as Mirana says it is, the last thing I want to do is sit around watching American history as second-rate smut.

I leave the theater for the lobby.

One of the talents of a successful thief and burglar is an

appreciation and understanding of architecture. Breaking in, getting to where the goods are, and getting out again are actions determined by the functions of structure, space, even safety. A good thief knows the difference between walls which simply divide rooms and walls which hold the place up. We know the requirements of fire codes, and where fire escapes, air shafts, heating ducts, electrical paths, gas lines, roof access, basement doors, or service entrances would logically be. Knowing how a building works saves a lot of time when moving through it. So it's with a thief's eye that I look around the lobby.

There's a curving stairway to the second floor. The theater doesn't have a mezzanine or balcony, so there's probably only an old projection booth up there from its movie house days, maybe some offices, possibly a few converted into dressing rooms for the stage show performers, and a bathroom or two. Any ventilation shafts would be cut into the ceiling and vent through the roof. So unless there's a hidden stairway, there wouldn't be any access from the second floor to the basement levels, and according to Mirana that's where the action is. The building isn't wide enough and its structural walls not deep enough to accommodate a hidden stairway. As a movie theater, there was probably never any need for one anyway, so there's no need for me to waste time on a fruitless search of the second floor.

I sharpen my focus on the lobby.

Except for the main entrance from the street and two curtained archways into the theater, there are no obvious doorways to anywhere. I move around the walls, looking and feeling for any not-so-obvious doorways.

Nothing. Not even an air shaft.

The only thing I figure out from the lobby gives me the willies: the place is a firetrap. Everyone in the building would have to either squeeze through the lobby or make their way backstage to a door to the street or the alley or fire escape, if there are any. Suddenly, all those people in the theater enjoying a smoke make me nervous.

But the lives of the exclusive and presumably high-paying clientele downstairs wouldn't be so cavalierly put in danger by whoever owns this place. Their money probably buys them not only a key to the door in the theater wall—and those entertainments I try not to think about—but it probably also buys them a fire exit to the street.

I walk outside.

The front of the building would be too public an escape route for a clientele whose money also buys them discretion. The alley, then, is my best shot.

The side and back of the theater are solid walls all the way up to the top—no windows, no backstage doors, no fire escapes. It looks like there used to be all of those elements when the place was built, but the current owners plastered over the doors and windows and got rid of fire escapes to keep any nonpaying customers from sneaking in. Whoever owns this place now is a coldhearted murderer, whether anyone's died yet in a fire here or not.

But there's a storm grate on the ground at the back of the alley, hidden by the shadow of the theater and the back wall of a building around the corner. It's a nice big checkerboard square of cast iron covering an opening large enough for a person to fit through. I pull on the grate. It gives.

I keep things as quiet as I can and count on the street noise to cover the sound of the grate scraping along the stone floor of the alley when I pull it away. I take out my lighter, hold the flame inside the opening to see what's what.

Bingo. The escape route for the privileged. There's a ladder built in to a side wall leading down below the street.

I snap my lighter shut and climb down, light it up again when I get to the bottom.

I'm in a tunnel leading off in two directions. One direction, the one that slopes down to the street, has walls and a floor of square stones carefully laid. It's likely a sluice tunnel and a passageway for workers who need access to the sewer system at the curb. The other direction is just a rough-hewn passage, with boards for a floor and boards propped against the sandy walls and ceiling. It ain't fancy, but fat cats in a hurry won't stop to question the decor.

I follow the floorboards until they arrive at a foundation wall of the building. There's a makeshift, badly hung door cut into it. A red-orange light seeps around the edges of the door.

Before I put my hand to the doorknob, I have to make a decision: If the door's locked, do I shoot it open, risk alerting the goons again, just so I can get inside? Or do I figure another way, if there is another way, which there probably isn't.

I put my hand on the doorknob but pull my gun just in case.

The doorknob turns. It's unlocked. Sure, it would be. The fat cats pay for the privilege of getting out fast.

I put my gun away, open the door, and step inside.

It's hot as hell inside, but something cold suddenly slams against the side of my head. The red-orange light changes to white sparks shooting through darkness as I feel myself slumping to the floor. And then there's just darkness.

A stinging slap against my cheek. A noise, a grunt-like bellow, shoots from my mouth. My eyes snap open.

All I see in the red-orange light is a dirty stone floor and two big feet next to me in black-and-white wingtips below brown pants cuffs. One of the wingtips is standing on my panama, crushing it. I'm on my knees, my hands pulled behind my back and hog-tied to my ankles with thick rope. Blood's dripping down the side of my face and seeping into the corner of my mouth. I hear a woman's voice say, "I warned you, Cantor. I told you not to stick your nose where it doesn't belong." It's a familiar voice. It's Agnes Cain.

It's hard to look up from my trussed-up position, but I manage just enough to see Agnes, still in her green and silver gown, the red-orange light glinting off her gold and ruby rings. She's holding my gun. "Hello, Agnes," I say. "Who's your friend?" I'm craning my head to the side to catch a glimpse of the owner of the wingtips and brown suit. He's a big guy, or maybe he just looks that way from the floor.

Agnes says, "He works for me. Say hello to Sammy."

"He doesn't look smart enough to work for you." That remark earns me a kick to the ribs from a wingtip.

A noise that sounds like a bark but feels like a gag bursts out of me when the shoe connects with my ribs. It takes a minute to force enough air back into my lungs, get back enough voice to be able to speak, and when I do, it's more of a croak. "Everybody here work for you, Agnes?"

"They do now."

Tough as it is between being hog-tied and the burning pain in my temple where I'm guessing Sammy must've slammed me when I came through the tunnel door, I tilt my head up to see Agnes. I need to see the face of the woman I'd mistakenly pegged as a class act, a streetwalker-makes-good success story, but who turns out to be rotten to the core. I need to see the look in her eyes, see past my gun in her hand to the lies she might tell me, or the truth she might finally admit. I need to see if she has a weak spot I can slip through and get out of this truss and get to the truth about Sophie. "How long has *now* been?" I say. "Who'd you buy or steal this paradise from?"

Her self-satisfied smile is so sharp I think it could sever my head. "Who says I bought it? Didn't steal it, either. Let's say I inherited it."

I let that roll through my brain, let it wander around like a pinball lighting up idea bulbs. "Then who'd you kill for it? Some big shot? Or one of the gang thugs?" But the pinball in my brain hits another bulb, a big, bright bulb which just might throw light into one of the shadows I'm trying to maneuver through, the one that matters to Santiago and Zamira. "Maybe this is where Pete Estrada comes in," I say, pushing my luck. "How about it, Agnes? Did Pete tumble from the gangster heights to become a big money smut operator? Did you kill him for this place?"

"Still with the questions, Cantor? Haven't you learned your lesson?"

"No, I'm a lousy student. C'mon, Agnes, either cut me loose or cut me a break and answer my questions before you finally kill me, which I believe is on your menu."

"I thought about it," she says with the nonchalance of someone trying to decide between ordering the steak or the fish, "when Sammy phoned me and let me know he'd caught someone coming through the tunnel. When he described who it was, I knew it was you. You're too clever for yourself, Cantor. So I'd like to know how you found this place, and who helped you."

"Or what? You'll have Sammy beat it out of me? Ask Tomas Santiago what happens when someone beats me up. It didn't do him and that girlfriend of his any good, either."

Agnes bends down to me, extends her arm, puts my own gun too close to my face for my liking. "I could kill you and finally be rid of you, Cantor. Maybe I should've pulled the trigger back in my office. But like I've been saying since I ran into you at the Callejón de los Burdeles, I'm a businesswoman, and you could be very good for business." She strokes the blood on my face with the barrel of my gun before she stands up again. There's something unsettling about seeing my own blood on the tip of my gun.

"And what business is that?" I say. "We both know I'd make a lousy streetwalker."

"Haven't you noticed, Cantor? We're in a theater. I'm talking about the entertainment business."

"I can't sing. Never could carry a tune."

"But I hear you're a very good dancer. Great rhythm."

"You've been misinformed."

"Oh no, Cantor. My information is strictly on the up-and-up. Veronica is a highly reliable source." There's that head-severing smile again, only now it's not just self-satisfied, it has a cold little laugh behind it. "I told you, I always want to know what my customers like."

"Do you always tell your girls to report back to you about your clients'…uh…performances?"

Still smiling, she says, "Think of it as office memos."

"Uh-huh. Agnes Cain, Incorporated. Purveyor of tattletale sex."

My humor laid an egg. Agnes isn't smiling anymore, her amusement replaced by an annoyed snap. "Okay, enough chatter.

Sammy, free her legs so she can stand up and walk, but keep her hands tied behind her."

Sammy pulls me up after he cuts my legs free. Standing on my feet isn't easy. My head hurts where Sammy slammed me; my legs are cramped and rubbery after being hog-tied. But I shake off Sammy anyway. I'm not about to give Agnes the satisfaction of appearing weak.

She puts the barrel of my gun into my side. "Let's go," she says and starts walking.

The red-orange room turns out to be a boxy hallway. "Taking me on a tour of whatever this place is?"

"You'll see what it is soon enough." She leads me through a door into a low-ceilinged passage lit by a sparse line of overhead light bulbs. Voices of groaning, gasping men and women, and the thin, heartbreaking tones of young girls, are among the sounds of smutty activity coming through doors on either side of the passage. Slow music punctuated by drums comes from somewhere ahead.

Toward the end of the passage, Agnes leads me away from the music and drums. We're in another passage with other doors. I say, "Care to tell me where we're going?" and then follow it with what's really on my mind. "Are you taking me to Sophie?"

Agnes tosses that away with a *tsk*. "Look, I told you I don't know anything about her. I've never heard of her, never met her, never seen her, so stop pestering me about her."

"I believed you in your office back at your house. I don't believe you now."

"Suit yourself. Now shut up."

A few feet later we turn another corner, walk about twenty feet, and turn again into a red carpeted hallway whose brass wall sconces are a better quality than the tired ones upstairs in the theater's lobby. Agnes leads me to a set of polished wood double doors which face another carpeted hallway with the same classy wall sconces.

I figure these carpeted hallways must be how the private clientele gets here. Agnes must've taken me along the service route.

She slides the double doors open.

We're at the top of an aisle leading down into a semicircular theater. Every seat in the place is filled, mostly with men but some women, too, everyone elegantly dressed as if attending a classy evening at the opera, quietly and intently watching a battle taking place in a sandpit.

It's not a battle I want to watch. It's a battle which makes me want to kill whoever set this up, even if it's Agnes Cain.

Two women—one a fair-skinned blonde, the other brown skinned and chestnut haired, both of them naked and bleeding from cuts all over their flesh—both have a long knife in one hand and a length of chain in the other. They're going at each other like two cats trapped in a sack, slashing at each other, blood spraying in grotesque arcs, bloodstained sand swirling beneath their feet, while each tries to lasso the other with their chains to yank them close for the final stab. This horror is a fight to the death.

Neither woman makes a sound, their unnatural silence adding to the horror. The women don't scream when slashed, barely grunt with each whip of the chains. Their faces, shiny with blood and sweat, grimace with teeth bared in desperation and terror. But the women stay as weirdly silent as the rapt audience.

Agnes whispers in my ear, "The fighters aren't allowed to make any sound. If either of them screams or cries or says a word during battle—you see that silver-haired gentleman in the tuxedo seated in the aisle seat in the first row on the right? That is Rinaldo Lopez. He's the manager of the pit. His gun has a silencer. He'll quietly shoot the woman who screams, and he'll shoot to kill."

I don't know what's worse: being brought here to watch the sadistic cruelty forced on the women in the pit, or my helplessness to do anything about it with my hands tied behind me and a gun in my side. "You're a monster, Agnes."

"Maybe. But a rich one. And about to be a lot richer. And by the way, I didn't kill Pete Estrada. I have no idea who did. When word got around that he was dead, I spent an hour or two on the phone, pulled strings, made deals. Remember I said I didn't care who wins Havana's wars? I have friends on all sides who owe me favors. They smoothed the way for me to make my move to take over this place. And you're right. It was Pete's. It was his last goldmine. It's my goldmine now."

"That was fast," I say, not bothering to hide my disgust, not that I could even if I tried, and I don't want to try. "Estrada's body's not even cold."

"Who was it who invented the telephone?" she says, enjoying herself far too much. "What was his name? Bell? Well, I owe it all to the time I spent with Mr. Bell's handy invention, and now here I am, first night on the new job. Ah, look"—she's pointing to the sandpit—"we're reaching the climax. The end will come soon."

She's nauseatingly correct, and I don't even have to wonder how she knows. Either she's a student of fight strategy, or, more likely, she's been supplying the place with women—probably part of that shopping she was doing when I ran into her at the Callejón de los Burdeles—and has been here often enough to understand the rhythm of death.

My heart is breaking for the two women in the pit.

There's a flash of chain as it arcs through the air and surrounds one woman's neck as she's tugged close to her killer. A final gush of blood spurts from the blonde's gut as her killer plunges the knife deep. The blonde goes down, her body in a last convulsion in the bloody sand.

The scene makes me sick. I have to fight to keep from both throwing up and bellowing in horror. But the audience doesn't even gasp. They don't even erupt in a perversity of cheers. They just politely applaud and chatter among themselves with the chilling decorum of patrons at an afternoon tea. I want to rip the heart out of every one of them, but I can't. They don't have hearts.

The winning fighter's flesh is covered in cuts and gashes and blood. The look on her face is tense with misery, relief, and a lurking, eerie air of triumph. She hunches over in pain and limps weakly out of the pit as three beefcakes walk in. Except for bulging silver satin loincloths that reveal more of the goods than they hide, they're naked and oiled, muscles rippling. Two have brooms and buckets of sand, which they pour onto the floor of the pit to refresh it with the brooms, covering the blood. The third piece of beef drags the dead blonde away.

While all this is going on, Agnes signals to Lopez and to another guy standing near him: my old pal Sammy of the black-and-white wingtips. As they make their way up the aisle, I get a better look at Lopez. He's younger than his silver hair would suggest, somewhere in the shallower wrinkles of middle age but still young enough to have the energy for whatever other nasty duties he has besides being a murderous master of ceremonies. His dark eyes show the sharp intelligence of a feral animal.

I get the feeling that as bad as the evening has already been, it's about to get a lot worse.

Agnes takes Sammy's handkerchief from his breast pocket, uses it to wipe the blood from my face, then says, "Hold her, I need to speak to Rinaldo." Handing me off to Sammy, who grips my arm as if his life depended on it, and in this joint, it just might, Agnes and Lopez move out of earshot.

Lipreading isn't in my bag of tricks, though I try as I watch Agnes's mouth open and close with words I can't hear. When she's finished, Lopez nods, walks down the aisle and into the center of the sand pit. "Señoras y señores, ladies and gentlemen," he says, quieting the chattering audience. "We have something special on the program."

A lot worse.

Sammy's hustled me backstage, where he tells two of the naked musclemen to hold me while he cuts my hands free, removes my suit jacket and my empty gun rig, and loosens my tie. It's clear where this is going.

Since beefcake isn't my cuppa tea, being held helpless by two naked specimens is lousy enough, but being stripped bare, including my socks, by a big thug is right at the edge of what I can stand.

But I have to stand it. I have to get through whatever horror show is coming if I hope to get back to my search for Sophie.

Sammy's looking me up and down like he's never seen a female form before. "You got muscles, for a dame," he says. "Could help you win in the pit. Here, this will help, too. Agnes says to make you mad." His grin alone is enough to make me mad as he runs his hands across my chest, down my belly, and grabs me in a place no male has grabbed me since grade school, which makes me plenty mad, yeah, as mad as when I flattened the kid whose hand went where I didn't want it.

I don't have that freedom now, which makes my fury even hotter and my frustration at my helplessness bitter as bile.

Sammy nods to the musclemen. He hands me over and they walk me out to the pit, where new sets of chains and knives have been set out at opposite sides, and where Lopez is finishing his spiel in Spanish and then launches into the English version. "Since this is a special match, the betting will start at one thousand American dollars. In a moment we will bring out our second contender, and you will pass your betting slips to our attendants in the aisles. As always, your debts and winnings will be settled in the cashier's room when you are ready to leave our establishment."

The glare of the stage lights keeps me from seeing Agnes, but I feel the audience's eyes on me, evaluating me, estimating my every muscle. I hear the whispered chatter of the crowd. I'm blind to a clear view of their faces, but I'm able to see a few of them in the rows nearest the pit. It's a mixed crowd of faces of every shade, from continents east and west, north and south, inscrutable faces who are able to hide their perversions behind money.

There are those back home who might say the same of me, that I can get away with my woman-love way of life because of the big money I make. It protects me, buys the connections and the high priced attorney who keeps the Law from deep-sixing me. Well, maybe they're right, at least a little. As far as I'm concerned, my preference for women is as legit as the typical boy-girl arrangement, but sure, I've bought a night of flesh from time to time, just last night as a matter of fact. But I have no taste for the perverse pleasure of someone's torture and death.

Agnes is forcing me to be an instrument of someone's death. Maybe even mine. Either way, she'll make a pile of cash. Yeah, she's a good businesswoman.

Lopez spreads his arms, says, "And now, señoras y señores, ladies and gentlemen, our contenders. You are looking at tonight's favorite, Cantor Gold. She is from America's biggest city, New York, where it is said she is very dangerous, feared for her prowess, which you can see in her strong body." My musclemen turn me around while the audience gives me their polite opera house applause. When I'm facing front again, Lopez continues, "And now for our second fighter." Two other oiled and muscled pieces of beef walk out from backstage holding a naked woman between them.

I want to scream.

CHAPTER SIXTEEN

L adies and gentlemen, meet the beautiful Veronica!"
      If I ever see Agnes Cain again, I'll rip her flesh from her
bones and toss it to the rabid mutts in the street.

It's not the assured Veronica of last night who stands in the
sandpit with me. It's Elspeth Beattie, the naive, small-town girl from
Galena, Ohio. I've never seen so much terror in anyone's eyes as I
see in hers. And I've never felt so much terror in my own soul as I
do now.

One of us is going to kill the other. One of us must kill in order
to live. Finding Sophie depends on me staying alive. Living with
myself will be hell.

But who's to say I'll be the one doing the killing? Sure, I'm
stronger than Elspeth, which I found out last night in Veronica's bed,
but she's younger, and she's damn agile, something else I found out
last night.

Lopez goes on with his spiel. "Veronica is also from America, a
sweet farm girl who has tasted the pleasures of our exciting Havana,
and she has offered those pleasures, too." The musclemen turn
Elspeth around for the audience's inspection and applause.

We're brought to our separate sides of the pit. Lopez takes his
seat in the first row on the aisle, pulls his gun—a big .45 revolver—
from a rig inside his jacket, and under the clear threat of getting shot
if we try to run, the musclemen let go of us and leave the pit.

With gaudy theatricality, Lopez calls to us from his seat, "You know the rules. You must not make a sound. You must bear your pain in silence. Now, take up your weapons!"

Our knives are long, our chains heavy.

"Fight!"

❖

We are bleeding. Elspeth from her face, legs, arms, and chest. Me, from my chin, shoulders, belly, and thighs. The wounds sting, the deep ones burn. We slash at each other through eyes filled with blood and tears, our cries of heartache and our bodies' pain trapped miserably in our throats.

Slowly, slowly, like a creeping animal obeying its hunger, the instinct to stay alive rises in the blood. I feel it in mine. I see it in Elspeth's widening glassy eyes. Our knives push deeper, we whip our chains with more speed. More blood oozes from us. Blood slides down our torn flesh and soaks the sand flying around our feet.

I'm fighting two people: Elspeth and myself, fighting off the savage urge to take her life and spare mine.

And still we keep lunging, the knives keep slashing, the blood keeps flowing.

The rage keeps building. Rage at Agnes Cain. Rage at whoever took Sophie. Rage at Meyer Lansky and Sig Loreale, just another couple of big shot guys with the arrogance to toss their promises away like so many potato peels. The rage burns in my bones, inflames my muscles, focuses my mind.

I love Sophie. I love life.

Elspeth-Veronica is sweet and desperate.

She is not my love.

My knife finds her heart.

❖

Backstage, a muscleman pours water over me, stinging my wounds. The sting's so bad when he rubs me down with a towel that

I snap it away from him, which he doesn't expect. He gives me a shrug that says, *It's your funeral*, and walks away.

But it won't be my funeral. Not tonight. Instead, tonight is the start of an anguish which will fester in my bones. Elspeth Beattie's dying eyes, their terror, will haunt me for the rest of my life.

But I see why my muscleman thinks I'm done for right now: Agnes is standing there, my gun in her hand, aimed at me.

She looks me over like I'm meat on a rack. "You are one juicy specimen, Cantor. You're going to earn me a lot of money. I might even make you my star attraction."

Every muscle in my aching body and raging mind wants to spit at her, curse her, and if it wasn't for that gun, I'd break her in half. She's not a human being to me anymore, she's a monster, a monster who forced me to do what I've sworn I'd never do: hurt a woman. She forced me to kill sweet Elspeth Beattie from Galena, Ohio, the Veronica who shared herself with me and gave me pleasure.

Agnes used her as bait.

But as long as Agnes has that gun, I need to keep her steady, keep her trigger finger from getting frisky. So I hide my fury, find my clothes and my empty gun rig on the floor, and get dressed again, while the monster looks on but doesn't shoot.

Dressed, but not bothering with my tie, just putting it into my jacket pocket, I wipe my face and neck with the towel I took from the muscleman as I approach Agnes. "So what's next?" I say. "Hide me away behind one of those doors we passed on the way here until the next night of murder? Or do you have something else in mind for me, maybe where I heard that music and drums. What goes on there, anyway?"

"That's a performance for another time," she says, "when you're ready."

Yeah, she means when my spirit's broken. It would have to be to make me do something worse than murder. I hate to think what's worse than murder.

"I could use a drink," I say, sliding the towel from my neck.

"I bet you do," she says, tilting her head back in a laugh. So she doesn't see it coming when I snap the towel across her face, unsteadying her as I wrench my gun from her hand.

"Agnes, you might be a lot richer since I pulled that same trick on you in your office, but you're still a lousy gunsel."

It takes her a minute to gather her wits, escape from her surprise and humiliation. Finally reorganizing her face from wounded shock to sneery scorn, she says, "You think you'll get out of here alive?"

"I'll have a better chance of staying alive running through the hallways than I did in that sandpit." Just talking about the pit rouses a vision of the last look of agony in Elspeth's eyes. It fills me with a misery so deep it threatens to choke my breath. I can't let it. Not now. Instead, I let my hatred of Agnes keep me going. "I'm going to turn the tables on you, Agnes," I say. "You used Veronica as bait. I'm going to use you as a shield. You and I are going to walk out of here together."

"And then what? You'll kill me before you walk out to the street?"

"I haven't made up my mind."

I hear, "What is going on here?" from somewhere behind me. It's Lopez. But before I turn around, I grab Agnes's arm and flip her around with me. She's between me and the silver-haired Lopez.

He reaches inside his tuxedo jacket for his .45.

"Don't do it, Lopez," I say. "I'm more than happy to shoot Agnes and take you along for the ride."

His hand slides back out of his jacket.

"Señor Lopez," I say, "where is the woman who fought before me? The woman who fought with the blonde? I'm taking her out of here with me. Getting her to a doctor."

"You cannot," he says. "She is already dead. Her wounds, they were too deep." If it wasn't for the natural music of his Habanero accent, his delivery of the bad news would have been absolutely flat. I don't know if he simply has no conscience or if it was ground out of him from years of working in this torture chamber. I do know, though, that he was perfectly willing to shoot to kill for the sin of crying in pain.

"How many other women and girls are being held here?" I say.

"The ones upstairs, too, in the stage shows."

"You think you can save them all?"

"I think I can try."

Agnes says, "You would, wouldn't you," the smirk in her voice sour as old cheese. "I pegged you right, Cantor. You're a romantic fool."

"You are brave, Cantor Gold," Lopez says. "I saw that in the pit. But your bravery will not be enough to accomplish this foolish thing. Even if you carried all of the women to safety, our members, the people who bet on your fight—"

"And the audience in that other room? The room with the music?"

"Sí, those people, too. They are powerful people. They can buy life and death. They will not let the women live free on the streets to tell of what they saw and did here. In time, all of the women will be found and silenced." He says it like he's tallying up numbers in a ledger. The lives here mean no more to him than that.

I say, "I guess I can expect they'll send someone to kill me, too."

"Once they know you are gone, yes."

"And I'm sure you'll be delighted to tell them."

"Not necessarily. You are not the type to be tamed, so you might be less trouble away from here. But if you plan to make trouble on the outside—" He finishes the thought with a quick threatening shrug.

I brush away his shrug with a smile. "Well, it wouldn't be the first time tough guys have come after me. I'm almost used to it."

"I am sure that is so. Right now, you are the one with the gun, so there is nothing I can do to stop you from leaving. But if you are going to leave here, I advise you to leave now, before someone looks for Señorita Agnes."

"I'm taking her with me," I say. "My insurance policy to get me out the door."

Agnes, stiffening against my gun, snaps, "Dammit, Rinaldo. Do something!"

"What can I do? She is the one with the gun."

"Which reminds me," I say, "give me yours, Lopez. And take it out very slowly."

"And if I do not?"

"I will shoot you."

"In that case," he says with a showy sigh and an oozy smile, "I will give you my gun." With my .38 still in Agnes's back, I keep my eyes tight on Lopez as he walks toward me, sliding his hand inside his jacket. I trust him about as much as I'd trust a used car salesman in an overstocked lot.

I see his gun slide slowly from his jacket: the grip, the trigger, the cylinder, and finally the barrel with the silencer at the end.

I open the palm of my free hand, say, "Okay, hand it over easy."

But Agnes pulls a fast one and reaches for the gun. The three of us—Agnes, me, Lopez—struggle for it, yanking it up and down and groaning like wild animals pawing at meat, until something jerks in my hand and there's that unmistakable pop of a silenced gunshot.

Agnes folds to the floor, blood spurting from her chest, ruining her green and silver gown.

Lopez's gun is in my hand.

Running his fingers through his silver hair, straightening it after our tussle for the gun, Lopez says, "Adiós, Señorita Agnes." There's no more emotion in it than if he'd said toodle-oo to the woman who'd just delivered his laundry. To me, he says, "You may give me my gun now."

"Why? So you can hold it to my head while you throw me into one of your slave chambers? I assume you'll take over the operation."

"I do not want you here," he says. "You would be trouble, rebellious, that is clear. And if I wish to secure my position here, I do not need trouble. I want you to leave. But I need to protect myself from others who will challenge me for this place, so I ask you to return my gun."

"This is the only way you'll get your gun, Lopez," I say, putting the barrel of his .45 hard under his chin. "Do you really think I'll let you keep this hellhole open? I've already killed someone tonight I didn't want to hurt at all. Killing you, on the other hand, will be easy. You're as much a monster as Agnes."

"Killing me will not close this place," he says, more coolheaded than a man with a gun at his throat should be. "If *I* do not run it, the members will appoint someone who will. Or maybe your American mobsters will take over. Some of them are members here, too. Oh, you are surprised? Oh no, Cantor Gold, you cannot be the avenging angel here. There are too many powerful devils in Havana. They will have their pleasure, and if you interfere, they will come looking for you." His face is like stone, its shallow wrinkles unmoving. His eyes stay on me, steady as steel rods. "You should go, run away, leave Havana quickly."

I take the gun from his throat but don't give it back. "I assume you'll take care of the problem at our feet?" I don't look down at Agnes, don't dare let Lopez out of my sight.

"Of course," he says. The man handles murder as if making small change for a pack of smokes. "And I will make sure that the women at her house are well cared for. I will keep that very profitable business running smooth. The women will not be brought here. This I promise you, which I am sure you are worried about. Now you will return my gun, por favor, and go."

"Not so fast," I say. "I have one last question for you, Lopez." I take out Sophie's photograph. "Have you seen this woman? Is she here? Has she ever been here?" It takes all the effort I can muster from my wounded, stinging, bleeding body not to let my voice crack with that terrifying question.

When he says, "I have seen this woman," I feel the air in my lungs start to burn.

"Here?"

"Yes, here. Ah, but do not worry, my friend. She was not a performer in the sandpit or in the Sala de Conquista."

"That room with the music and—"

"Drums, sí," he says with a smile so cold it could freeze my eyes. But at least the air in my lungs cools.

"This woman," he says, "she was a performer upstairs, on the stage. Señor Estrada did not want her harmed. He'd found her starving in the street, you know? Oh, you did not know she was Pedro's woman? At least until she was gone."

I push the .45 back up to his throat, fast, the action automatic, unthinking, an act of pure anger, if not at Lopez then at the words that came up from that throat. "What do you mean, gone?"

With the barrel of my gun deep in his flesh, his icy calm almost breaks, but he holds on. "She became too troublesome, always trying to push him away. He felt humiliated, after he'd saved her life, saved her from starving. Finally, he did not want to see her face, not even down here, so he sold her. I understand she brought him good money."

"Sold her? To whom? Wasn't he afraid she'd tell what she knew about this place?"

"A burdel operator would not care, and neither would the clients. Such a story might even add to her allure. And anyway, she would not be free to tell any nosy reformers, or those crazy revolucionarios who want to make Cuba a place without sin or fun. No, Cantor Gold, whoever he sold her to would not care."

My guts twist with every word out of his mouth. The pain of Sophie's suffering, the pain she might still be suffering, hurts more than all the bleeding wounds on my body. "Where is she, Lopez? Who did he sell her to?"

"Please, the gun in my neck, it makes it difficult to speak."

I ease up the pressure against his throat but don't take the gun away. "You can talk now. Where is she?"

"I am not sure," he says. "He only told me he sold her to a burdel, but he said the place is popular with local Americans—you know, the norteamericanos who no longer live in your country. So go find your Yanqui compatriots. Maybe they can help you. Now, if you will please, give me my gun."

I pull it away from his throat, but a second later push it back again. "Señor Lopez, I'm going to go into the Sala de Conquista. If you are lying, and I see Sophie there, so help me—"

"She is not there. I promise you. Just leave this place. And do not go into the Sala de Conquista. You will not like what you see there, and you will never sleep again."

Chapter Seventeen

Sleep. I'd like to dive into sleep. I'd like to curl up in this rented Olds and sleep away the pain in my flesh and the horrors in my memory. But if I shut my eyes I'll find only nightmares, miserable apparitions of torn bodies and dying eyes. And besides, if I curl up here in the car, the hotel's rental desk will charge me an arm and a leg for bleeding right through the nice white upholstery, just like I'm bleeding through my clothes.

By the time I reach Nilo's place, my shirt is soaked.

It's Isabel who comes to the door. She's in a pink nightgown and white terrycloth robe, her hair disheveled from bed, her sleepy eyes widening at the blood drenched sight of me. "Madre de Dios, Cantor. Quickly, come in!"

I practically fall inside the door.

Isabel props me up against her, puts her arm around my waist, and walks me to the kitchen. Her strength is reassuring, and surprising, until I remember her pulling those heavy potted plants across her veranda and schooling me on what it takes to carry around three children. *A mother is strong inside and out*, she'd said.

Yeah, a little bit of strong mothering would hit the spot right now.

Settling me in a chair in the bright kitchen, its yellow walls cheery as a noontime picnic, Isabel takes first aid supplies from a cabinet and brings them to the table. She helps me off with my jacket, my gun and rig, and then my shirt and undershirt, the last two tossed aside as beyond the salvation of laundry soap. "Trousers, too," she says, noticing the bloodstain along a thigh.

Only my skivvies keep me from being buck naked for the second time tonight.

There's something disconcerting about the married and motherly Isabel touching almost as much of me as Veronica did; Veronica, last night's woman of shared pleasure and tonight's terrified warrior, dead by my hand. But the medicinal sting of whatever Isabel poured on the cloth she's pressing against the wounds on my body and the gash on my chin burns away drowsy thoughts about the two recent sets of female hands on me. The stinging cloth brings me abruptly back to the reality of pain. But this is the searing sting of life, not the flesh-tearing pain of the sandpit death.

Securing bandages to my deepest wounds, her hands and fingers strong and efficient, Isabel says, "You did not listen to me, Cantor. What am I going to do with you? Did I not tell you to stay out of the way of dangerous people? What has happened to you? Who did this to you? Put your trousers on."

"You know I won't stop until I find Sophie," I say, zipping up, putting my jacket on, "no matter how many knives or bullets come at me."

I button my jacket as I hear Nilo say, "Someone is shooting at you?" as he walks into the kitchen, tying a seersucker robe over his red pajamas.

Isabel says, "Shhh, Nilo. Not so loud. You will wake the girls."

"I checked on them, querida. They are sleeping the peaceful sleep of angels." Seeing my bloody shirt and undershirt on the floor, Nilo's eyes, like Isabel's when I arrived at the door, go from sleepy to spooked.

"Look, you two," I say, "I'm sorry to wake you. But I couldn't walk into my hotel at three in the morning bleeding all over the lobby. They'd call the house dick, who'd probably muscle me out the door. Besides, I managed to get some new information and I could use your help figuring it all out. And I really need a drink."

Isabel, taking three glasses from a kitchen cabinet and

motioning Nilo to the living room for the whiskey, says, "What kind of information?"

"About Sophie," I say. "I might have a lead on where she could be."

Nilo walks in with a bottle of scotch and a bottle of rum. "This is good news, yes?"

"It might be," I say, as Isabel and Nilo join me at the kitchen table and he pours the booze: scotch for me and Nilo, rum for Isabel. I down my drink in one desperately needed gulp, let the whiskey pump some gusto back into the blood in my veins, and let its heat soothe my stinging flesh and battered bones. Feeling more human now and less like butchered meat, I say, "Listen, is there a burdel in Havana that's especially popular with Americans?"

Isabel, looking at Nilo and then at me, says, "Well, Sloppy Joe's Bar is popular with Americans, especially your sailors. It is a good place for them to find women. And there are the new casinos and nightclubs opening in Marianao near the racetrack, the fancy new Tropicana, the Sans Souci. Big spots that cater to Yanqui dollars."

Nilo adds, "I have done business in those new places. I could ask—"

"Uh-uh, not the tourist joints. I mean places where the local Americans might gather. The expats." I pour myself another scotch.

Isabel says, "You think your Sophie is in such a place?"

"That's what the guy said."

"Who said this to you?"

"A guy named Lopez. Rinaldo Lopez." The reactions on their faces make it clear they've heard of him, where he works and what he does. Both of them stare at me as if shocked I'm not dead. But Isabel's face also carries disapproval, her brow furrowed, the folds sharp, chilling the usual warmth of her eyes. I guess it's the mothering instinct; she's concerned about the company I keep.

"Cantor," she says, placing her hand on mine, "I know you love your Sophie, but if she has come through that place, El Teatro de Arte, then even if she is alive—"

"She's alive."

"Okay, but she will not be the Sophie you knew. Maybe it is best if you leave this alone, even if it breaks your heart."

But Nilo answers for me. "She cannot leave it alone, Isabel. I could not leave such a thing alone if it was you I was looking for. I would swim through the fire river of Hell to find you, mi amor."

I never knew until now that Nilo is the more romantic half of the couple. Sure, Isabel smiles at his chivalrous remark, but the smile has an impatient edge. "And maybe leave our daughters with two parents dead?" she says.

"Nilo is right," I say. "I survived one hell and would go through more to find Sophie. And I know in my bones that she's still the same woman I've always loved. I know because of how she rejected and humiliated Pete Estrada. Yeah," I add, almost choking on the little word, "Pete lied to me when I showed him her photograph. He said he couldn't help me. The bastard didn't even admit he knew her. Did you know he owned El Teatro de Arte? His last chance at being a big shot in Havana. If I'd known he'd ever had her, I might've killed him myself."

Isabel says, "Then you should be glad he is dead."

"Yeah, I'm glad. But his killing is getting in the way of my search for Sophie. It's poured gasoline on the fire of the gang rivalries, and gotten lowlifes like Rudi Hidalgo and American big shots like Lansky involved. I'm tripping over gangsters and dodging knives and bullets wherever I go."

I down my third scotch, an amount I can usually handle like it's just water quenching my thirst, but my beat-up body and horror-harassed mind are starting to buckle. "Isabel, Nilo, can I borrow your couch?"

❖

I'm asleep one minute, only half asleep the next, drifting in and out of consciousness, in and out of dreams of Sophie, of nights we spent together in each other's arms, days in each other's eyes, laughing, talking, enjoying the silences of just being together. I hear her through my clouding dreams, hear her whisper, *Cantor,* through invading nightmares of Elspeth Beattie and Agnes Cain and Rinaldo Lopez and knives and chains and bloody sand. Blood under the bodies of Pete Estrada and his man Armando. The gruesome butchery of Pilar's severed lips and tongue, Lansky wagging his finger at them. A knife in Charlie Ossatura's chest. Santiago slamming me across my face. In and out of consciousness, moving through all the violence that follows me wherever I go.

Violence took Sophie from me. It's in violence I will find her.

❖

Sometime after dawn and far too little sleep, the sun through the living room window drills through my eyelids. I dredge up every ounce of willpower to open my eyes and get up from the couch.

In the kitchen, Isabel gives me a kiss on the cheek and extra bandages, Nilo gives me a shirt, and after the mule-kick strength of Isabel's café Cubano, I'm able to drive away.

Somehow, I make it back to my hotel by nine a.m. without running over a pedestrian or slamming the car into a palm tree.

A hot shower, the fresh bandages, my dove gray suit over a clean shirt of pale yellow, and a room service breakfast with a carafe of Cuban coffee almost as strong as Isabel's help stabilize me a little more, in body at any rate. My spirit is still taking a beating. Unless I figure out what or where this American hangout is, I'm no closer to finding Sophie than I was when I first stepped off the plane in Havana.

Getting ready to leave, I load the chambers of my .38, put my penknife and rounds of ammo in my pants pocket, when there's a knock at my door. I'm in no mood for company and could kick myself for not hanging the Do Not Disturb sign on the doorknob when I came in. I'm about to tell the housemaid who's probably holding a bundle of towels and fresh sheets outside in the hall to come back later, but I figure it's time for me to hit the streets anyway. So I call out, "Un momento," instead, put my gun into my shoulder rig, close my suit jacket, and go to the door.

I'm just about there when the familiar nerve tingling, heart racing daydream kicks in. Back in New York, it's the daydream that the knock on my door means Sophie's escaped her captors, found her way home, found her way back to me. Here in Havana, the daydream says that word of my search has filtered through the Cuban underworld; Sophie knows I'm here, she's found me.

Her name's on my lips when I open the door.

I hear, "Cantor"—

—and see Zamira, who doesn't notice my disappointment because it's buried under my surprise.

She's fresh as a daisy in a swirly skirted floral-print cotton dress under a lightweight red sweater thrown around her shoulders, her blond hair mildly windblown from the street, her red straw handbag suspended from her arm. But there's surprise in her snake's eyes, too, surprise at the sight of my bruised face and gashed chin. "What happened to you?"

"Those shadows you sent me to find, that's what's happened to me. What are you doing here, Zamira?"

"We must talk," she says, sashaying past me and into my room.

After pausing by the mirror to fix her mussed hair, Zamira sits down in the club chair near the window, leaving me the chair at the desk but providing me with an interesting view of her legs as she crosses them, her red toenail polish like blood drops peeking through her open-toed straw wedgies. I might normally enjoy such a tantalizing view, but enjoying anything about Zamira is a dangerous game. "So go ahead and talk," I say.

"This Estrada business," she says with an impatient wave of her hand. "You promised you'd take care of it, and you must do it quickly."

"Zamira, it's been less than twelve hours since I saw you. What's the rush?"

"This," she says, taking an envelope from her bag. "A messenger came this morning and gave this to Consuelo when she opened the hat shop."

"Consuelo is the woman at the counter?"

"Sí. The messenger said it was for Tomas. But I have read it, too."

"Yeah, I bet you did. Which is why you're here and he's not. It doesn't take a genius to figure he's the muscle but you're the brains, Zamira. Why do you let him take all the credit? Wait, never mind. Stupid question."

The Zamira sitting across from me is suddenly a very different Zamira than the heartless dame in the hat shop basement or the chilly chanteuse at the Café La Dulce Noche. This Zamira has a different beauty, a sadder one but even more fierce with ambition and something else that shines in her eyes even as she narrows them: curiosity. It's curiosity which lifts her out of the chair and onto my lap, letting her sweater fall from her bare shoulders as she takes my face in her hands and kisses me.

I have to say it's a helluva kiss, loaded with appetite for exploration and adventure. I could enjoy its power, lounge around in its heat, if it wasn't for the venomous heart fueling it.

So with unaccustomed reluctance, my body lets my brain take over and get out from under Zamira's rather delicious lips. "Another world," I say, "another life, maybe. But in the here and now, just tell me what's in that note."

Disappointment with a touch of anger spikes her sigh. "Ah, sí, your world is more free than mine. Or maybe you just live that way." She gives my face a last silky stroke before getting up from my lap and returning to the club chair, sliding her sweater back onto her shoulders. She hands me the note.

There's no signature, just a blood drip at the bottom of the handwritten message, which includes my name. "My Spanish is a little rusty," I say, "but I think it's telling you not to help me find Estrada's killer."

"Sí, on pain of death. That is in the drop of blood, an ancient sign. Only Cubanos of the old heritage use it."

"Any idea who might have sent it?"

With a shake of her head, she says, "It could be anyone. I know many such people in Havana, even people who do business with Tomas and me."

"But who might have a reason to warn you off? Who wouldn't want Estrada's killing solved? Maybe someone in a rival gang?"

"I do not think so. Most of them are trash, soulless trash," she adds with a spit.

"Uh-huh. Not like the two aristocratic Angry Dogs who brought me down to the hat shop basement. One of them stank so bad he nearly choked off my breath from ten feet away."

"Every army needs stupid soldiers as well as smart ones. They are the most useful, and loyal. Tomas and I make sure they are loyal. But enough about my business. I am here to talk about the business you promised. We must figure out who is behind this note, who sent this threat. I wonder…" she says, more to herself than to me. "Perhaps this warning is not about Pedro Estrada. Maybe someone does not want me to help you find your woman." Her words come out softly, mere wisps of thought, but they hit me with the force of a punch.

It's an idea I hadn't thought about in all my running around. It's all just felt like I've been running through alleys and shadows and bumping up against people and crashing into walls. What if someone is actually putting up those walls? Who'd care about me finding Sophie?

I run my mind through everyone I've dealt with since arriving in Havana—Lansky, Estrada, Agnes, Hidalgo, Charlie Ossatura, Tomas Santiago, Mirana at Taberna Escorpión, Rinaldo Lopez at El Teatro de Arte, even Isabel and Nilo, and not one of them has any reason to care if I find Sophie or not. Maybe Estrada, out of resentment, or even Ossatura, angry she got away. But during the last twenty-four hours, neither of them was in any position to stop me. The dead can't build walls.

"I don't think so," I finally say. "I think this is about Estrada. Let's face it, his killing made a lot of people mad."

"Then you must take care of it quickly, without angering whoever wrote this note."

"C'mon, Zamira, we both know you're a smart cookie. So how many times do I need to remind you that neither of us does something for nothing. You must help me, too."

Those eyes of hers, like a viper considering where to sink her fangs, stay on me, but she says nothing. Just shrugs.

"Okay," I say, slipping the note in my pocket, "I'm glad we understand each other. You can start by answering a question. Do you know a place, maybe a saloon, maybe a burdel, that's popular with Americans. Not tourist Americans. Local expats."

A smile, slow and cunning, spreads across her face. "Doesn't everybody?"

CHAPTER EIGHTEEN

Hatless, my panama having been crushed by Agnes Cain's wingtipped gorilla back at that torture chamber called El Teatro de Arte, Havana's soft breeze runs through my hair and soothes my bruised face as I drive along the Prado with the car's convertible top down, Zamira by my side. I'm sure the breeze is playing havoc with my hair, making it even more of an unruly mop than it usually is. Sophie loved to kid me about my untamable locks, but with a twinkle in her eye. Zamira, though, is taking no pleasure from the open air and Havana sun, covering her short hairstyle under a blue kerchief and hiding her eyes behind dark glasses. Funny, I'd pegged her as a more sensual sort, the kind of woman who enjoys even the most delicate of physical pleasures. But once again I'm face-to-face with the puzzle of women, which is okay by me. A surprise now and then keeps life interesting.

Even at this bright hour of late morning, the Prado is up and running with money-spending tourists, well-dressed locals, the glitzy hotels and casinos already throwing their colorful neon glare all over the street. But we're not going into any of the Prado's joints. At the north end of the boulevard, near the seaside Malecón, Zamira tells me to make a right onto Calle Costera, a small street of pastel colored Cuban-Spanish Baroque two- and three-story villas with narrow service alleys between. Light coming off the nearby sea dapples the ornate carved decoration along the rooflines and windows, sparkles up the curlicued painted iron balconies gracing the facades. The houses on Calle Costera are as pretty as pastries lined up in shop windows.

"Park here," Zamira says when we're near an aqua two-story spot. There's no sign out front or on the pale pink door, nothing to indicate the place is anything other than a private house. But I know damn well it's a brothel, another flesh joint in the string that's been holding Sophie captive.

"Who owns this place?" I say.

"You will see."

"Zamira, I'm in no mood for games."

Taking off her dark glasses and kerchief, putting them into her handbag with the slow rhythm of someone who's not sure you've earned the privilege of their time, she says, "I am not playing games with you. But if you want my help in getting you inside this house, you must not ask so many questions." As I get out of the car, she adds, "And if you are going to dress in ropa de caballero—you know, gentleman's clothing—you will give me a gentleman's manners." Drumming her fingers on the armrest with the arrogant impatience of a gangland diva, she remains in the passenger seat and waits for me to come around to her side of the car.

"Did you think I wouldn't?" I say, opening her door.

"I do not know what you are, so I do not know what you do." She extends her hand, and I help her out of the car. She slithers up from the seat, graceful as a boa constrictor sliding up a leg.

But it's not Zamira's enticing charms that are sending the shakes through me. It's the possibility that Sophie is very near, somewhere behind that rosy pink door or the pink shutters on the windows. I take a few deep breaths to steady myself, quiet the storm inside me that's built up over the years of wild hopes, crazy dreams, and miserable nights of silence. Standing here on this quiet street, a street too pretty for the degradation likely going on behind that pink door, warmth suddenly spreads through me. The warmth is slow to start but speeds up into a heat of need for the love stolen from me. The heat coils through my veins, burning now with anger at what Sophie's been made to suffer, might still be suffering. My heart and soul are crying, but my body is tensing into a tight spring, ready to jump, kick, spit at, slap around, slam against, or kill anyone who tries to keep me from reaching my stolen love and taking her home.

Zamira says, "You will let me do the talking, yes?" The intrusion of her voice breaks me out of my thoughts.

"I thought this is an American hangout. I can speak for myself. I'm pretty good with English."

"Do not be smart, Cantor. The people here do not know you. They know me."

"Is that so? What's your connection here?"

"Have you not yet learned that my Angry Dogs are everywhere in Havana? You see this street?" she says, opening her arms slowly to take in the whole scene, her swaying red handbag like a smear of blood in the air. "You hear how quiet it is? You do not see us or hear us, but Tomas's soldiers are here. We are paid very well to keep this street peaceful, to keep the Animas Boys and the other gangs from muscling in and taking over, and to keep the wrong people away."

"People like me."

"We shall see."

We walk to the front door, which I now see has a small glass peephole. Zamira positions herself in front of the peephole and knocks lightly. A short time later, the door's opened by a middle-aged woman who looks more like a no-nonsense executive secretary of a stodgy corporation than the operator of an expat watering hole. Her graying brown hair is stiff as coiled wire, her cheeks are bony, and her gray pinstripe business suit rigid as a lead pipe, the skirt ending in that prim place mid-shin. When she says, "Why are you here, Zamira? We made our regular protection payment," her voice is as flat and cold as a Midwest prairie in a hard frost. Looking past Zamira to me, her blue eyes sharp with suspicious curiosity but empty of any other feeling, she says, "And who is this?"

I start, "I'm—"

"We are not here about your payment, Ida." Zamira cuts me off. "But we must get inside the house and off the street."

Ida—a name too motherly for the hard case wearing it—stands

aside and lets us enter. I get a good look at her as I walk by, especially at the bulge under her jacket. It's not just the swell of female flesh, it's the bump from a holstered gun. I really should give her the name of my tailor.

We're in a spacious vestibule that's more Park Avenue clubby than Havana tropical. Instead of pastel walls, there's dark wood paneling. Instead of rattan furniture, there's a few leather upholstered club chairs. Only the big, slow overhead fan that keeps the air gently moving gives the game away.

Through an archway at the end of the vestibule is a hallway running right and left with more dark wood paneling and brass wall sconces. Very upper-crust Yankee. Maybe that's the clientele here. Or maybe it's how the clientele passes itself off, gives itself some class it never had, and gets away with it a thousand miles from dusty small towns or stinking slums or just plain boring neighborhoods.

But there's nothing else for me to see in the hallway. Whatever goes on here is well out of sight of my prying eyes.

Ida says, "What's your business here, Zamira?"

But I decide it's time to take charge of the conversation, take my turn to do the talking, and I make it fast, before Zamira has a chance to open her mouth. "I'm looking for someone I have reason to believe is here."

"A member? It's still too early for members to arrive," Ida says.

"A woman," I say. "This woman." As I reach into my jacket for Sophie's picture, an ice-eyed Ida snaps her fingers and two guys with guns step out from either side of the hallway. The guys are as corporately suited as Ida. The guns, though, are strictly gangland, big .45 revolvers. "Whoa!" I say, sliding the photograph from inside my jacket. "I'm just taking a picture from my pocket." With a side glance at Zamira and a nod to the gunmen, I say, "Two of your Dogs?"

Zamira, annoyed, says, "I told you, our soldiers are invisible. And do you not remember I said you must let me do the talking, Cantor?"

Ida, her eyes narrowed like slits in a rock face of rough stone, says to me, "Just a minute. Your name is Cantor? You're Cantor Gold?"

"Yeah. Who told you?"

"Your name's been getting around. Word is you've been making trouble all over Havana, people meeting a bad end everywhere you go. I don't want your trouble here. These gentlemen will make sure you leave now," she says with a nod toward the guys with guns. There's movement in the hallway beyond the vestibule as she says this, a shadow, followed by a dark-haired young woman wearing nothing but white hosiery held up by black garters. Seeing what's going on in the vestibule, she hurries away, smart enough to not make a sound.

It wasn't Sophie. But my worst fears claw at me, unleashing my urge to kill whoever stands in my way of finding her, starting with Ida, whose bones I'd happily snap to splinters.

"I'm not leaving until I find this woman," I say and hold Sophie's picture up to Ida's face. "Is she here? I understand you got her from Pete Estrada."

Zamira snaps, "Cantor!" practically choking on my name. "You did not tell me! I should kill you!"

Ida says, "Not before I do," checking her watch. "But there's no time. It's noon, and the street is about to open for business. Zamira, get Gold out of here. You and I will deal with this later. Or you can kill her if you like."

Never mind the guys with guns. Never mind Ida's threat. I put myself right in her face, slide my hand fast into my jacket, pull my gun, and press it against Ida's ribs. "I said, *is this woman here?*"

A small, tight smile, colder than ice, cracks across Ida's thin mouth. "Kill me and you'll die, too. These gentlemen will gun you down," she says with no emotion at all, which makes her smile even more chilling.

"No one has to die if you just tell me if Sophie is here and bring her to me."

But the guys with guns are close now, their weapons aimed straight at my face. They needn't have bothered. The business end of a handgun is against the back of my head. It doesn't feel like a very big gun, small enough to fit into a red handbag. But Zamira could blow my brains out with it just the same.

"Cantor," she says, turning it into a hiss. "We have business. We are leaving."

❖

Outside, the street's changed. It's still quiet, but it's the quiet of murmured conversation among well-dressed men in tropical suits and panama hats or straw trilbies, even a derby here and there. Some of the men speak Spanish, some English, others various tongues from various places. Everyone is walking to the pastel villas along the street or getting out of expensive cars, mostly late-model American luxury numbers—bulky Cadillacs and Lincolns heavy with chrome—but a few stately British jobs quietly roll along the curb. There are higher, sweeter voices, too, of women dressed in colorfully elegant day wear, standing outside the houses and softly calling to the men, conversing with them before they enter any of the houses.

I should've known. Calle Costera, this street of pretty buildings, is just a higher priced meat market than the slummy Callejón de los Burdeles.

Zamira says, "They play cards, too, the men who come here," as she slips her little Browning .25 pistol into her handbag and leans against my car. "A few houses even have full casinos. Ida's casino is very fancy. You must be a member to get into her house, and it is strictly for rich Americanos. You see?" She's nodding toward the pink door.

Yeah, I see. I see a lovely blonde in a chic yellow sundress, fresh and wholesome as a Kansas cornfield, walking out of Ida's house and greeting a linen-suited old guy who's just stepped out of a chauffeured dark blue Caddy. The woman's English is perfect but slightly accented, giving spice to her farm-girl-chaste-act allure. The old guy, smiling, is eating it up as the woman deftly sends him through the door before greeting another arriving gent, younger this time, and cooler in his susceptibility to the blonde's charms. Maybe his tastes run more to brunettes, or maybe he's just here for a card game.

I have to get back in there. I have to see if Sophie is in that house.

"Whatever it is you are thinking," Zamira says, noticing me stare at the building's facade, studying the structure, the slatted windows, the routes to the balcony, "you must not try to get in there again. You will be killed, either by Ida's men, or my Angry Dogs. Remember, our soldiers are here," she adds, glancing along the street and up to the rooftops, "and we see everything."

"And what about you, Zamira?" I say, angry and growling. "Are you going to kill me, too?" I've got her by the arm, my grip tight and twisting.

"You are hurting me! Is this how you handle your women?"

"You pulled a gun on me, honey. You were ready to spatter my brains all over those classy wood walls. I should rip your heart out."

"And you lied to me! You did not tell me you had information about Pedro Estrada."

"The only information I had was that he knew Sophie, sent her here after using her like a rag, and that he lied to me about it. I still have no idea who killed him."

"Then you are stupid. I should spit in your face." She starts to, but my tightening grip changes her mind, so she just goes on with her rant. "You got close to his people and learned nothing. Nothing! You will not make the same mistake again, chica. I will tell our soldiers to follow you everywhere, but you will never see them. Tomas has made them into las guerrillas, remember? You will do as you promised, or you will die."

"And where will that leave you and Tomas? In the middle of a gang war with no end, that's where. The Animas Boys will still want revenge for Estrada's killing. Believe me, they will be coming for you when they're good and ready. You and Tomas will be facing those boys and any other gangs who resent your Angry Dogs' growing power and your alliance with Lansky. You're plenty smart, Zamira, smart enough to make your Perros Enojados the richest and strongest outfit in Havana, smart enough to get the backing of Meyer Lansky and the American Mob, but that's where your smarts end. You know how to outplay your enemies, but you don't know how to make them go away."

"And you do?"

"Maybe. Maybe there's a solution to both our problems. You need a lesson in strategic warfare, and I need an American power broker to get me back into this American place. Get in the car."

Chapter Nineteen

Only one of my favorite thugs, the well-dressed guy who could pass for a politician's bodyguard, is at his usual post outside Lansky's penthouse door. The missing one, Mr. House Dick, is dead from a slashed throat at Charlie Ossatura's Rumba Room. Instead of giving me the once-over, Mr. Politician's Bodyguard gives the eye to Zamira. He doesn't seem to know who she is, but he sure as hell likes her swaying curves strolling along the hall.

I say, "Tell Lansky I'm here with—uh, tell him I'm here with an associate he's done business with."

"This cute little associate got a name?"

Zamira, ever the gangster princess, says, "You do not have the right to know my name. I will speak only to Señor Lansky, not his... his lacayo." If her nose went any higher in the air, she'd sniff the ceiling.

I start to translate, address the guy's puzzled expression, but think better of it. Mr. Politician's Bodyguard might not take kindly to being called a flunky, and I don't want to waste time smoothing things over. Instead, I stick to bland business. "Look, just tell him we're here. Let him decide if he wants to see us."

"You just missed him. He went down for lunch."

"Where? Here in the hotel?"

It was established on my first morning in Havana that this guy would rather smash me against a wall than talk to me. But it's also been established that I've already been Lansky's guest on two occasions, that I'm connected to kingpin Sig Loreale, and any friend of the big man in New York is a friend of the Little Man in Havana.

Just as I'm wondering if I'll have to play the Loreale-Lansky card, Mr. Politician's Bodyguard says, "He's having lunch down at the hotel's pool." I guess he remembered that card is in my deck.

❖

Poolside at the Hotel Nacional is a palm tree fringed panorama of the pampered, the privileged, and those who play at it, everyone sunning themselves on chaise lounges, enjoying drinks under umbrellas, or floating around in the kidney-shaped pool's excessively blue water. Oiled skin glares in the sun, while dark glasses hide secrets of who's ogling who. Skittering through all this luxe leisure, white-jacket waiters, trays in hand, serve drinks and delicacies.

It's not hard to spot Lansky. He's the guy bookended by a couple of bodyguards in straw trilbies and seersucker jackets over flowered shirts while the boss, preferring to remain businesslike in a tan linen suit, lunches at a table next to a cabana.

Zamira says, "But he is so small."

"Oh, right, you've never met him. But hasn't Tomas? Don't they have business?"

"Tomas has spoken to him on the telephone. That is all."

"Well, don't let his size fool you. There's a lot of dangerous power in that little container."

One of the bodyguards, all bulk and menace, walks toward us as Zamira and I near the table. Lansky calls him back and motions us over. His little V-shaped smile couldn't be more charming if he was greeting dear old pals, but then again, he's not looking at me.

"Cantor," he says, "to what do I owe the pleasure? And won't you introduce me to your friend?" He's still not looking at me. I wonder if he ever looked at his wife the way he's looking at Zamira. I wonder if he even remembers he has a wife.

"Mr. Lansky, this is the real brains behind the Angry Dogs. This is—"

"Zamira," he says, pleased to finally meet Tomas Santiago's mysterious consort. But Lansky's smile, though still charming, is a little tighter, the V a little harder edged, its points sharp with vigilance. Her hand on her hip, the red handbag sways from Zamira's elbow, her posture a curve of swagger. "So you know of me," she says, somewhere between flattered and suspicious.

"Only recently," Lansky says, and then finally glances at me. "So, what brings you here?" He gestures for us to sit down. "You want some lunch? I've just started my ropa vieja. I promise you, the food at this hotel is first rate. I know the chef personally."

I bet he does. And if the chef overcooks a dish, could be he's out of a job or ends up encased in cement. "No thanks," I say, "but I'll take a Chivas, neat."

"What about you, Miss Zamira? Maybe some fruit to cool the blood on this warm afternoon?"

"Sí, gracias. And a mojito, por favor," she adds with a shrug that's not as easygoing as she'd like it to be. Her eyes are tight at the corners, the floral pattern of her sundress stretches around her shoulders. She's as wary of Lansky as he is of her, two serpents eyeing each other.

Lansky signals for a waiter. The guy arrives so fast I bet he's exclusively assigned to the American mobster.

After Lansky gives the order for our drinks, including another glass of seltzer for himself and a large fruit plate for the table— "You should eat a little something with that scotch, Cantor, or you'll get an upset stomach"—the waiter scurries away. Lansky takes a forkful of his ropa vieja, chewing the shredded meat and vegetable stew slowly while he looks at Zamira, then at me, then at Zamira again. The twinkle in his eye is brighter when he looks at Zamira.

The drinks and fruit plate arrive by the time Lansky's swallowed his forkful of stew. The waiter scurries away again. Far away.

"So," Lansky says, "which one of you is going to enlighten me about this surprise visit?" He catches Zamira glancing up over the rim of her mojito at the two bodyguards. I don't blame her. Lansky might own their ears but Zamira and I don't, and neither of us wants our stories rattling around in ears or settling in mouths we can't control.

Not that we can control Lansky's. But he didn't get where he is by spilling secrets. The guy knows how to win trust, and he pulls it off now with a wave of his hand, saying, "Give us some room, boys."

The boys back up, and then back up some more until Lansky puts his hand down.

Holding another forkful of stew, he says, "Okay, children. It's time we get down to business. Miss Zamira, how about if we start with you."

The mojito seems to have settled her, given her a good dose of her brass back. She relaxes in her chair, staring at Lansky while he eats his meal, and she takes his measure. When she doesn't answer him right away, he gives her a sharp glance, holding his eyes on her until she finally—in her own sweet, arrogant time—says, "I want to know who killed Pedro Estrada, and I want to defeat my enemies."

"Yes, I'm sure you do, on both counts. But why come to me?"

"Because the enemies of my Perros Enojados are your enemies, too, Señor Lansky. And Pedro's killing makes trouble for both of us. There is vengeance building in the streets, and it will explode very soon. Such violence is not good for your business, you would agree? So it is important that Tomas and I win this war for Havana's streets, a war *you* want us to win, too, yes?"

"That would be desirable. My associates and I have invested a lot of effort in you and Mr. Santiago."

Zamira gives him a nod, but that's all the appreciation he'll get. Brave girl. "But there is new trouble, too, Señor." Nodding to me, she says, "Cantor, the note in your pocket, show it to Señor Lansky." When I hand it to Lansky, she says, "Someone is—how do you say?—pulling the strings? Someone we do not know, and I think is not known to you, either. Someone deep in the dark."

"Miss Zamira," Lansky says, handing the note back to me and taking up a forkful of stew, "the only thing I understand in that note are the words *Cantor* and *Gold*."

"Ah, my apologies, Señor Lansky. I will tell you. The note

warns not to help Cantor find Pedro Estrada's murderer. The blood drop means on pain of death."

Lansky puts down his fork before the stew reaches his mouth, the corners of his smile crawling up almost to his eyes. "You see why I enjoy doing business in Havana? You Habaneros have plenty of spirit. That blood drop!" He's almost laughing. "Sort of romantic, you know? Like the old days on the Lower East Side, remember, Cantor? Reminds me of the evil eye that scared the daylights outta my parents with their primitive old-country ways. Well," he says, stretching the word with a musical New York drawl, enjoying the last of his nostalgia before putting it away and taking up the forkful of stew, "someone certainly has an interest in poor Pete Estrada's demise. So tell me, Cantor, have you gotten anywhere in finding the killer?"

But I'm chewing on a mango slice, chasing it with a swallow of scotch, and thinking.

"Cantor?" he says again. "The Estrada matter. Any new information?"

"Uh, no. But—"

"Un momento, Señor Lansky," Zamira cuts in, "I want to know about Pedro, yes, but we have not finished talking about the war for control of Havana. Even if our soldiers fight and win in the streets, I understand such a victory might not be enough. Cantor tells me that you are an expert in making enemies go away. I want the enemies of Los Perros Enojados to go away."

Slowly, taking his time because he owns the time, Lansky finishes his last forkful of stew, followed by a long sip of his seltzer. He takes a pack of Camels from his pocket, lights a smoke, and finally looks at Zamira, eyeballing her as if seeing past her tawny skin and snakelike beauty, right through her eyes and into her mind. "I see why Cantor figures you're the brains of Santiago's outfit. Listen, Miss Zamira, there are only two ways of making your enemies go away. You can kill them all, but that's only a temporary solution. Their children will grow up with vengeance in their bones, and they will come after you. You will have to fight the war all over again. That's not a future you want."

"No, Señor, I do not."

"And I don't want it, either. The better solution is to turn your enemies into, well, if not friends, then into business partners. But first, sure, you have to win the streets, and then you have to find a way to make your defeated enemies understand that holding a grudge and plotting against you is not in their interest. You have to convince them that working *with* you is best for everyone. But then you've got to be willing to let your new partners have profits of their own, territories of their own. You can't take everything and expect loyalty." Leaning across the table, he adds, "This is why my associates and I let you run your street trade while we move in on the hotels and casinos. Do you understand?"

She's been put in her place, and she knows it, finally giving him a nod of obedience. "But that is difficult with Habaneros," she says. "Everything with us is to the death."

"So I'm finding out," Lansky says, with an annoyed wave, "but not impossible, which I'm also finding out. Listen, there are people in Havana who cling to the old ways and the old tribes, sure. But there are other people who understand that more modern ways are coming, that people like me and my associates will bring modern methods to Havana, and if they want to profit, they must not stand in our way." He ends his lecture with twinkling eyes and one of his charming smiles, and adds, "Even you and Mr. Santiago, and his friends in the hills—oh yes, we know all about Santiago's adventure with the radicals. None of you must stand in our way." His smile is slightly less charming.

I have to hand it to Zamira; she doesn't buckle or bat an eye at Lansky's implied threat. She just finishes her mojito and says, "You are a very interesting man, Señor Lansky."

"I'm just a businessman, Miss Zamira. Now, what about you, Cantor? Are you here about Estrada?"

"In a way. It seems the sonovabitch knew Sophie—"

"The woman you're looking for."

"Yeah, that's right." I have to squash the urge to remind him he'd promised to help me find her. Today, though, that's old news. I have more immediate needs now. "It seems Pete owned a sex trap called El Teatro de Arte—oh, you know the place," I say, seeing the looks on Lansky's and Zamira's faces: amused but slightly disgusted recognition on Lansky's face, less amused but more sly recognition on Zamira's. "Yeah, he kept Sophie there." I nearly choke on the statement but feel better when I say, "But she gave him a hard time. That's when he sold her to a members-only joint on Calle Costera patronized by rich American expats."

Lansky says, "Stop there, Cantor," and stubs out his smoke in the last of the stew.

"So you do know the place? I could use your help to get back inside."

"It's time you went back to New York, Cantor. And Miss Zamira, tell Tomas to use whatever means necessary to win the streets. I will not stand in his way. But remember what I told you about what to do afterward. Play it smart, and you and I can do business. Act stupid, and well…" He shrugs, then waves his hand for his straw-hatted bodyguards to move in. The next thing I know, Zamira and I are lifted out of our chairs. The boys hand us off to two waiters, each taking one of our arms. They couldn't be more polite as they toss us out of the hotel.

CHAPTER TWENTY

Outside, Zamira struts and spits with the rage of a wounded animal. "You Americanos! All big talk, big plans, and crazy threats. No wonder we Cubanos don't like you. And you know what? You don't even like each other. Your Señor Lansky does not like you, Cantor Gold."

I'm running out of patience with this arrogant diva demanding I jump when she snaps her fingers. But that's not all that's bothering me as I hustle Zamira to my car. Lots of thoughts run around in my head and I don't like any of them. I've had sand kicked in my face since my first day in Havana, and everyone's trying to fling me around, throw me off from whatever's going on. But Zamira's right about one thing: someone in the shadows is manipulating all of us, making everyone maneuver around everyone else, and none of it has anything to do with Sophie.

And yet...

"You want to know who killed Pete Estrada?" I say. "Then give me some room. Right now, get in the car. I'll drive you home."

❖

After dropping Zamira at La Dulce Noche—it turns out that she and Santiago live in an apartment above the café—I'm back in my hotel room. If I'm ever going to untangle the knot of thoughts in my head, I'll need some information, some tidbit which could help me pull just the right string that will unravel the whole stinking business.

It's time to call home.

I dial the hotel switchboard, ask the sweet-voiced operator to get me an international line to New York. She says she'll call me back.

I make another call, to the hotel's room service, tell them to send up a bottle of Chivas scotch.

While I wait for the operator and the whiskey, I light a smoke and take out the photograph of Sophie.

Her face has haunted me for more than three and a half years. Even after it became too painful to see the photograph on my desk every day and I hid it away in my office safe, it ripped my heart out when I'd go into the safe for some cash or a spare gun and I'd see a smiling Sophie cheek to cheek with a lovestruck me. I'm gone from the photo now, torn away by Agnes Cain's cruel fingers. All that's left is Sophie, and I swear her eyes look back at me with new and terrible urgency. I swear I hear a plea through her smile: *Find me.*

A knock at the door jolts me back into my own skin. It's the room service kid with the scotch. I give him a couple of bucks American; he gives me a grin as I close the door.

I take a glass from the bathroom, pour myself a stiff belt, pull up a chair to the phone, and settle in. I'm already pouring a second one when the phone rings. The international operator is on the line. I give her my office number in New York.

I'm calling Judson Zane, my young guy Friday who keeps my office running smooth as a slick road, and whose ability to keep secrets rivals any spy's. But Judson's real talent is finding people deep in the underworld and getting them to provide certain services without asking pesky questions. He's also just as good at getting people to tell him things. His network of traded favors is as extensive as a railroad map.

It's a little after two thirty in the afternoon here in Havana, and the same time in New York. If Judson's true to form, he's working at his desk, his wire-rimmed glasses sliding down the bridge of his nose. He's either making sure the books are balanced—and written in a code that would make a cryptographer's eyes cross—or taking calls from clients who want me to steal a painting, a sculpture, or some other treasure, or he's making calls to dig his underworld network even deeper, spread it wider.

I hope I don't get a busy signal.

He answers on the second ring.

"Judson, it's me."

Not one for chitchat or to waste time with greetings, he gets right to, "How's it going in Havana?"

"In circles. Maybe two circles. Maybe they're connected, maybe not, but I need you to get information that will help me crack them open."

"Is Sophie in one of those circles?"

"Yeah, I think so. I think she might be held at a private watering hole owned by an American woman named Ida."

"Got a last name?"

"Uh-uh, but the place is on Calle Costera and it's patronized by big shot Americans living in Havana or doing business here. No tourists. Try to find out anything you can about this Ida and her operation. Find out who the members are, what connections they have. And listen, Meyer Lansky might be connected to it in some way, which means maybe Sig Loreale, too."

Judson is silent at the mention of those two familiar names, except for a noticeably deep breath.

"Okay," I say, "that's the first circle. The other has to do with a general who's who in the Havana crime operations, but go deep, into the shadows deep."

"Have you spoken to Nilo and Isabel Anaya? Can't they help you out with that?"

"Yeah, I'm sure they can, but it's better if I keep things close and quiet for a while, Judson. The circles are getting too tight around my neck."

"I'll call you back later," he says and hangs up.

Now what? I could try to barge back into Ida's place, or follow one of the knotted strings in my brain and barge in someplace else. But the first would get me killed by either Ida's muscle or the unseen army of the Angry Dogs, and the second could make those circles I've been running around in even more dangerous, especially if I'm wrong, or worse, if I'm right.

So until Judson calls me back with hard information I can use to break out of the circles and rescue Sophie, there's nothing much I can do except pace the floor, drink the whiskey, look at Sophie's photograph, and cry.

❖

The ringing phone shakes me awake, my eyes popping open in a dark room except for streetlight slanting through the blinds. Still in the chair, I jerk my body around to the phone and pick it up. "Yeah?" comes out in a rasp.

"Cantor? It's Judson."

"Go ahead," I say past a tongue that tastes and feels like dry steel wool. I turn on a lamp, but the light claws at my eyes, and I turn the lamp off again. "Tell me what you found out."

"Listen, Ida is one Ida McNamee, and she's on the nastier side of nasty. Originally from a factory town in Wisconsin, but moved to St. Louis when she was eighteen, got involved with a gunman in the St. Louis Mob during Prohibition days. He wound up on the wrong side of one of the city's periodic gang wars, and figuring she'd save her own skin, she killed him, put a bullet in his head. But the cops were on to her, and things got too hot in St. Louis, so she scrammed to New York where she opened a basement gambling joint. It's where she met Lansky when he was on his way up."

"They were an item?"

"Nah, nothing like that. It seems she impressed him with her head for business, and her tightfisted control of who came into her joint."

"Yeah," I say, "she's still picky."

"I don't doubt it. Anyway, Lansky set her up in various enterprises, most of them involving gambling and flesh. They made tons of money. After the War, when Lansky re-established the Mob's activities in Cuba, he brought her down to Havana in '49 to open the place on Calle Costera. The street was becoming the place to go for high end sex and high stakes gambling. Ida's joint really rakes in the cash. But here's where it gets interesting, Cantor."

About time. Up to now it's just the same old American crime world tale of small town monster makes good.

Judson goes on, "Lansky allows Ida to keep the Calle Costera profits, because what he's really interested in is who goes there. And you're right, it's rich Yanks with connections to politicians and big corporations in Cuba *and* stateside. You know, the big sugar processors and fruit companies, and all the other outfits coming down to do business there. Ida passes their names to Lansky, who exploits them, even blackmails them into providing a legal front that washes the cash for the Mob's operations in Havana and back in the States. But it's all done on the quiet. Ida assesses who's ripe for Lansky's picking. She doesn't feed him just anybody, and none of her house's other members know it's happening."

"What about Sig? Is he connected to the place, too? Maybe has a financial interest?"

"Not that I can see. It appears to be strictly a Lansky operation. Which would make sense. While Lansky covers Havana, Sig keeps control here in New York."

"What about the members? Anybody I can use to get me in? Anybody vulnerable to pressure?"

Through a sigh signaling that he hates giving me bad news, Judson says, "Doubtful. Some of those guys are too well protected, too powerful, even for Lansky's threats. And the others are already owned by him, which means he'd hear about any play you tried with them."

The thing about bad news is you can toss it, not waste time on plans that won't work. I'll have to figure another way of getting past Ida. Right now, though, I just move on. "Okay, what about who's who in Havana? Anyone making chess moves from the shadows?"

Judson gives me another sigh, then says, "Maybe."

Chapter Twenty-one

Yeah, it's that string, the one that if plucked will make the circles open up and the tangles unravel.

But to pluck it I'll have to make a deal, a deal I don't like.

I clean myself up, get the taste of stale booze out of my mouth, put on a fresh shirt, a blue one with a light brown tie, and my suit jacket. Before leaving my hotel room, I check my gun, put it back into my rig, and check the extra rounds in my pocket. I hope I won't need them. I'm prepared to use them all.

❖

It's almost seven o'clock when I pull up in front of Café La Dulce Noche.

Inside, the crowd's still thin, too early for night reveling Habaneros. The waiters aren't hurrying with their trays, the musicians play easygoing Latin tunes, saving the heat for later. The snooty maître d' remembers me and isn't so snooty this time when I ask to see Zamira and Tomas. He politely telephones upstairs to their apartment, "Cantor Gold está aquí," he says, nodding like an obedient puppy as he listens to instructions, then hangs up. "There is a stairway there, you see?" he tells me, pointing to an archway about twenty feet past his station.

I give him a "Gracias," and head for the archway.

There's a door at the top of the landing. It's opened by Tomas before I'm even at the top step. He's almost dressed for the evening—

tuxedo trousers, a white shirt with the sleeves rolled up, his bow tie still untied—while he chews on a chicken leg, his handsome face greasy around his pretty mouth. "So, Cantor Gold," he says, his broken voice coming through a chew of chicken. "You have brought us news?"

"Maybe," I say, reaching the door. "I've brought you a deal."

Stepping inside, I'm in a small, softly lit dining room that's more old-fashioned than I imagined it would be, classier than I'd give its occupants credit for, but with an element of gangster life plain as day. The old-fashioned is in the red-orange walls covered with family photographs, small landscape paintings in carved old-timey frames, and a big mirror in an ornate frame of white and gold. There's a heavy, deeply carved walnut sideboard with a matching dining table and four chairs, all of which would be right at home in an old colonial Spanish hacienda. The classy is in the quality of all the stuff, nothing shoddy or knockoff among the lot. But the gangster element is as obvious as a thumb in the eye: on the table, next to a pack of American Lucky Strike cigarettes, a box of Cuban Montecristo cigars, and a book of matches, there's a .45 auto, a .38 revolver, Zamira's little .25, and boxes of bullets.

Zamira, slithering from the living room through glass paned French doors, is dolled up for her evening's torch song stints. Her cream satin dress, cut low enough to inspire intoxicating imagination, hugs every curve of her body like hands enjoying a feel. Her lipstick's the color of a hot summer sunset, and her blond hair's sporting a dark Spanish comb studded with rhinestones. She looks delicious, and deadly. But she always does.

She says, "What is this I heard you say about a deal? What is there to deal? I do not want a deal. I want information about Estrada's killer."

"I might be able to do better than just information," I say, which elicits a tilt of Zamira's head, a widening of her eyes, and a suspicious stare from Tomas. "But as we keep reminding each other, you don't get something for nothing. If you two want Estrada's killer, I want something from you. That's the deal."

Tomas finishes his chicken leg, tosses the bone onto a plate on the table, and pours himself a drink from a bottle of rum on the sideboard. "And what is it you want?" he says and takes a deep pull of the rum.

I say, "You remember what you told me in that basement, Tomas? That you're not a brute, that you're, uh, a gentleman? A gentleman would offer his guest—and his lady—a drink."

The handsome face does its best not to snarl and more or less succeeds, except for the trace of a sneer Tomas can't quite muzzle.

"Zamira does not drink before a show," he says.

"Uh-huh. Well, I'll take a scotch, thanks. Chivas if you've got it."

"Sí, but of course," he says, with mock sincerity as he pours the scotch. "As you say, I am not a brute." He hands me the glass, smiling as if he'd like to kill me.

"By the way," I say, "Zamira's going to miss the early show. She's coming with me."

She says, "And where is it you think you are taking me?"

"Ida's place on Calle Costera. One way or another, you're going to get me in there again, and Tomas is going to call off your street army of Angry Dogs so that all I'll have to worry about are Ida's thugs."

"But they are Señor Lansky's people. We cannot give them orders, and we dare not oppose them."

"I'm not asking you to. Let me worry about them. If Sophie is at Ida's joint—and I'm counting on it that she is—you're going to tell your soldiers to let us get away. Once Sophie is safe, you and I are going to put the noose around Estrada's killer."

Tomas spits, "No! No one turns my soldiers into sheep!"

But Zamira says, "Be quiet, Tomas. There is nothing wrong with Cantor's deal, except that it is backward. We will take care of the Estrada business first, Cantor, and then we will see about your woman. What is it you Americans say? Ah, I remember: take it or leave it."

❖

The tangled streets in this part of Old Havana have plenty of seductive charm, especially at night, when moonlight barely filters through the grand old palm trees, their fronds rustling in the sweet, soft breeze.

But the perfumed air and the big trees want to suffocate me tonight, as heavy on my breath as my thoughts are heavy on my heart. Thoughts about Old Cuba, old families, old traditions, old friends.

Zamira's very quiet in the passenger seat of the car, her hands tight around the satin evening bag on her lap. Tension snaps from her like flashes of heat lightening before a storm.

I finally pull into the familiar little street and park the Olds in the shadow of a tall palm.

Zamira says, "You look a little sad, like you have lost your best friend." Then she adds, with a small, sly laugh, "I thought *I* was your best friend, querida."

I slide her a look that says she's not funny.

She dismisses my glance with a shrug, says, "So who lives here?"

"My best friends."

"I do not understand. I thought you were taking me to whoever killed Pedro Estrada, not making a social call."

"Sometimes, Zamira, a social call can help catch a killer." I get out of the car and walk around to open her door.

As Zamira steps out, a sliver of moonlight streaks along the Spanish comb in her hair and slides across her face, her eyes bright with suspicion and cunning. She grabs my arm, holds us by the car. "Who are these friends? Do you trust them?"

"I've trusted them for years. Come on, let's go."

"Aren't you going to tell me who they are?" she says as we walk from the car, her evening bag under her arm. "What are their names?"

"Nilo and Isabel Anaya."

"Anaya," she says, her eyes narrowing. "I know that name. I have never met these people, but I am sure I have heard the name Anaya."

"I'm not surprised," I say and knock on their door. "Nilo has connections all over Cuba and South America."

This information seems to annoy Zamira, provoking a sneer. "Then I am surprised they have not done business with us. Los Perros Enojados own the streets, yes? Well, most of the streets. But soon we will own all of them."

"Sorry to disappoint you, Zamira, but Nilo's street hustling days are long gone."

"Huh, a snob, like you and your Señor Lansky. So since your friend is so well connected, he will take us to Estrada's killer?"

"Well, we'll see, won't we."

The words are barely out of my mouth when Nilo opens the door. "Cantor!" he says. "You are always a surprise. But always a welcome one. And I see you are not alone. Please come in, and introduce me to your lovely friend." Nilo takes in Zamira from top to bottom and back again with zest. I never knew this professed happily married man had such hungry eyes.

"Nilo Anaya, this is Zamira—" It occurs to me that among the many things I don't know about Zamira, I don't know her last name.

Rescuing me from my hapless introduction, she says, "Fernández."

Nilo says, "Welcome to my house, Señorita Fernández." He takes her hands between his. His gesture is almost fatherly. His smile isn't. Both the handshake and the smile are more awkward than is the habit of the usually congenial Nilo. But I've learned never to underestimate the effect Zamira has on people. Her beauty could seduce anyone, while her eyes bite you and draw blood.

She smiles back but slides her hands free of Nilo's. Her smile's less awkward than his, but cagier.

It's time to get past Nilo and Zamira's little drama and raise the curtain on the drama I've come here to play. "I need to talk to you and Isabel, Nilo."

"Of course, of course. Isabel is in the kitchen. She is just putting the supper dishes away. I was about to go upstairs to see if my daughters are doing their homework, so I will join you in a few minutes." He leaves us and heads upstairs.

I take Zamira's elbow, guide her to the cheery kitchen, where not too many hours ago Isabel's gentle fingers patched up my wounds.

Surprised to see me, Isabel's taking off her apron when we walk in. She's even more surprised to see me with a woman who looks nothing like the woman she saw in the photo I showed her of Sophie. Surprised, but not displeased. "Cantor," she says, her smile wide with her usual warmth, "so you have taken my advice and chosen to embrace our famous Havana hospitality instead of chasing a ghost? Good! Now please introduce me to this beautiful woman on your arm."

"Isabel, this is Zamira Fernández. I believe you wrote her a note."

Zamira's sudden, sharp breath cuts across the kitchen.

Still smiling, Isabel hangs her apron on a hook on the wall. "But I have never met this woman, Cantor. Why would I write her a note?"

"Oh yeah, I forgot, you wrote it to Tomas Santiago. But Zamira has special privileges with Santiago, like reading his mail."

Zamira, silent and smooth as a serpent, opens her handbag, reaches inside and pulls out her .25.

"Put it down, Miss Zamira." It's Nilo, stepping into the kitchen. "Put your gun and your handbag on the table. Do as I say. You see, the gun I am holding is much bigger than your little one."

Zamira, her mouth tight, her body suddenly stiff, reluctantly puts the gun and her handbag on the kitchen table.

"Now you, Cantor, take out the gun I know you are carrying—the gun I gave you, yes?"

"The gun I paid you good money for."

"Sí, you are right, of course. But please, take it out and put it on the table."

His big .45 leaves me no choice. I put my gun on the table.

"Gracias," he says, joining his wife. He's the jovial, smoothly charming Nilo I've known for years, except for the pained frown on his face, and that gun aimed at me. "Ah, Cantor, my friend, we tried to warn you off, but you would not listen. We told you when you first came to my house and we shared those sweet merenguitos that you were entering dangerous waters, but no, you would not listen. And again last night, when my Isabel so tenderly cared for you, she told you not to pursue this foolish adventure. And still you did not listen. So we thought to work through someone who would understand the meaning of our warning. You, Miss Zamira, and your man Tomas Santiago, you are Habaneros. You would understand."

"Sí, I understand that Cantor was foolish to trust you."

Isabel looks at me, the expression on her face almost pleading. "Cantor, please, we are friends for a long time. Nilo and I love you. Let's all sit down, we can talk about this."

"Start by telling me which one of you killed Pete Estrada," I say, "and why. But talk fast. There's a woman I need to rescue tonight."

Isabel snaps her fingers, accompanies it with a disgusted *tsk*. "Estrada, Estrada. He was nothing. A pig. He was even evil to your woman, your Sophie. Why do you care who killed him?"

But it's Zamira who answers, "Because *I* care, Señora. And now that you know who I am, maybe you know that Pedro Estrada's killing will make trouble for me and Tomas and our Perros Enojados. It will bring vengeance from our rivals, there will be blood in the streets, and it will upset a very delicate arrangement we have with— with important people."

Nilo, his .45 still aiming at me and Zamira, says, "Your Angry Dogs mean nothing to us. And your business with Meyer Lansky— please, do not be coy with us, Miss Zamira. Your business with the Americans is no secret. I think you may be in over your pretty head. But you, Cantor, like my Isabel says, we are friends. We are colleagues. We care much about you. Why are you involved with this cheap gangster's woman?"

If Nilo wasn't holding that gun, I'm sure Zamira would silence his insult by clawing his eyes out. Instead she just spits out, "Because Cantor and I have made a deal! She would take me to Pedro Estrada's killer and I will take her to her Sophie."

Deep in the heart of the double-crossing Isabel, who trampled my affection and poisoned my trust, is the warm hostess. Opening her arms like a Madonna dispensing love, she says, "Everyone, calm yourselves. Please, we can sit down, have coffee or maybe a drink, while we talk about what is to be done. No one has to die tonight."

CHAPTER TWENTY-TWO

The only gun on the kitchen table now is Nilo's. It's right in front of him, in case he gets a hankering to prove his wife wrong and someone has to die. Isabel's put my .38 and Zamira's .25 on a kitchen counter, out of our reach.

Nilo and I are drinking scotch. Isabel and Zamira are sipping rum. I'm smoking a cigarette, Nilo's smoking a cigar. Anyone walking in would think were just a bunch of old pals gathered at a kitchen table getting ready for a hand of canasta—except for that .45 pointed at me and Zamira.

"It was the little things," I say. "A bunch of tiny itches. Taken one by one, I could scratch them away, but they eventually gathered into a rash. That's what happens when trust and friendship numbs you, until that itchy rash wakes you up and drives you crazy."

Isabel, refreshing my scotch, says, "You can be so colorful, Cantor. I have always enjoyed that about you. Itches!" she says with a laugh that rubs me like sandpaper.

"Those itches started to add up, Isabel. Got to me pretty bad. One of them was all those promises you and Nilo made about helping me get information about Sophie, but you never came up with anything. Nothing but friendly advice. Yeah, such friendly, loving advice to stay out of Havana's dangers."

"Cantor, my friend," Nilo says, the cigar between his teeth, "our advice was sincere. We did not want harm to come to you. When you first came to my house, you did not speak of Pedro

Estrada. All you wanted was a clean gun, some local money, and information about your woman. But once you started poking around in the Estrada business…" A shrug finishes the thought.

"Okay, the advice was sincere," I say, "but so were the lies. You've got contacts all over Cuba, Nilo, in all sorts of places high and low. I bet you could've found out where Sophie is with just a few phone calls. You can find out the whereabouts of a stray cockroach in a dark alley. I should've been wise to your lies early on, but I trusted both of you too much." There's a lump in my throat when I say it, a pain I try to wash away with a deep swallow of scotch. But it doesn't wash it away. It stays with me, makes everything I need to say even harder. "And you knew about El Teatro de Arte, about what goes on there. You even wondered how I got out alive."

Zamira, frowning as if warding off evil, whispers, "Madre de Dios."

"Yeah, that's right, Zamira, you didn't know about my adventure in that hellhole. I barely got out with my skin. But Isabel, Nilo, you two knew all about the place. You even knew about Rinaldo Lopez, and that's where you slipped up, because if you knew about Lopez, you knew Estrada owned the joint."

There's a particular kind of wince that cramps people's faces when you throw a story at them they can't deny, can't wiggle out of. On Isabel, it tightens the smile she's trying too hard to maintain. On Nilo, it forces him to take his cigar from his teeth before he chews right through it.

I keep going, keep pressing. "When I told you Sophie had been held at El Teatro de Arte until Estrada sold her to an American place, you both played it stupid, said you had no idea where American expats take their pleasure, and like a sap I believed you. Of course you knew. It seems everyone in Havana knows about Ida McNamee's private playground on Calle Costera. But you know what finally put it together for me? The itch that finally exploded into a raw rash? Romance."

Isabel's head tilts in curiosity. Nilo looks confused. Zamira, privy to the story behind what I said, laughs.

As I reach into my jacket pocket, Nilo's quick to raise the .45 and aim it at my head.

"Relax, Nilo," I say, sliding Isabel's note from my pocket. "My own gun's on the other side of the room. The only weapon I have is this little piece of paper. But it's a pretty sharp weapon. It can cut you and Isabel in half."

Nilo grabs it from my hand.

"Go ahead," I say, "take it. It finally told me all I need to know. At first, I didn't understand the blood spot. It could have been a smudge after someone nicked themselves shaving, for all I knew. Zamira understood, though. But even when she explained to me that it's an ancient warning used by Cuba's old clans, I still didn't connect it to you, Isabel, even though you're a Habanero from way back before the conquistadors. My trust in you, my trust in our friendship, surrounded me like a cement wall. It took the most powerful guy in town to smash that wall. It took Meyer Lansky laughing at the blood spot and saying how much he loved Havana because of the romance in the Habanero soul. Romance, yeah, that's what finally scratched all those itches. That's when I started thinking you might've written the note, Isabel."

Nilo says, "Do not talk such stories, Cantor."

"Then don't keep denying that the two of you have been yanking me around. Yanking everyone around, as a matter of fact—me, Zamira and Tomas, the Animas Boys, even Lansky. You remember my office guy in New York, Judson Zane? Well, he has this talent to find things out people don't want found out, and what he found out started to look like the two of you have been playing everyone against everyone else, even *before* I showed up. With your deep connections in Cuba, you could snarl things plenty while you wait to make your move. You've been scheming for your piece of the new Havana, and stupid, trusting me never saw it. But what I don't know is, which one of you killed Pete Estrada? And why?"

Zamira fidgets a little in her seat. I guess we're finally getting to the part that interests her.

Isabel says, "Does it matter, Cantor? I think it is best you leave it alone now."

"Why? Either you'll kill me tonight or you won't. But do an old friend a favor. If I have to die, don't let me die ignorant."

Zamira fidgets again, says, "Please, I need el baño."

Nilo, raising his gun again, says, "You will stay right where you are, Miss Zamira."

"But I cannot. Do you want me to pee on your nice kitchen chair?"

Isabel gets up, takes my .38 from the counter, says to Nilo, "I will take her, mi amor. You stay here with Cantor. You," she says to Zamira, "open your handbag and empty it on the table."

Zamira spills the contents: a tube of lipstick, a red and gold compact, a comb, a white linen handkerchief with floral embroidery around the edges, a clip with American dollars and her driver's license, a few loose Cuban bills, and a change purse of white leather. Very girly.

Satisfied that there's no hidden weapons in Zamira's handbag, Isabel says, "Now stand up and come around the table slowly. Remember that I am holding a gun and I will use it."

She means it. So I can't resist asking, "Are you as handy with a knife as you are with a gun, Isabel? Did you knife Estrada and his henchman?"

"You think I can fight off two men?"

"One at a time, sure. First Estrada, and then Armando when he came in to see what was going on. You're as strong as an ox, Isabel. I remember you pulling those great big heavy potted palms across the veranda without breaking a sweat. Mothers are strong, you said. Yeah, that was another itch."

Zamira's around the other side of the table now, where Isabel grabs her by the arm, saying, "The bathroom is very near."

They walk out of the kitchen. I pour myself another scotch, keeping an eye on Nilo and that .45. Somehow I have to get it away from him. If I want to live to get out of here and find Sophie, I have to get hold of that gun.

But Nilo's no fool. He's got me figured and slides his chair a little distance back from the table, putting him and the gun out of my reach. "Cantor, this is not how I want things to be. I have known you a long time, and we are friends. What are we to do?" There's a shuffle at the kitchen door, and Zamira says, "Put Cantor's gun on the table, Señora Anaya." One arm is around Isabel's waist and her other hand holds a knife to her throat. "And you, Señor Anaya, put your gun on the floor and kick it away, or I will slice your wife. Ah, you did not know I had a knife under my dress? It was in my garter, against my leg, this sweet knife. You are a stupid man, Señor Anaya. You let a woman's curves blind you."

Nilo raises his .45, aims it at Zamira.

But she's ready for him, hurting him in his heart as she pricks Isabel's neck with the point of the knife, drawing blood from the flesh and a sharp gasp of pain from Isabel.

I'm ready for Nilo, too. With his attention distracted by Zamira, I've grabbed my gun from the kitchen counter, aimed it at my old friend.

Shrugging defeat, he crouches down to put the gun on the floor, slides it away, and stands up again, eyeballing me with his every move.

Zamira says, "Which one of you killed Pedro Estrada?"

I add, "And why?"

Zamira starts, "I do not care—"

But a young girl's voice comes from elsewhere in the house and then into the kitchen. "Papi, por favor. My English lesson, it—" A girl of about fourteen wearing a blue cotton nightdress stops cold at the kitchen door, horrified at the scene of grownups with guns and a knife at her mother's throat.

I'm horrified, too; this must be the child I remember as a four-year-old ten years ago, the Anayas' firstborn. Maricela. It's cruel enough that she's walked in on a nightmare of violence, but it eats me alive to realize it's not the first cruelty she's endured. Scars are carved into the girl's face, marking up her cheeks, disfiguring an eye.

Someone hated her. Someone cut her bad.

The four adults in the room and the one child are all frozen where we stand.

"Zamira," I finally say, as easygoing as I can, "put the knife down."

She lowers her knife, slowly, not happy about losing control of Isabel, but understanding that this is no scene for a child.

Nilo rushes to his daughter, takes her in his arms. "Maricela, mi amor."

I slip my gun into my rig inside my jacket, pick up Nilo's .45 from the floor, and put it into my trouser pocket. "Nilo, maybe you should go help your daughter with her lessons."

"Sí," he says as if in a daze. "Sí. Come, Maricela."

The minute father and daughter are gone from the kitchen, Zamira wastes no time grabbing Isabel again and bringing the knife back to her throat, the point pricking the open wound. "I am sorry your daughter saw such things, but we have business, Señora. Which one of you killed Pedro Estrada? You or your husband!"

Quiet tears fall from Isabel's eyes, run down her cheeks. "What does it matter?" she says. I've never heard the elegant Isabel Anaya sound so pitiful. I might even feel sorry for her, but that was yesterday, before she broke my heart. "Estrada was a monster," she says through the tears. "Cantor, tell her. You saw his terrible place, what happened to the women there, the young girls he used. Even you are happy he is dead!"

Zamira says, "I do not care what kind of man he was. I care only to wipe the streets clean of his death so that Los Perros Enojados can rule them. Surely you understand such things, Señora Anaya." She scratches the point of the knife against the wound in Isabel's neck. "So you will tell me, who killed Pedro Estrada? You, or your husband? Maybe you killed him together?"

Isabel, blood running down her neck, gasping in pain, manages a rough shout, "No! You will leave Nilo alone. I killed Estrada. You saw my daughter, my Maricela? *He* did that. Estrada did that!" Her tears are coming faster now, her agony for her daughter choking Isabel's every word. "Do you know how that monster found his little girls for his theater? He hunted them when they walked out of school. That is how he took my Maricela. He stole her off the street. Nilo and I were wild with worry. We did not know where she was, even with our connections all over Cuba. But she finally was able to run away. It was not easy, but just like your Sophie who escaped Ossatura, my Maricela is strong and smart, and after many weeks she saw a chance, a small, dangerous chance, to slip away from that terrible place. When she came home, her face—" With the knife drawing blood and her story tearing her apart, Isabel can barely speak now.

I'm tempted to tell Zamira to put down the knife, relieve some of Isabel's suffering, but my broken trust silences me.

After a struggling breath, Isabel manages, "She told us it was Pedro Estrada who cut her because she was disobedient. But he was not finished with her. He told her that with her cut face she would no longer be pleasing to men, so he turned her into a servant. I wanted to kill him, cut him like he cut my daughter. But he was still an important man, with many powerful friends protecting him. I had to wait until he was weak, with only that one man, that servant, in his house. Months I waited, wishing every day that I could put my knife into his dirty heart. And finally I did. I went to his house. I told him, *I am Maricela's mother*. He just laughed at me. He did not expect the knife I took from my pocket. It felt good to kill him. Very good! And killing his man felt good, too. But, Cantor, I did not know you would be there that same night. When you first came here, you did not tell us you had business at his villa. You must believe me. I did not want you framed for this."

"But you would have let it happen," I say. "You kept warning me of danger, but you did nothing to keep me out of everyone's crosshairs."

"So you are going to let this—this Zamira, this woman of the gutter—kill me? You would take away my children's mother?"

Her last, desperate question stings me like a hard slap.

But Zamira isn't the sentimental type. "You are dead, Señora," she says and puts the full blade of the knife across Isabel's throat, ready to slice.

I pull the .45 from my pocket, fast. "Stop, Zamira. If you kill her, I'll shoot you down."

She glares at me, The knife doesn't move.

I raise the .45. "I'm aiming right between your eyes, Zamira. Put the knife down or your brains will be a bloody mess on the floor."

"You will let a murderer go free?"

"Tonight, yes. Tonight, the Anaya children will not lose their mother. After I'm gone from Havana, you two tigresses can maul each other until there's nothing but shredded skin on bone. I won't be around to cry over either of you." The .45's still aimed at Zamira's head.

The sharp smile spreading across her face could strip the leaves from all the palm trees in Cuba. She lets Isabel go, careful to keep the knife out of reach of her former prey.

I take my first full breath since we walked through the Anayas' door. "Where's your telephone, Isabel?"

Putting a napkin to her bleeding neck, she says, "In the living room."

I keep the .45 pointed at both women, march everyone to the phone. "Zamira, call Tomas. You know what to tell him. And then you and I are going to Calle Costera."

Chapter Twenty-three

Zamira doesn't say a word as I drive through Havana, which is fine by me. The gut-wrenching drama with Isabel and Nilo rattled me up pretty hard, and now I need the peace and quiet of the drive. I have a lot to think about, scenarios to work through, figure every danger that could play out when I make my move to secure Sophie's freedom.

I'm crazy with anticipation of finally seeing Sophie again. It makes it tough to keep my mind focused. My heart's pounding fast; my blood feels like it's about to explode from my veins.

Zamira finally breaks her silence a few blocks from Calle Costera, shaking me out of my churning deliberations. "Tomas was not happy," she says.

"Yeah, so I gathered when you were on the phone with him. Your Spanish sounded like you were gnawing a bone. But you convinced him, yes?"

"Sí, he will do as he is told."

"Uh-huh, because a deal is a deal."

"As you say, a deal is a deal." She says it with all the enthusiasm of someone giving a eulogy for a distant relative nobody liked. "Our soldiers will not interfere with you. I am sure Tomas has passed the word to them by now."

Trusting Tomas Santiago and Zamira Fernández is about as safe a bet as giving money to a bookie whose bags are packed. But it's a chance I have to take. I have no choice.

❖

Fancy cars are jockeying for position when I turn onto Calle Costera, some so chromed up they glare in the streetlights, others more tasteful, letting the stylish curves of the Caddies and Lincolns and Buicks speak of their owners' good breeding and fat bank accounts. Tonight, the people stepping out of the cars include women as well as men, everyone dressed for the evening.

The sight pounds me with twin rages: the rage of fear for Sophie's safety in the pawing hands of a man, and the rage of jealousy at the idea she could be bedded by a woman other than me.

I calm down by reminding myself that there's likely as much gambling as sex going on inside Ida's place. Maybe a client, male or female, just wants Sophie to blow on their dice.

Zamira says, "You are sure your woman is here?"

Maneuvering into a parking spot saves me from answering. I have to keep believing Sophie is here, that she'll see me, get to me. I have to believe we'll make our escape.

My .38's in my shoulder rig, Nilo's .45 is in my trouser pocket, my suit jacket covering the bulge. I ask Zamira, "Your gun's in your handbag?" as I help her from the car.

"Of course. And my knife is on my leg again. Do not worry, chica. We are our own little army, and I am your loyal soldier." Her sneery laugh is small but it slices right down to my marrow.

"It's not you I'm worried about," I say.

That kills her laugh, but not the sarcastic sneer. "Well, gracias, Cantor Gold. I am walking with you into danger and my life means so little to you? Listen, my Yanqui friend, you cannot make a move without me. You need me."

"Sure, I need you. But don't confuse needing you with trusting you. I don't." I take her arm. It's as much to keep her from having second thoughts about helping me get through the door as to present ourselves as a couple looking for an interesting evening.

It's a little past nine thirty when we join the crowd arriving at

Ida McNamee's place. The woman greeting people at the door is a young brunette elegantly dressed in silver lamé. Her skin glows with womanly health; her hair is softly styled and shines in the moonlight. All in all, she's done up like a Hollywood movie star. Elizabeth Taylor comes to mind. Ida sure keeps the advertising classy.

The brunette stops us at the door. "New faces? I need to see your membership credentials." Her accent is as American as a Georgia peach pie.

Zamira says, "Listen, querida, I am Zamira Fernández. My soldiers protect you. I am sure you know they are all over the street, even though you do not see them. Without me, you could be dead. Do you understand?"

The brunette's skin goes white as milk, the womanly glow gone, and the flesh of her face now stiff. She stares at Zamira as if confronted with the arrival of the Grim Reaper. She doesn't know the Angry Dogs are keeping low and quiet tonight, and I'm not about to tell her.

But I have another use for her.

"What's your name?" I say. "I don't care if it's real."

"Giselle," she says, the sound barely eking from her throat.

"Well, Giselle. I want to show you something." I take out the photo. *Okay, my love, here we go,* I say silently to Sophie, but when I show it to Giselle and ask, "Is this woman here?" my throat's tight as a twisted nerve.

She looks at the picture, then looks at me, but says nothing, too scared from Zamira's little threat, and maybe fear of Ida's retribution. I slide my jacket open just enough to show her my gun. "Miss Fernández will not be able to protect you from me," I say, giving her a vicious act I don't entirely feel. I'm not in the habit of hurting women—the memory of Elspeth Beattie in the El Teatro de Arte sandpit suddenly chills me—but I'm betting that terrifying poor Giselle even more than she already is will shake her tongue loose. I say again, with all the hammer blows I can put into it, "Is this woman here?"

She still doesn't answer, her tongue dead in her mouth.

The crowd is starting to push me and Zamira to let them through. But the crowd be damned. Giselle be damned. "Listen, girlie," I say, "I'm not budging until you tell me what I want to know. I don't care if everyone behind me starts a riot, and I don't care how scared you are. So I'll ask you again: Is the woman in the picture inside this house?"

Looking at me, then at the restless, simmering crowd, she hands me back the photograph. "Yes."

I swallow hard to keep my breath from bursting out of me, keep my knees from buckling. Years of misery, of fear, of hellish sleepless nights are suddenly squeezed into a tight, tiny ball about to explode.

But I don't dare let it. Not yet.

Somehow I manage to dredge up a bit of kindness in my voice to soothe the terrified Giselle. "Okay, where is she?"

"Upstairs," she says.

Zamira says, "In a game room, or one of the bed—"

I don't want to hear the rest. "We're going in," I say to Giselle. "Don't press any buttons, don't sound any alarms or give any signals, understand?"

She nods again but says, "You'll never get up there. The upstairs floor is only for very special members. The stairs are heavily guarded. Ida's men will take you away quietly—and kill you."

Zamira says, "We can handle such men."

"No," I say. "Let's go, Zamira." I take her arm, guide her away from the door.

Shocked, she says, "What is wrong with you, Cantor? You are giving up?"

"Don't be stupid. I'll get Sophie out or die trying, but I won't waste time with a battle for a stairway. I have another play. You promise your Angry Dogs have orders not to interfere with me?"

"Didn't we say a deal is a deal? I do not break deals. But I do not know what you are going to do. What is your play?"

"Architecture."

❖

After putting the convertible top up on the Oldsmobile and telling Zamira to stay inside, be as inconspicuous as possible until I get back, I leave her and walk around the block to Calle Sol. I have no idea if she'll still be there when Sophie and I make our run to the car. I wouldn't put it past Zamira to steal the car. I've got the keys but there's not a doubt in my mind she knows how to hot-wire it.

But if Zamira's going to bail out on me, that's a problem for later. Right now, I have to find an opening here on Calle Sol that gets me into Ida's place.

Calle Sol looks a lot like Calle Costera, minus the women beckoning at the doors and minus the crowds. Lights are on here and there in the houses, where residents, maybe families, are evidently enjoying an evening at home.

Like Calle Costera, narrow service alleys separate the houses. The alleys don't go all the way through to Calle Costera but are closed off by concrete walls. The wall in the alley of the house behind Ida's place is pretty high, I'd say about twelve feet, too high for me to scale without gear. And there aren't any garbage cans or crates I can stand on and boost myself up.

But the wall at the end of the alley between houses two doors down looks promising. It's still a little high to scale, about ten feet, but it's damaged. Part of the wall has crumbled, with a sizeable scoop gouged out of the top.

It'll do.

I'll have to scale the wall without making a sound. The last thing I need are a bunch of alarmed citizens calling la policía de la Habana. Those boys have even less mercy for people like me than the badge bullies back home in New York.

Without the soft step of my crepe soled shoes, I'd better walk as quietly as I can along the alley. Any little click of leather soles on pavement could send a panicked resident to the phone. But I've learned to step light and fast over the years, and I make it to the wall without anyone peeking out a window, a telephone to their ear.

The lowest point in the scooped out section of the wall is just above my head, in easy reach.

Okay, this is it. Time to put a plan into action. Time to go get Sophie and bring her home.

I reach up and grab a scooped area of the wall, pull myself up, ignoring the broken, jagged concrete scratching the palms of my hands. I put my feet against the wall, push off to help propel me to the top, careful to keep the scrape of my shoes quiet.

The wall is only about four inches thick, too narrow to walk along. But the house at the right side of the alley is a one-story job, the roofline only a few feet above the wall. I slide my way over to the house, where the ornately carved roofline has plenty of places to grip. Grabbing a couple of fancy flowers at the end of twisting vines, I scramble up.

From the roof of the house, I see the rooftops of the Calle Costera.

In order to get to Ida's place, I'll have to make a small jump from this building to the back of its Calle Costera counterpart, and then make the longer leap across an alley to Ida's rooftop. Without my crepe soled shoes, there's no way to keep those jumps quiet, avoid the risk of alerting the neighbors or the hidden gunmen of the Angry Dogs. I don't see any Dogs, but I bet they're around. I guess I'll find out if a deal really is a deal.

I make the first jump, an easy stretch from roof to roof. Two guys on the rooftop where I land unfold up from the shadows, stand up and turn around, their big rifles snapped fast in my direction. Sure, Los Perros Enojados. The soldiers of Tomas and Zamira's Angry Dogs. The rest of the gunmen must be hunkered down in the shadows of the other rooftops, their guns aimed discreetly down to the street, guarding the action against any rival gangs who have big ideas about moving in and taking over.

I put my hands up, walk toward the two Dogs nice and easy. "Me llamo Cantor Gold," I say, just loud enough to be heard, not so loud to alert the neighbors behind me on Calle Sol. "Hablas inglés?"

One of the guys says, "I do, sí. Cantor Gold, we were told to let you pass, but you were to be on the street, not on the roof."

"Change of plan," I say. "The street was getting a little crowded. But the deal's the same, yes?"

My nerves twist and my fists clench while the guy thinks things over until I guess he figures his bosses' decisions are above his head. He finally shrugs, says, "Okay," and jerks his thumb for me to move along.

"Gracias," I say.

The other guy keeps his rifle on me, though.

My English speaking pal says, "But if trouble comes to you, we cannot help you." Moonlight catches his smile. It's not friendly.

I make the longer leap to Ida's roof, landing with a thud and a tumble. Two more guys with two more rifles unfold from the shadows, but my English speaker gives them a wave, and they take their aim away from me and back to the street, lying low in the shadows again.

The ornate roofline of Ida's house provides handy places to grab on to as I climb down to the second floor balcony. The window shutters are closed, mercifully keeping me in the shadows, but I can't see inside, can't get even a glimpse to see if Sophie is nearby.

The shutters are also locked.

I take out my penknife, open the blade, and as I slide it in and under the inside latch, I hear a man's shout from the street, "Up there!"

Dammit! My play's crashed.

People start to swarm in the street, pointing up at me. The rooftop Dogs are suddenly up and aiming their rifles, some at the street, some at me.

I can't go up and I can't go down.

The only place I can go is inside, but I have to get these damn shutters open, fast, find Sophie, and get past any thugs who try to stop me. I've got my .38 and Nilo's .45, and with that kind of firepower I stand a decent chance of getting out with Sophie.

I've got to get inside.

I slide the blade back into the shutters, finagle it under the latch, try to work fast, try to get the shutters open

There's more commotion in the street, with people coming out of Ida's place and the other houses along Calle Costera to see what the hoopla is all about. People are shouting in Spanish and English and half a dozen other languages. I try not to let them rattle me as I work the knife.

But one shout does get through: "*Cantor?*"

I know that voice. Its music is a little ragged, a little worn, but it still enchants me, still becomes part of my breath. Sophie's voice.

I look down to the street. There she is, my Sophie, in a flowing, flowery Japanese robe that she clutches around her the way a refugee clutches their only coat. Her dark hair still brushes her shoulders. Her face is turned up to me, the same beautiful face, the same beautiful dark eyes but sadder, tearing at my heart with their look of disbelief, desperation, and hope. The glint of light along her cheek is a tear. She's crying.

"Sophie!" I climb off the balcony, shimmy down the drainpipe along the corner of the building. As I hit the street, I extend my hand, shout, "Sophie! Come on, I'm getting us out of here!"

Her eyes wide, she reaches for me, but she's still more than ten feet away with the crowd surging all over the street, pushing us farther apart.

I hear her call out, "Cantor!" and see Sophie try to push her way toward me through the crowd.

I shove people left and right to get to her, shout, "Sophie! I'm coming!" over and over. I'm almost there, close enough to see her face through the crowd, see the tears and panic in her eyes. I'm just about close enough to grasp her outstretched hand—

But the air suddenly cracks with gunfire, followed by screams that rip through my ears. The street's wild with panicked people running all over the place as more shots ring out from every direction, pouring down from rooftops, engulfing Calle Costera.

I hear my name again, "Cantor!" but it's not Sophie calling me this time. It's Zamira. "Cantor, we must get out of here! I think we have been betrayed. Someone must have snitched about my Angry Dogs standing down tonight. The Animas Boys, they are here and they are attacking!" She grabs my arm, tries to pull me toward the car.

"I'm not leaving without Sophie!" I shake Zamira off, pull

out the .45 from my pocket, push my way back through the crowd. People are screaming as bullets ricochet all over the street.

The gun out, I don't dare shoot even though I see Sophie trying to push her way through the swirling mass to reach me. If I shoot, there's too much danger I'd kill a bystander, or even hit Sophie in the mayhem. Her face appears in and out of the surging crowd, between the falling bodies of the wounded and the dead shot down by the gangs' gunfire. I see Sophie's eyes try to find me and hold me. Her mouth opens, calling my name.

I hear the gunfire, hear the screams, see Sophie's eyes widen, see blood spurt—near her? Behind her? *Hers?*

I can't see her now. I shout her name as I push through the chaos of the crowd, the .45 raised but useless. Everyone is running to escape the gunfire coming from everywhere. Bullets rain from above and crisscross the street. But Zamira's back at my side, pulling at me, screaming, "Cantor, we must go!"

"No! I have to get to Sophie!"

"You are crazy!"

Zamira's still grabbing me as I push toward the spot where I saw the blood fly. I look between the petrified faces of the crowd, look down between their feet, past the dead bodies…and see the ripple of the Japanese robe.

Zamira sees her, too. "If that is your woman on the street, it is too late, Cantor. She is dead. We must leave here or we will be killed!"

"Get away from me, Zamira! Sophie is not dead. She can't be dead. I have to get to her, bring her home!" A bullet whizzes past my head before I even finish talking. There's more gunfire, more bullets, more death all around us. The gang war rages.

I keep calling, "Sophie!" even as blood spurting from people near me sprays my face and mingles with my tears. I hear no answer.

Zamira, screaming, pulls at me again. "Cantor, you cannot get to her. There is only one way out of here. Please, come with me!"

More bullets whiz around me. One nicks the arm of my jacket. Another ricochets off the pavement, sends concrete shards flying. I drop to the ground, try to crawl my way through the rushing tangle of feet, stay under the gunfire. But bullets tear up the pavement, send concrete shards against my face. Blinding dust flies in my eyes.

The gunfire between me and Sophie grows thicker, the deafening crack of bullets comes faster, a firestorm devouring everyone in their path.

I can't let it devour me. I'll crawl through Hell before I leave Sophie on the street. If she's hurt, I need to get her to safety. If she's dead—

"No!" I can feel my scream bursting from my throat but can't hear it through the gunfire, the shrieking crowd, the pavement blasting around me. Chunks of exploded concrete crash down on me, pummel my back, slash at my head. I crawl forward, or try to. I can't tell if I'm moving. If I am, it's by inches, less than inches, stopped by rushing feet, bullets pouring down, the street blasted to smithereens, bodies falling on top of me, pressing me hard against the pavement.

Burying me.

CHAPTER TWENTY-FOUR

Cantor's apartment, New York City
A week later, early evening

Days and nights of whiskey and I'm still not blotto enough to kill the pain. The pain digs deep, doing its best to claw the life out of me.

It's getting dark in my living room, maybe I should turn on a light, though just thinking about it gives me a headache. I'd rather have another drink. I reach for the bottle of Chivas on the side table next to my chair, my big red club chair that's been holding me in its upholstered embrace since I don't know when. But the bottle's not on the table. It's on the floor, lodged between my bare feet.

Bending down to pick it up is no easy business. The living room is shimmying around me, making it tough to settle my shaking hand in the dark, get my fingers around the bottle. But I finally grab it, lift it to my lips for a swig. Maybe this one will finally blot out the horror of spurting blood, of Elspeth Beattie's dying eyes, of Sophie, my Sophie, lying in the street…

The bottle's empty. Crap.

If I want another drink, I'll need another bottle, and if I want another bottle, I have to go get it. So I get up from my chair, or try to, but my body doesn't want to be bothered. I can't feel my flesh or my bones. Dammit. Why are my bones numb but my mind burns? I want to be as numb as my bones. I want my head to be empty. I want this constant horror movie in my head of Sophie on the ground,

Sophie out of my reach, to end. I want to stop reliving waking up sick and battered on the floor of a fishing skiff that brought me out of Havana to Key West, courtesy of Zamira and Tomas, or so the captain said.

Okay, Gold, everyone thinks you're tough. Let's see how tough you are. If you want your whiskey, get up and get the hell outta this chair.

My little pep talk does the trick. I'm on my feet, more or less, swaying like a boat in the wind.

It's a good thing I didn't turn on a light. The swaying stripes of my bathrobe would probably make me dizzy.

My toes press down on the carpet while I hold on to the edge of the side table to keep from falling over, but my foot stubs against something else: my gun. What the hell is it doing on the floor? How long has it been there? Maybe I should forget about the whiskey and just blow my brains out. Maybe I already tried. What stopped me?

Maybe I can figure it out if I have another drink.

I manage to stumble across the living room to the credenza, fumble around for the last bottle of Chivas. When that's gone, I can either call the liquor store and have them send over a few more bottles, or I could just switch to whatever's in the cabinet. I haven't had bourbon in a long time. Might be fun.

I open the Chivas, take a swig, carry the bottle with me to the window. *C'mon, whiskey. Do your goddamned job. Take the pain away. Blot out the nightmares in my head.*

New York's lights are just coming on, beating the stars in the sky at their own game. The neon signs and theater marquees from nearby Broadway splash their colors all over the streets and buildings, smear across my window. Their sales pitch of good times and snappy nights is like a slap in my face. Broadway's good times, its glamorous stage stars and chorus girls, its sensational shows and jazzy cabarets, are for other people. For me, without Sophie, without hope of seeing her again, there's just darkness and booze.

But Broadway's lights are pretty.

Another swig of whiskey and I start to laugh. Yeah, Broadway's lights are sure pretty, lures for suckers and sharpies alike, invitations to drop a lot of cash for a night on the town, show your wife or your best girl a high time. Hah! If those good-time Charlies only knew! A lot of that cash finds its way into the pockets of guys like Sig Loreale and the other gangsters who dip their fingers into New York's wallets. From time to time, some of that cash even winds up in my money clip. Easy dough. Not as flush as my smuggling racket, but showbiz money has its charms. Leggy showgirl sort of charms.

Yeah, those colored lights—

The phone interrupts my Broadway boogie musings, its ring spiking into my head. I raise the bottle of scotch to throw it at the phone, kill its ringing, but stop myself before I toss the bottle and lose the booze.

I mumble, "All right, all right, cut it out," as I wobble back to the credenza and the phone. I slap the receiver from its cradle, silencing the ring, and carry the bottle of scotch back to the window and the pretty lights of New York.

But I can hear the old woman's familiar voice come through the phone. It's Mom Sheinbaum, her singsong Lower East Side accent full of Old World music and underworld guts. "Hello? Cantor? Are you there? What's the matter, you don't answer your phone for days?"

Days? I didn't hear the damn phone for days?

"Cantor, so nu? Where are you? Pick up the goddamn phone. It's Esther Sheinbaum. Listen, mommaleh, there's an item I want you to get your hands on for a client who'll pay big for a fancy-schmancy little statue by some famous dead person whose name I can't pronounce. Right up your alley. Cantor? Come to my house tomorrow morning and I'll tell you all about it."

Yeah, New York's lights sure are pretty.

About the Author

Ann Aptaker's debut novel, *Criminal Gold*, was a 2014 Goldie Award finalist. Her second book, *Tarnished Gold*, was a 2015 Lambda Literary ("Lammy") Award and Goldie Award winner. Her third book, *Genuine Gold*, was a Goldie winner. Ann's books have earned excellent reviews from *Curve* Magazine, *Crimepieces*, *Rainbow Reads*, and other print and internet venues. Her Cantor Gold crime series celebrates her favorite themes: dangerous women and crime and mystery fiction. Like her protagonist, Cantor Gold, Ann resides in her beloved hometown, New York, where she is an adjunct professor of art and art history at New York Institute of Technology.

Facebook: Ann Aptaker, Author
Twitter: @AnnAptaker
Instagram: ann_aptaker

Books Available From Bold Strokes Books

Against All Odds by Kris Bryant, Maggie Cummings, and M. Ullrich. Peyton and Tory escaped death once, but will they survive when Bradley's determined to make his kill rate 100 percent? (978-1-163555-193-8)

Autumn's Light by Aurora Rey. Casual hookups aren't supposed to include romantic dinners and meeting the family. Can Mat Pero see beyond the heartbreak that led her to keep her worlds so separate, and will Graham Connor be waiting if she does? (978-1-163555-272-0)

Breaking the Rules by Larkin Rose. When Virginia and Carmen are thrown together by an embarrassing mistake, they find out their stubborn determination isn't so heroic after all. (978-1-163555-261-4)

Broad Awakening by Mickey Brent. In the sequel to *Underwater Vibes*, Hélène and Sylvie find ruts in their road to eternal bliss. (978-1-163555-270-6)

Broken Vows by MJ Williamz. Sister Mary Margaret must reconcile her divided heart or risk losing a love that just might be heaven sent. (978-1-163555-022-1)

Flesh and Gold by Ann Aptaker. Havana, 1952, where art thief and smuggler Cantor Gold dodges gangland bullets and mobsters' schemes while she searches Havana's steamy red light district for her kidnapped love. (978-1-163555-153-2)

Isle of Broken Years by Jane Fletcher. Spanish noblewoman Catalina de Valasco is in peril, even before the pirates holding her for ransom sail into seas destined to become known as the Bermuda Triangle. (978-1-163555-175-4)

Love Like This by Melissa Brayden. Hadley Cooper and Spencer Adair set out to take the fashion world by storm. If only they knew their hearts were about to be taken. (978-1-163555-018-4)

Secrets On the Clock by Nicole Disney. Jenna and Danielle love their jobs helping endangered children, but that might not be enough to stop them from breaking the rules by falling in love. (978-1-163555-292-8)

Unexpected Partners by Michelle Larkin. Dr. Chloe Maddox tries desperately to deny her attraction for Detective Dana Blake as they flee from a serial killer who's hunting them both. (978-1-163555-203-4)

A Fighting Chance by T. L. Hayes. Will Lou be able to come to terms with her past to give love a fighting chance? (978-1-163555-257-7)

Chosen by Brey Willows. When the choice is adapt or die, can love save us all? (978-1-163555-110-5)

Gnarled Hollow by Charlotte Greene. After they are invited to study a secluded nineteenth-century estate, a former English professor and a group of historians discover that they will have to fight against the unknown if they have any hope of staying alive. (978-1-163555-235-5)

Jacob's Grace by C.P. Rowlands. Captain Tag Becket wants to keep her head down and her past behind her, but her feelings for AJ's second-in-command, Grace Fields, makes keeping secrets next to impossible. (978-1-163555-187-7)

On the Fly by PJ Trebelhorn. Hockey player Courtney Abbott is content with her solitary life until visiting concert violinist Lana Caruso makes her second-guess everything she always thought she wanted. (978-1-163555-255-3)

Passionate Rivals by Radclyffe. Professional rivalry and long-simmering passions create a combustible combination when Emmet McCabe and Sydney Stevens are forced to work together, especially when past attractions won't stay buried. (978-1-63555-231-7)

Proxima Five by Missouri Vaun. When geologist Leah Warren crash-lands on a preindustrial planet and is claimed by its tyrant, Tiago, will clan warrior Keegan's love for Leah give her the strength to defeat him? (978-1-163555-122-8)

Shadowboxer by Jessica L. Webb. Jordan McAddie is prepared to keep her street kids safe from a dangerous underground protest group, but she isn't prepared for her first love to walk back into her life. (978-1-163555-267-6)